MAKING TROUBLE

Just as Joe and Betsy finished their second round, Lieutenant Connors and another named Falvey, a recent arrival to the post, came in through the doorway. Connors glanced around, not searching for anything, just sizing up the bar and its customers. When his eyes landed on Betsy and Joe Holly, he walked over to the table. His left eyebrow was raised and he had an evil-looking smirk on his face.

"Well, well, if it isn't Mr. Holly drinking with the captain's wife," Connor said. "The captain will be interested that the charges he brought against you are reinforced."

"Connors, I think you had better find another place to go," Joe said, rising to his feet.

Connors ignored Joe and turned toward Betsy.

"Mrs. Willoughby, do you realize you are sitting at a table with a man who was drummed out of the army?"

Joe could feel himself begin to tremble with anger.

"Lieutenant Connors," Betsy said as if she were talking to a child, "why don't you be a good little boy and mind your own business?"

"I am minding my own business, Mrs. Willoughby. I am loyal to your husband as any officer in the army should be. Your friend, Holly, is a disgrace to the uniform."

Joe's first punch landed in Connors's stomach. . . .

Other *Leisure* books by John Duncklee:
GRACIELA OF THE BORDER
GENEVIEVE OF TOMBSTONE

DOUBLE VENGEANCE

John Duncklee

LEISURE BOOKS NEW YORK CITY

To Penny, my wife and first editor

A LEISURE BOOK®

October 2001

Published by

Dorchester Publishing Co., Inc.
276 Fifth Avenue
New York, NY 10001

ISBN 0-8439-4929-5

Visit us on the web at www.dorchesterpub.com.

DOUBLE
VENGEANCE

Chapter One

Scowling down at the stacks of paperwork partially covering his mahogany desk, the colonel stood with his arms crossed. He looked up and dropped his arms to his sides when the knock sounded on his office door. "Come in," he snarled.

The brass knob turned and an officer with embroidered lieutenant bars stitched onto the shoulders of his blue cavalry uniform let himself in, came to attention, saluted snappily, and said, "Good morning, Colonel Haynes."

Haynes returned the lieutenant's salute with a slight touch to his forehead, his ruddy face and trimmed gray mustache turning into a smile. "Good morning, Holly. Take a seat. I have a lot to tell you."

Holly, a long-muscled man at five feet ten inches, sat in one of the three leather-upholstered chairs that faced the front of the colonel's desk. He looked straight at the officer through clear hazel eyes, separated by a long, thin nose that complemented his angular face down to the slight cleft on his pointed chin. The lieutenant could not be considered handsome, but he had a ruggedness that gave him the look of power and determination.

"I'm sure you are wondering why I sent for you, so I will come right to the point," the colonel said, still standing and smoothing his thinning gray hair with both hands. "The payroll wagon to Camp Huachuca has been held up and robbed three times within the past year. Major Armbruster, commandant at Camp Huachuca, was in my class at West Point and is a conscientious, methodical man. He has tried everything he can to discover why these robberies are taking place so easily. He thinks there might be someone inside the post who may be in cahoots with the robbers."

"That's happened before," Holly remarked.

"Ned Armbruster is a fine officer, very capable and tough as nails. He has his hands full with Apache raiders, so he cannot give his full attention to this payroll robbery problem. I'm sending you to Camp Huachuca. I've been watching you closely, Joe. Your father and I were at Gettysburg together. He might have been sitting at this desk had that rebel bullet not shattered his right arm."

"I remember when he came home with his sleeve empty."

"I didn't mean to bring up sad memories for you. You have the makings of the same kind of fine officer that your father had. This mission, if you can solve the mystery, will guarantee your captaincy."

Joe's thoughts flew back to his father. *He might have been a good army officer, but he was not much of a father to me.*

"Is there anything wrong? Do you understand your

8

mission?" the colonel asked, noticing the look on Joe's face.

"No, nothing's wrong. I'll do my best, Colonel."

"I've looked through your records and found that none of the officers presently at Camp Huachuca should know you. The enlisted men are all Buffalo Soldiers. You may have been with a few of those men at Fort Riley, but I don't think that will hinder your mission."

"Will Major Armbruster know the nature of my mission?" Holly asked.

"Only you and I know your mission. You will be on your own except you will have regular duties like the rest of the officers at the camp. Fighting Apache raiding parties will probably be part of them. I am hoping you will be able to discover who, if anyone, at Camp Huachuca, is working with the robbers. Hopefully, Ned Armbruster is wrong, but I know him for being a shrewd judge of situations."

"I understand the need for secrecy, Colonel, but suppose I find the culprit and Major Armbruster doesn't believe me?"

"You will contact me. We will use a code for communication because one cannot always trust telegraphers these days. When and if you discover who is behind the robberies, telegraph me the words 'inside the fence' if it is someone inside the camp."

"What if Major Armbruster is wrong about the robberies being an inside situation?"

If the informant is not military, wire the words, 'outside the fence.' I will send an officer to contact you personally to relay your information to me. Don't trust anyone in Tombstone. There are more crooks there than anywhere in the country."

"Thank you for the warning, Colonel," Holly said, and smiled.

"Good luck, and be careful."

"I'll do my best, Colonel," Holly replied, rising from the chair, saluting the district commandant, and leaving for the bachelor officers' quarters.

While packing his belongings for the ride to Camp Huachuca, Joe laughed to himself at the general's remarks. Joe Holly had grown tired of army life after only a few months. Had he anything else in mind from which to make a living, he would have resigned the commission his father, with his army connections, had engineered.

Life on the Maine horse farm under his dictatorial father had become oppressive to twenty-year-old Joe. It had become increasingly obvious as time passed that his father favored his oldest son, Edward, over Joe. When Major Holly had expressed his desire for Joe to become a cavalry officer, Joe had jumped at the chance to make his own way in the world. However, he soon discovered that he had traded one oppressive environment for another. Despite his disappointment with army life, Holly never expressed his feelings to his fellow officers, who regarded him as an esteemed colleague, especially for his knowledge about horses and horsemanship.

Hoping he would find army life in the West less stringent than the spit and polish requirements around the District of Columbia, he had requested a transfer to Fort Riley, Kansas. After only six months' service on the frontier, he wondered why he had received orders to report to Fort Lowell, near Tucson, Arizona Territory.

As he reported to the commandant of Fort Riley prior

to leaving for his new assignment, the colonel had no reason to offer concerning the transfer. "You will find Colonel Haynes to be a fine officer who commands respect from his troops. Please give him my very best regards, Lieutenant Holly."

"I will, sir. It has been a pleasure serving under your command," Joe said.

"You have the makings of a fine officer, Holly. Keep up the good work and you will have your captaincy in no time."

"Thank you, Colonel."

"There is a supply train leaving for New Mexico Territory the day after tomorrow. You will find another going to Tucson once you are in Santa Fe. Good luck and godspeed to Fort Lowell."

Holly wondered about his new assignment in Arizona Territory. He had heard that the summers were hot and houses were made of mud. *Poor Edward. He may be the favored son, but he is stuck there with a life that is determined by our father. This army life may not be what I want, but it will have to do until I find something else.*

After weeks of riding with supply trains through mountains and plains, Joe arrived at Fort Lowell during the blistering heat of Tucson's summer, just before the monsoon winds from the south began bringing in the billowing white thunderheads loaded with the summer rains.

Packed and ready for the three-day ride from Fort Lowell to Camp Huachuca, Joe Holly saddled his bay gelding, tossed the loaded saddlebags behind the cantle and tied them on snugly with leather thongs. Mounted, he waved good-bye to the corporal on duty at the stables. Before joining the supply train to Camp Huachuca, Joe rode into Tucson to buy a more suitable mount for the rough Arizona mountain country than the tall thoroughbred bay gelding that belonged to the army.

The hot, dusty streets of Tucson were almost deserted during the afternoon siesta as he rode toward the corrals owned by J.Z. Tyler. As usual, J.Z. sat on the rough-hewn wooden bench outside the small adobe building he called his office. Except when some prospective buyer showed up, J.Z. spent most of his days whittling. He always seemed disinterested in his business, but it was all part of his knack for selling horses. He wore a bushy, black mustache flecked with gray. When talking, he automatically stroked the mustache so that it hung down over fat jowls that shook when he spoke.

The horse trader continued to whittle a piece of cottonwood as Joe rode up and dismounted. "Mr. Tyler, I am told you might have a horse suitable for riding in mountain country."

"I reckon there's a few back in the corrals that'll do you."

"Would you mind showing me?" Joe asked, wondering if J.Z. Tyler did all his trading from the bench.

"Just go on down the alley and look 'em over. I'll be out there in a bit."

Before looking over the horses in the corrals, Joe tied the bay to a hitchrack. Having a good eye for horseflesh, he glanced into the first corral and saw most of the horses there were past their prime. Too many had white spots around their withers, telling Joe they had once suffered saddle sores. The horses milling around the second corral showed more promise. Joe spotted a sorrel gelding with a white star on its forehead. Opening the corral gate, he entered, closed the gate behind him and eased his way across the enclosure to get a better look at the sorrel.

Except for the star on its forehead the horse had no other white markings. His hooves were a slate-gray color that Joe knew would mean hardness. Yellowish white hooves beneath white stockings on a horse meant softer hooves that often split when the horse traveled over rocky country.

Joe liked the slope of the gelding's shoulder and its long hips. Its chest was wider than the thoroughbreds Joe was used to and inside its hind legs were well-muscled gaskins. Satisfied that he would like to give the gelding a ride, he turned to leave the corral and saw J.Z. at the gate with a halter in his hand. "Take this halter and catch him. He'll run you a bit till you get him cornered."

Joe approached the sorrel with the halter in his right hand. The horse sensed Joe was after it and shied away to the far end of the corral. Joe followed the sorrel and finally cornered it away from the rest of the horses. Placing the halter on the horse's head, he led it out into the alley between the corrals. "What do you know about this one, Mr. Tyler?"

"The feller I bought him from claimed he was a Steel-dust. He's green broke. Prob'ly had ten saddlin's."

"Do you mind if I saddle him and give him a try?"

"Go right ahead. I wouldn't want you to buy a horse you hadn't rode."

Joe led the sorrel over to the hitchrack where he transferred his saddle from the bay to the sorrel. J.Z. waddled over carrying a hackamore in his hand. "He don't know a bit yet, but he'll do all right with this hackamore."

Knowing the horse was green broke, Joe mounted carefully and his right foot found the off stirrup quickly. He kept a tight enough rein to discourage the horse from putting his head down to buck. At Joe's gentle urging, the sorrel headed out along the road.

After a ten-minute ride Joe felt satisfied with the horse, returned to the hitchrack, dismounted and tied the sorrel next to the bay. He looked over at J.Z., who had returned to his bench to whittle. "I think the sorrel will do," Joe said. "He still needs a lot of work reining. What are you asking?"

"Thirty," J.Z. said without looking up from his whittling project.

"That's a mite high for a green broke horse, isn't it, Mr. Tyler?"

"Helluva good horse that Steeldust. He's prob'ly got a bunch of cowsense besides bein' a good lookin' sorrel."

"Cowsense makes little difference to me."

"It will if'n you go to sellin' him."

"I'll give you twenty-five, Mr. Tyler."

"I'll tell ya what, Lieutenant. I won't go down to twenty-five, but I'll toss in the hackamore. You'll need it till you can get him bit-wise."

"I guess you've sold the sorrel," Joe said, and reached into his pocket for the money. "I do need a bill of sale, Mr. Tyler."

"What's your name?"

"Joe Holly."

Tyler shoved himself up from the bench and went into his office. A few minutes later, he handed Joe the bill of sale and put the gold coins in his pocket. "That Steeldust horse will do you a good job in rough country," J.Z. said. "Tell your friends I've got a bunch more."

"I'll do that, Mr. Tyler."

Joe mounted the sorrel and, leading the bay gelding, rode back toward town to find the supply train for Camp Huachuca.

Chapter Two

The train of four wagons had an escort of a sergeant and eight troopers in case of an attack by either Apache raiders or local highwaymen. Being unacquainted with the trail leading south and east from Tucson, and in no hurry to arrive at his new assignment, Holly had a good opportunity to observe the desert and mountain ranges.

The sergeant, a grizzled veteran of the Apache Wars, spoke freely about the greatest problem facing the settlers in Arizona Territory. "Those Apache devils are a helluva lot tougher to fight than most savages," he said. "They'll swoop in on a ranch, run off with as many horses and cattle as they can find, then disappear. We try to follow them, but they won't stand and fight. We had most of them put away on reservations until Geronimo decided to break out and go to raiding again."

"I understand they prefer horses to cattle," Joe said.

"An Apache would rather eat horsemeat to beef anytime. They use horses to ride, but lots of times they raid on foot. Those rascals can hide themselves so well, a man can ride within ten yards of one and never see the devil. You'll have fun riding after them from Camp Huachuca. That renegade Geronimo won't stay put anywhere. Just when the army thinks they have him, he disappears into the Sierra Madres down in Mexico."

Joe watched the billowing white thunderheads fill the July sky. By noon they had begun to turn black on their undersides and converge with one another. "Looks like we'll have some rain," he said to the sergeant.

"You never know about these summer storms around here. They're real spotty. A storm can come up and start dumping rain in one place and the ground will be powder dry right next to it. By the looks of those clouds I'd say it will rain some place nearby."

A huge, brown dust storm swept through the desert toward them. Without stopping the wagons, the mule skinners donned their slickers. At the sergeant's command, the troopers halted, dismounted and put on their rain gear. Holly did the same. Mounted once again, the escort trotted back to retake their positions. Joe noted with approval the sergeant's precaution against spooking any of the saddle horses by not trying to put on flapping slickers while mounted.

The blinding dust cloud hurled millions of stinging sand particles at the men and animals. Lightning bolts streaked through the dark, ominous sky quickly followed by thunder claps, booming and echoing. Shielding their faces with their free arms, they felt and heard the first large raindrops slamming at their rain gear. Then, as if someone had turned on a giant valve, the storm hit with full fury, quickly filling the sandy top layer of the desert loam. The lightning and thunder became simultaneous. Rivulets began running in the tracks of the wagon trail. The mule skinners bellowed at their charges to keep them going. Almost as quickly as it had begun, the storm ended. The afternoon sun blazed down. The pungent smell of wet greasewood filled the humid air. To Joe, the wet shrubs smelled like the rain had been laced with horse liniment. When the slickers had dried, the sergeant ordered the troopers to dismount again to take off their slickers, roll them into bundles and tie them in back of the cantles on their McClelland saddles.

Away from the perimeter of the storm, the mules, horses and wagon wheels again churned up the fine, dry dust into a cloud that Holly judged could be seen for miles by Apaches or bandits with positions on the surrounding hills and mountains.

The horses and mules lathered in the afternoon heat. The gradual climb from desert shrub to the grasslands slowed the mules pulling the heavily loaded wagons. Arriving at the Posta Quemada Stage Station, twenty-six miles from Fort Lowell, an hour before sunset, the mule skinners stopped their mules and began unhitching them from the wagons. Before unsaddling their mounts, the troopers led them to the long, wooden water trough in the corral.

The freighters took care of their mules before retiring to the stage stop for a supper of beef and beans. The army escort, including Holly, camped a short distance away.

After three days on the slow, arduous trail, and another summer thunderstorm, they arrived at Camp Huachuca in the middle of the afternoon. Joe was glad the temperature in Huachuca Canyon felt a lot cooler than the baking heat of Fort Lowell and Tucson.

After taking care of his horses, he reported for duty in the commandant's office near the parade ground. Major Armbruster, a thickset man with wavy black hair and piercing green eyes, returned Holly's snappy salute without rising from his chair. "Lieutenant Holly, you are replacing a man who didn't get along with the colored troops. He took his company out on patrol against the Apache, and he was the only one killed. Therefore, I suggest that you do not let any prejudice interfere with the manner by which you treat those under your command."

"You have no need to worry on that score, Major," Holly said. "I found the colored troops at Fort Riley to be excellent soldiers. Besides, I am from Maine not South Carolina."

"Very well, Lieutenant. You have been traveling for quite a time. I suggest you take some time off. You may be curious about Tombstone. Should you decide to look the town over, be careful. There are more gunmen per square foot in Tombstone than anywhere in the country."

"Yes, sir. Thank you for your consideration."

"Report to Captain Willoughby in four days. You will be under his command," Armbruster said, and lowered his eyes to the stack of papers in front of him.

"Yes, sir," Holly replied, and left to get settled in the bachelor officers' quarters.

Remembering the words of Colonel Haynes at Fort Lowell, praising Major Armbruster as a fine officer, Holly wondered if below the cold, hard demeanor the major showed in his office there was something else about the man that had impressed Haynes.

Early the next morning, after a deep sleep and a good breakfast, Joe decided to ride to Tombstone to see what that town with the reputation for being so wild had to offer in the way of recreation.

Arriving in the middle of the afternoon, he rode to the livery stable to put up his horse before selecting a hotel for his two-night stay in the booming silver-mining town. From the descriptions he had heard, he thought there would be more people out and around. Once settled in his room in the Grand Hotel, Joe changed into a clean uniform and left for the Oriental Cafe and Bar.

Several miners stood at the long bar. Joe ordered a whiskey from the bartender, a man with a serious, almost scowling face with a long, bushy black mustache that had been carefully waxed and twisted.

After downing the shot of whiskey, Joe left to stroll around the town. He observed the conglomeration of businesses, mostly saloons or restaurants on Allen and Fremont streets. Passing by part of the red-light district on Sixth Street, Joe smiled at the invitations, and contemplated entering one of the parlor houses. Instead, he looked around for a restaurant.

After sunset and a hearty meal of beefsteak, he visited several saloons before retiring for the night in his hotel room. Before falling asleep, Joe Holly pondered how he would go about fulfilling his mission for Colonel Haynes.

Returning from Tombstone in time for supper, he dined with the other bachelor officers and retired early. The next morning before muster, he reported to Captain Willoughby.

"Welcome to Camp Huachuca, Lieutenant. The commandant informed me that he had assigned you to my command. I trust you have rested from your travels sufficiently to help train these soldiers. I am not sure which have less discipline, the Apaches or the colored troops."

Holly wondered if Willoughby's pompous-sounding greeting indicated that the captain was like another West Pointer he had known at Fort Riley. As for Willoughby's statement about the discipline of colored troops, it was Joe's opinion that they were proud of their service and never questioned orders. *In fact, I'm probably less disciplined than they are.* "I am ready for any orders you may give me, sir."

"Good, Lieutenant. After breakfast, have the troops saddled and ready for parade drill." Before dismissing the Buffalo Soldiers for breakfast, Willoughby introduced them to Holly. Then the captain went to his house on Officers' Row.

When the troops had finished saddling their horses, Joe introduced himself to each soldier and tried to remember their names. Willoughby arrived, taking Joe aside. "Lieutenant Holly, I'm leaving the troop under your command for this morning's drill. With my assignment as the post's financial officer, I have a mountain of paperwork to get finished. Drill them hard. These troops could use more discipline."

"Yes, sir," Joe replied. Having learned of Willoughby's duty as financial officer, Joe wondered if he might be the one who was giving information to those who robbed the payroll wagons.

"Corporal Handley," Joe said. "Mount the troop in a column of twos."

"Yes, sir, Lieutenant," Mose Handley replied, and turned to face the soldiers. "Troop B, prepare to

John Duncklee

mount." Already in place, the soldiers took their reins in their left hands by their horses' withers. "Mount."

After two manuevers on the parade ground, Joe saw that Troop B knew what it was doing. He wondered again about Willoughby's remark that the troopers needed discipline. When Joe unsaddled his horse after the afternoon session, Willoughby approached him in the stable area. "Lieutenant Holly, when you have dismissed the troop, stop at my house for a cocktail."

"Very well, Captain," Joe replied. "I will be there as soon as I get my horse cooled."

Having grown up around horses, Joe always took care of his own mounts instead of turning them over to enlisted men as some officers were in the habit of doing. By doing this he became better acquainted with the troopers. One of the aspects of army life he had come to dislike intensely was the chasm between the officers and enlisted ranks.

Willoughby met him at the front door. "Come in, Lieutenant."

"Thank you, sir," Joe said, almost swallowing his words as a beautiful red-haired woman came into the foyer.

"This is Mrs. Willoughby, Lieutenant. Betsy, this is Lieutenant Holly. He has joined my troop."

"My pleasure, Lieutenant Holly."

"It's nice to meet you, Mrs. Willoughby," Joe said. The coquettish look in Betsy Willoughby's eyes captured him, yet made him feel uneasy.

"Shall we adjourn to the parlor for cocktails?" Willoughby suggested. "What's your poison, Lieutenant?"

"Whiskey will be fine, Captain," Joe replied, amused and confused by Willoughby's sudden friendliness after the cold welcome he had received that morning.

"Betsy, be a dear and have Sam bring the lieutenant a whiskey. I'll have my usual."

Willoughby sat in an overstuffed arm chair, obviously his favorite. Joe chose a wooden armchair with a leather seat and back. After returning from her errand, Betsy sat on a love seat embroidered with roses opposite Joe. A small end table separated Joe from the captain. Sam, the captain's orderly, brought in a tray with the drinks.

"Thank you, Sam," Betsy said.

"You is welcome, missus," Sam said, and returned to the kitchen.

"Well, to the capture of all the renegade Apache," Willoughby said, raising his glass.

Joe joined the toast. Willoughby asked Joe about his background. As he responded, Joe saw that Betsy listened intently. Willoughby one-sidedly continued the conversation, telling Joe about where he had been and what battles he had fought. Sam came in with another round of drinks. As Willoughby rambled on Joe glanced occasionally toward Betsy. Each time, he noticed that she was not looking toward her husband but at him. Joe got the impression that Betsy Willoughby was trying to seduce him with her eyes. He looked away from her, attempting to keep his attention directed toward the captain. Oblivious of his wife's attraction to Joe Holly, Willoughby stared at the ceiling as he spoke.

After three rounds, Willoughby began slurring his words. "Lieutenant, I noticed you don't take advantage of your position. You don't have to cool your mount. Let a trooper do it. That's what they're here for."

Joe didn't respond to Willoughby's remark, and excused himself from the cocktail session. The captain remained seated as Betsy showed Joe to the door.

"Good night, Lieutenant Joe Holly," she said, taking his arm. "I look forward to seeing you again soon."

"Thank you, Mrs. Willoughby. I appreciate your kind hospitality."

Chapter Three

Two weeks later, Major Armbruster dispatched three companies to cover the waterholes along the Mexican border. Geronimo had raided the Peck Ranch in the Santa Cruz Valley, south of Tucson near the Mexican border and west of Camp Huachuca. He had murdered Peck's pregnant wife and infant son along with an acquaintance. The raiding party had captured Peck and his wife's niece. But believing Peck to be insane, the Indians turned him loose and headed south with the young girl to the Sierra Madres in Mexico.

The mission of the Camp Huachuca troops was to ensure that Geronimo and his raiders would not cross the border from Mexico into the United States.

Not a part of the chase after the renegade, Holly and Troop B found guarding water holes a boring assignment. Joe used the time to become well acquainted with his troopers, especially Corporal Mose Handley, an Alabama native, and the Apache scout called Frog Eyes.

One evening as B Troop bivouacked near a water hole, Holly asked Mose why he had joined the army. "I figured it was better than cowboyin' or choppin' cotton," Mose replied. "How come you to join, Lieutenant?"

"My father thought it would be best for me. He thought I was too happy-go-lucky to be a Maine horse farmer."

Frog Eyes, whose Apache name meant Man With Eyes of Eagle, was seated nearby. "I join to keep from getting hunted all the time. And, money buy whiskey," Frog Eyes remarked. "I am Arivaipa, not from clan of Geronimo or Chiricahua."

"I reckon we're all here for some reason or other," Joe said.

In the afternoon of the fifth day of the bivouac, Willoughby informed Joe about his plans to return to Camp Huachuca the following morning. "I don't want to get too far behind with the paperwork connected with my duties as financial officer of the post."

Just then, the soldier posted on lookout well above the spring feeding the water hole sounded the alarm. He had spotted four horsemen driving a herd of about fifty head of cattle from the south.

Willoughby ordered Joe to assemble the troopers in case the drovers might be Apache raiders. The riders turned out to be a rough-looking crew of Anglos. With the troop in formation near the water hole, the cattle, a mixed bunch of steers and heifers, hesitated. The nearest rider called out. "These cattle need to drink. Move outa the way. You people are too close to the water."

"Where are you coming from?" Willoughby demanded.

"Mexico," the same man answered. "Just get your troopers away from the waterhole."

"Lieutenant Holly," Willoughby said. "Move the men away."

Joe ordered the troopers to lead their mounts aside until he saw the cattle approach the water hole and begin drinking. When the cattle had gotten their fill, the drovers rode their horses to the water's edge, slackened their reins and let them drink. Willoughby motioned to Joe to bring the troopers back to their former position.

The rider who had spoken rode up to where Willoughby stood. "Those critters have been all day without water."

The captain noticed he had a scar across his left cheek and long curly hair springing from under his floppy old felt hat. "I must inquire what you are doing with them. Do you realize that Geronimo is on the loose again and may be heading this direction?"

"I bought these cattle from the Sierra Quebrada Ranch and am headin' for Tucson with 'em."

"Do you have any proof with you?"

"I got a bill of sale."

"Show me," Willoughby said.

The man reached into his shirt pocket, withdrew a folded piece of paper and leaned down to hand it to the captain. Willoughby unfolded the grimy sheet and read the handwritten scrawl. "Is Humberto Morales the former owner?"

"Sure is, Captain."

"This bill of sale says eighty head of steers. I counted fifty-seven as you drove them in."

"I have to go back for the others in a couple of months. They were too wild to put with these. I have to get them moving out, Captain."

"You'd better be on the lookout for Apaches. I can't escort you because I have orders to guard this water hole."

"See you around, Captain."

The drovers started their herd down the trail to Tucson. The steers filled with water and wanting rest were at first reluctant to leave the water hole. The drovers yelled and slapped the steers' rumps with reatas. Willoughby took Joe aside. "The leader of that bunch looks like he might be Curly Bill Brocius, the rustler and bandit."

"Why not detain him and the cattle?" Joe asked.

"When you are around here longer you will find out it doesn't pay to go looking for trouble, Lieutenant."

"We wouldn't have to go looking for trouble; it came right to the water hole."

"He had a bill of sale for the cattle," Willoughby said defensively.

"Did the bill of sale have a date on it?"

"You know, I never noticed."

"I'd bet a month's pay that the man who showed you the bill of sale signed it himself."

"Lieutenant Holly, some things are better left alone, and that's one of those things."

Puzzled, Joe moved off to think about just what kind of man Willoughby might be in a skirmish with the Indians.

The next morning, Willoughby and four troopers left for Camp Huachuca. Joe Holly was not sad to see the captain leave. When they were out of hearing, Frog

Eyes approached. "Now you know why the troopers call him 'chicken captain.' "

Joe looked at Frog Eyes and grinned.

The next morning, the lookout again yelled down that riders were approaching. Joe waited by the water hole with eight of the troopers, ready for the visitors. There were seven Mexicans. The obvious leader, a handsome man riding a good-looking gray stallion, held up his right hand in salutation. "Good morning," he said, using good English. "I am Ernesto Carbajal. We have tracked our stolen cattle here. Have you seen them?"

"They came through here yesterday," Joe said. "They showed the captain a bill of sale from a man named Humberto Morales."

"I'm acquainted with every cattleman in Sonora. I do not know a man named Humberto Morales. Those men are cattle thieves."

"I don't know what to tell you. The captain left. He didn't wish to detain the men. They said they were heading for Tucson."

"I will try to reach them before they reach Tucson. Of course, they are probably lying."

"Good luck to you, sir," Joe said, feeling both powerless and foolish under Willoughby's apparent ineffective command. He watched as the Mexicans watered their horses and took off in the direction the stolen herd had gone.

Soon after the troops had returned from the border, Joe received an announcement of a party at the commandant's house on the post. He noted that Captain Willoughby was on the guest list. It was an invitation, but from the commandant it was really an order. It was bad enough for Joe to be forced to work with Captain Arnold Willoughby; the prospect of socializing with the West Pointer was almost too much for him to take.

Even before the assignment to the border, Joe had learned that blond and beady-eyed Willoughby was thirty-three years old and very possessive of beautiful Betsy, ten years younger. Joe had overheard some of the enlisted men refer to Willoughby as the chicken captain. There had already been several incidents that made Joe distance himself from the man. Even before the incident with Curly Bill at the water hole, Joe understood why the enlisted men had dubbed their commander the chicken captain. The week before the troop rode out to the border, Joe had given a weekend pass to Mose Handley. Willoughby had rescinded it to have Mose work around his house. Joe had also been puzzled by Willoughby's reluctance to pursue a group of raiding Apaches farther than the foothills of the Dragoon Mountains. Remembering the grizzled sergeant's conversation about the Apache not wanting to make a stand and fight, Holly wondered if that was Willoughby's reasoning or if it was plain fear that caused his attitude.

There was also Betsy Willoughby. Holly found her attractive. But, married to the captain, she was not fair game in Joe's eyes. However, Betsy seemed to have other thoughts, and openly flirted with Joe at the frequent post parties over the two months he had been at Camp Huachuca. He found himself feeling extremely uncomfortable around the vivacious, red-haired beauty.

The parlor of the Armbrusters' house was crowded when Joe arrived. He apologized for his tardiness to the commandant and his wife. After making his way from the door to the refreshment table, Joe asked the Buffalo Soldier in charge of making drinks for a straight mescal. As he turned to mingle with the group, he faced Betsy Willoughby, dressed in a low-cut green gown, her eyes sparkling with delight at finding her target.

"Joe, please come outside with me. I need to speak to you alone."

"Mrs. Willoughby, I don't think that's wise," Joe replied.

"Don't worry about Arnold, he's off in the corner with his cronies."

Reluctantly, Joe followed Betsy Willoughby through the kitchen and out the backdoor into the yard where they were alone.

"Joe, I need to see you away from this awful place. I'll be in Tombstone alone next weekend. Meet me at the Grand Hotel Saturday evening."

"Mrs. Willoughby, I think that would be asking for a lot of trouble."

"Please stop calling me Mrs. Willoughby. I'm Betsy. I cannot bear being Mrs. Willoughby any longer. Can you possibly understand that I need you, Joe Holly?"

Suddenly she threw her arms around his neck and began kissing him fervently. Joe's back was to the door. Just then Captain Willoughby came running through the doorway and grabbed Joe by the shoulders, jerking him away from Betsy.

"What the hell are you doing kissing my wife, Lieutenant!" He roared like a wounded bull.

Joe stood wide-eyed with a shocked look on his face. "I'm not kissing your wife, Captain. She's kissing me."

Willoughby cocked his arm back and threw a punch at Joe Holly's head. But Joe ducked quickly and the blow did nothing but make the captain lose his balance. Automatically, Joe countered with a swift punch to the captain's midriff knocking him to the ground and leaving him gasping for air.

Joe stood over the captain, fists still clenched. Willoughby finally got his wind back.

"Lieutenant, you have struck a superior officer. You will face charges of conduct unbecoming an officer and a gentleman," Willoughby snarled between gasps. "I'll make sure you get drummed out of the army with dishonor. Whoever commissioned you must have been out of his mind."

He pushed himself up from the ground. As he brushed off his dress uniform, he snapped at his wife.

"Betsy, I think you had better join the others inside."

"Arnold, you go straight to hell. I'm going home," Betsy retorted.

"Then I'll join you. I'm not leaving you alone at home with this scoundrel of a lieutenant on the loose. How long has this been going on?"

"Arnold, shut up," Betsy said, with loathing in her voice. "Good night, Lieutenant Holly," she said, smiling coyly at Joe.

"Good night, Mrs. Willoughby," Joe said, touching his forehead with his right index finger, and turned toward the commandant's parlor for another drink of mescal.

Joe's head-throbbing, mescal hangover was worse after he was informed that he was restricted to his quarters pending a court-martial. He thought about his chances against the West Point officer. He knew that West Pointers always seemed to get the best deals in the army.

Double Vengeance

The commandant of the camp did not waste any time convening the court-martial for Joe's trial. When asked about who he wanted to represent him, Joe answered that he would represent himself. The entire situation made Joe Holly so angry he became reckless. He no longer cared about what the outcome of the court-martial might be.

The prosecuting officer was a West Pointer and, like Willoughby, a captain. The commandant, Major Ned Armbruster, was sitting in the middle chair behind the long table when Holly was escorted into the room. He stood at attention as the commandant began the session.

"Lieutenant Joseph Holly, you are charged with behavior unbecoming an officer and gentleman in the United States Army. You have chosen to represent yourself in this court-martial. How do you plead, Lieutenant?"

"Not guilty, sir."

"Captain Banner, as prosecutor in this case, you may make your opening statement at this time," the commandant said.

"Thank you, Major. The charges against Lieutenant Holly are the direct result of the lieutenant striking Captain Arnold Willoughby, the defendant's superior officer. This assault occurred when Captain Willoughby discovered the lieutenant embracing Mrs. Willoughby. The act of striking a superior officer cannot be tolerated in the United States Army. It is against Army regulations. It also lowers the morale of the enlisted ranks, setting a poor example for discipline. The matter of embracing a superior officer's wife, though not specifically against army regulations, is unbecoming an officer and a gentleman. The prosecution recommends punishment to the fullest extent possible at the discretion of this court."

The prosecutor returned to his desk and sat down, never giving so much as a glance toward Joe Holly.

"Lieutenant Holly," the major said. "It is your turn to make your opening statement."

Joe stood, pausing a few moments before speaking. He looked over to the prosecutor, turned his back on the assembled court-martial members, and glared angrily at Arnold Willoughby who was sitting at the rear of the room. He turned toward the commandant.

"Major, these charges against me are unwarranted. I was not kissing Mrs. Willoughby. She was kissing me! Furthermore, Captain Willoughby swung at me first. I was only defending myself. I am requesting Mrs. Willoughby's presence to testify in my behalf. She was the only witness."

"Since Captain Willoughby brought the charges against you, it would be irregular for his wife to testify on your behalf, Lieutenant Holly," the commandant said, sternly. "Do you have anything further to say?"

"No."

"I think 'no, sir' is more appropriate, Lieutenant."

Holly stood without saying another word. Then he returned to his chair.

"Captain Banner, does the prosecution have any witnesses it wishes to call?"

"Thank you, Major. I would like to call Captain Arnold Willoughby."

"Captain, will you please come forward?" Armbruster said.

Willoughby walked to the witness chair and sat down after the commandant gave him the oath, swearing to tell the truth.

"Captain Willoughby," Banner began. "How long have you been in the United States Army?"

"Fifteen years, since I was appointed to the United States Military Academy at West Point."

"In all those years has anyone ever struck you as Lieutenant Holly did on the occasion of the commandant's party?"

"Never."

"Please explain to the court-martial board how this incident came about."

"I had come from the study inside the commandant's home. I did not see Mrs. Willoughby so I inquired after her whereabouts from another officer. He informed me that she had left through the back door of the house. When I went through the doorway, I saw Lieutenant Holly embracing Mrs. Willoughby. I hurried over, put my hands on his shoulders to pull him away from my wife. He turned and struck me in the abdomen, knocking the breath out of me. I fell to the ground."

"How many times did the Lieutenant strike you, Captain?"

"Just once, but I was afraid he would continue his attack."

"Thank you, Captain. You may question the witness, Lieutenant Holly."

"I want to question Mrs. Willoughby, not her husband," Joe said, still seated in his chair.

"Lieutenant Holly," the Commandant admonished. "You have already been denied questioning Mrs. Willoughby."

Joe Holly stood up. "Colonel, this is not a fair trial. I have only one witness, and I have been denied asking her any questions. It is now my word against his, and I won't have a chance against a West Pointer."

"Lieutenant, you will refrain from judging the fairness of this court-martial board. If you have no one to question, the room will now be cleared to allow deliberations on this case."

Everyone, except the officers sitting behind the long table, left the room. Joe Holly walked slowly out to the parade ground in front of the headquarters building. The corporal assigned as his escort followed him. Walking toward him was Betsy Willoughby clad in a low-cut dress that clung to her curvaceous body.

"How is it going?" Betsy asked, as she stopped in front of Joe.

"They went after me and they got me. I wanted to call you as a witness, but they wouldn't allow it. That kiss you gave me sure has tossed me into a den of lions."

"I wish they had called me. I could have told them that my stupid husband deserved that punch you gave him. What a night that was. Arnold came close to striking me. I know I gave him good reason, but I'm tired of everything about the army except you."

"I wonder what I would do if I found my wife in some other man's arms."

Betsy looked away with an impatient look on her face. "Look, Joe. I don't know what's going to happen, but I still want to meet you in Tombstone as soon as you can get away from this horrible place."

"I guess I'll have to wait and see what happens when the court-martial is through with my hide. I think you should think about what might happen if your husband knew about you meeting me in Tombstone."

She waved her hand in the air as if chasing away a fly. "I'll get word to you somehow. Good luck."

"Thanks, Mrs. Willoughby. I'll need all the luck I can muster to come through this unscathed."

"God, Joe Holly, when are you going to call me Betsy?"

"I don't know."

"I hope soon," Betsy replied, coquettishly tilting her head. "And I hope we can meet in Tombstone."

Holly wasn't sure he wanted to see Betsy Willoughby in Tombstone. There wasn't a doubt in his mind that she was an attractive woman who would be fun to spend the night with, but she was married. He had been brought up to respect marriage and certainly not to chase after married women. However, Besty was chasing him. Holly did not know what to do about it.

The sergeant-at-arms called from the porch of the headquarters building. The court-martial board had reached its decision. Joe and the corporal left the parade ground and went into the building to discover what was in Joe's future. Joe felt himself become tense with anger as the commandant ordered him to stand at attention in front of the long table.

"Lieutenant Joseph Holly, you have been charged and tried by this court-martial board for behavior unbecoming an officer in the United States Army. Striking a superior officer cannot be tolerated. Therefore, this court-martial board has found you guilty as charged. Do you have any statement you would care to make at this time?"

Joe stood for a moment as all kinds of angry thoughts buzzed through his mind.

"Major Armbruster," Joe said, relaxing from standing at attention. "This court-martial board is a goddamn joke and you know it. You and your goddamn cronies have no sense of justice. You have lost any respect I might have had for you."

"Lieutenant Holly, that will be enough. Stand at attention when you address this court-martial board."

"Just get on with your railroading, Major. I can hear you just the way I am standing."

Major Armbruster stood, turned and huddled with the rest of the court-martial board. Once again, the other officers looked out over the audience impassively. Armbruster remained standing with a deep scowl on his face as he addressed Joe. "Lieutenant Holly, you leave me little choice. The board had decided to put you under post restriction for six months. However, you have just demonstrated that you are not fit to be an officer in the United States Army. As commandant of Camp Huachuca and judge advocate of this court-martial board, I order you drummed out of the army at sunrise, tomorrow morning. You will report accordingly. In the meantime you will be confined to the stockade. This court-martial board is adjourned."

Joe stood silently after the gavel thudded on the long table. Then he turned to the corporal.

"I reckon I can call you Mose now, Corporal Handley."

"You can call me anything you wants to, Lieutenant Holly."

"Well, Mose, best you and I get to the stockade. I wouldn't want you to get into trouble."

"Lieutenant Holly, I won't be gettin' in trouble. I got less than a week to go on my enlistment, an' this chile is puttin' on civilian clothes."

Their conversation continued as they ambled toward the stockade.

"What are you planning to do once you're out of the army, Mose?"

"I don't know. But I just made up my mind to get out."

"What caused you to decide that?"

" 'Cause I listened to what happened to you in there. You is a good man an' a good officer, Lieutenant. There ain't one of us Buffalo Soldiers that don't have a passel of respect for you."

"What happened to me won't necessarily happen to you, Mose. I remember the time down by the border when you said you joined the army because it was better than cowboyin' or chopping cotton."

"It's probably still better than choppin' cotton or cowboyin', but I ain't thinkin' 'bout neither. I just want to get shed a that chicken captain. I don't trust that man, and I sure don't like him. He's the army for me, so I is gettin' out."

"Well, Mose, I'll be out before you are. One more night and I'll be a civilian."

"What is you plannin' to do, Lieutenant?"

"First off, I'm going to get myself to Tombstone."

Moses Handley turned to Joe and grinned.

"I think I knows why, Lieutenant."

"Even though I didn't kiss Mrs. Willoughby?"

They reached the stockade. The guard opened the gate. Joe turned to Mose.

"I'll see you at sunrise, Mose."

"I be proud to see you, Lieutenant," he said, and left Joe in the custody of the soldier on duty.

Joe unbuckled the sheath holding his sabre and handed it to the guard.

"Lieutenant, I feels bad for you, suh," the guard said.

"Thank you, Trooper Jameson. But just think how nice it will be for me to be a civilian again."

"I gots two years before I can think 'bout bein' a civilian, suh."

"You'll make it fine, Trooper."

John Duncklee

Joe sauntered over to sit under the ramada in the middle of the stockade. There were two troopers sitting there in the shade. They rose when Joe approached, but he told them to remain seated. They chatted away the rest of the afternoon. Supper was beans with a small chunk of beef. Joe finished what was on his plate, and retired to his bunk in the cell made of adobe. It was not long before the fatigue from the day's happenings allowed him to fall asleep.

Chapter Four

Before early morning light, the guard brought Joe his breakfast of beef and beans. When he had finished eating, Joe ambled over to the gate, and watched the entire regiment begin assembling on the parade ground. A young lieutenant with two troopers marched stiffly over to the stockade. The guard opened the gate.

"Lieutenant Joseph Holly, I have been ordered to escort you to the parade ground for the ceremony," the officer said, solemnly. "Trooper Jameson, return the lieutenant's sabre."

Jameson went into the guard house by the stockade gate, retrieved Joe's sheathed sabre, and handed it to him. Joe buckled it to his belt.

"Lead on, Lieutenant Connors," Joe said.

Connors turned around in front of Joe. The two troopers stood behind.

"Forward march," Connors barked, and began marching to the parade ground.

Joe did not march. He walked with a sullen grin on his face. The commandant stood at attention facing the troop. Connors marched within four paces in front of Armbruster and barked, "Detail, halt." He did a right face, strutted forward two paces and did another right face. Another strut brought him parallel with the two troopers.

"Troopers, about face," he barked again. "Forward, march."

Ten paces behind Joe, Connors halted the troopers, had them execute another about-face. Then he marched over to stand in front of the armed escort.

With a sarcastic twinkle in his eyes, Joe looked straight into the commandant's eyes as the major nodded to the sergeant standing at attention in front of the troop.

"Drummer, sound off," the sergeant ordered.

Joe heard the drum begin to roll as the drummer began beating with his drumsticks. Armbruster stepped toward Joe, took a small penknife from his pocket, and reached over to Joe's shoulders to loosen the threads holding the golden yellow embroidered lieutenant's stripes to his uniform.

"Try not to draw any more blood, Major," Joe sneered.

"Hold your tongue, Lietenant Holly. This is a serious business."

Joe held the smirk on his mouth as the commandant severed the threads on the back of the bars, and ripped them off. The cloth insignia dropped to the ground at Joe's feet.

Next, after pocketing his penknife, Armbruster grabbed Joe's sabre and unsheathed it. Stepping backward a pace, he leaned over, and snapped the blade across his left knee. Coming to attention again, he tossed the broken sabre aside. The drumming stopped.

"You are now a civilian, Mister Holly."

Joe looked straight into the major's eyes and spat on the ground in front of him.

"Lieutenant Connors, escort Mr. Holly to the stockade. Holly, you will remain in the stockade until further notice."

"Wait just a minute, Major Armbruster. I'm no longer in the army. You have no jurisdiction over me now," Joe snarled.

"I am commandant of this camp, Holly. As long as you are on this post you are under my jurisdiction. Sergeant, dismiss the troop!"

Joe unbuckled the sheath that had once held his sabre, and tossed it onto the snapped halves on the ground.

Lieutenant Connors escorted a very angry Joe Holly back to the stockade. Trooper Jameson opened the gate after Connors explained the commandant's orders. Joe ambled through the gate over to the ramada.

"It looks like the good major wants to keep feeding me," he said to the two troopers sitting under the ramada as they had the day before.

Arnold Willoughby stopped at his house before reporting back to his morning's work of inspecting the horses after his troopers had cleaned and groomed them. Betsy sat at the kitchen table sipping coffee.

"Well," Willoughby said to his wife. "Your smart aleck Lieutenant is now a civilian and got himself thrown back in the stockade. I hope Ned keeps him there for a year."

"How can the major put Joe Holly in the stockade when he's a civilian?"

"The idiot spat on the ground in front of him after the drumming-out ceremony ended."

"I think Joe Holly could use a good civilian lawyer," Betsy said.

"He will pay hell getting a civilian lawyer to come way out here. What are your plans for today? Are you still going to Tombstone shopping tomorrow?"

Betsy Willoughby suddenly knew what she had to do. Joe Holly needed a lawyer badly and she would go to Tombstone immediately and hire one.

"I changed my plans, Arnold. I'm going to go shopping today. I will spend the night and come home tomorrow."

"Will Sara be going to town with you?"

"I don't know yet."

Willoughby leaned over and gave his wife a peck on her cheek.

"Try not to spend too much of my pay, dear," he said, and gave out a false-sounding chuckle.

"Arnold, be a dear man and have my buggy readied."

"I'll have the troopers bring it around in fifteen minutes."

"That's all right. I'll get it at the stables."

Willoughby left the house and proceeded to the stable area. Betsy changed into her town clothes and hurried over to get the buggy. The horse was harnessed and two troopers were hitching him to the vehicle as she arrived. One of the troopers put her overnight valise into the back and helped Betsy step into the buggy. She thanked the men and urged the horse into a trot to the main gate of the post. As she passed through the gate, Betsy waved at the guard and kept the horse moving.

It was late afternoon when she arrived at the office of Horatio Upton, attorney at law. She climbed down from the buggy, tied the horse to the hitchrack, and went to the front door of the lawyer's office. Upton answered her knock and opened the door.

"What may I do for you, Madam?" he asked.

"I have an important matter that needs attending to. It demands your immediate attention."

"Tell me what this is all about, Mrs. . . ."

"Willoughby. Betsy Willoughby. I live at Camp Huachuca. There is a man named Joe Holly who was drummed out of the army at sunrise today. I am told that right after the commandant stripped his rank from his shoulders and broke his sabre, Joe Holly spat on the ground in front of the major. He had Joe thrown in the stockade. I want to hire you to get Joe Holly released from the stockade. His court-martial was a travesty of justice."

"What were the charges against him?"

"Striking a superior officer. My husband."

"Getting Mr. Holly released doesn't present much of a problem. He's no longer under army jurisdiction. It sounds to me as if the commandant may be overstepping his authority. I will explain the situation to the judge in the morning. I see no reason why the judge wouldn't grant me a court order. I'll research the law on this to make sure.

"I can probably take care of Mr. Holly's release, but I will have to go to the camp."

"I appreciate this very much, Mr. Upton. When shall I meet you in the morning?"

"The judge is an early riser. I can see him before

breakfast. I will meet you here at eight o'clock."

Betsy left the lawyer's office and drove the buggy to the livery stable. She ate supper at the Oriental Cafe and Bar. By the time she finished her meal, she wanted to go to bed and retired to her room in the Grand Hotel.

After an early breakfast. Betsy went to the livery stable, and had the buggy hitched up for the trip back to the camp. Upton had everything in order by eight o'clock and was ready to leave when Betsy drove up to his office in the buggy.

"Good morning, Mrs. Willoughby."

"Good morning to you, Mr. Upton. We need to get going if I am to get you back here before midnight."

Placing his leather briefcase in the buggy, Upton climbed in and sat next to Betsy. She reined the horse around, and headed the buggy for Camp Huachuca at a trot.

The guard at the main gate to the camp waved them through after recognizing Mrs. Willoughby. She stopped the buggy in front of the commandant's head-quarters. A trooper came off the porch and tied the horse to the long hitchrack. Betsy and Upton entered the building. A trooper sitting at a desk in the foyer rose at her approach and asked what her business was.

"We are here to see the commandant."

"One moment, please. I will see if he is available."

The trooper went over to the door marked COMMAN-DANT in gold-leaf. He knocked softly. The voice within said, "Enter."

The trooper opened the door and informed the major that he had visitors.

"Show them in, Trooper," the commandant said.

The soldier motioned to Betsy and Upton that they could enter the office.

"Why, Betsy, what a nice surprise," the major said.

"You may not think it is such a nice surprise when you learn why I am here, Major Armbruster. I would like you to meet Horatio Upton. He is Joe Holly's lawyer."

"How do you do, sir," Upton said. "I have a court order from Judge Langsworth for the release of Joseph Holly from your stockade. I hope this will not create any problem for you, Major."

Upton handed the paper to Armbruster, who read its contents.

"I see no reason why I should comply with this, Mr. Upton. I am commandant of this post. Therefore, I have jurisdiction over anyone who may be here."

"I'm sorry to inform you, Major, you have no jurisdiction over civilians who have not committed any criminal act. Spitting on the ground is not a criminal act."

Armbruster turned in his chair and looked out the window as he tapped his index finger on the desktop. After contemplating the situation, he turned back to face the lawyer. "I suppose it would be best if I did release Holly. I doubt if time in the stockade will teach him anything. However, I insist that he be in your custody until he is away from this post."

"That is perfectly agreeable, Major. And thank you for your cooperation."

"I will send word to the stockade. You may pick up Mr. Holly in fifteen minutes."

Chapter Five

Joe hurried to the bachelor officers' quarters, packed his belongings, including his Colt .44 revolver, into his warbag and returned to the entrance of the stockade. Betsy drove up and stopped the buggy.

"Do you have anything you want to get from your quarters, Joe?"

"I've retrieved everything I want, Mrs. Willoughby. If you'll be kind enough to wait until I get my horse saddled, I'll join you shortly."

"We'll be happy to wait for you, Joe,"

Joe tossed his warbag into the buggy and hurried over to the stable area. After saddling his sorrel gelding, he returned to the buggy and tied the halter rope to the frame at the rear of the vehicle. Climbing aboard the buggy, he sat down, wedging himself in next to Horatio Upton. Betsy slapped the reins on the rump of the buggy horse.

"I heard what you two did, and I sure appreciate it,"

Joe said, as they headed toward the main gate of the post.

"Well, Joe Holly, I couldn't stand to see you rot in that horrible place. You are now a civilian and free of the army. How does it feel?"

"I haven't had time to figure that out," Joe said. "I know I'm glad to be away from it."

Betsy waved to the guard at the main gate, and kept the horse at a trot most of the way to Tombstone. When they arrived an hour after sundown the horse was well lathered. She drove directly to the hotel where the desk clerk carried her valise and Joe Holly's warbag into the lobby. Then, at the livery stable, she instructed the horse handler to cool her horse before putting him up for the night. From the way people attended Betsy, it became obvious to Joe that she was a frequent visitor to Tombstone.

Horatio Upton took his leave and walked to his office with his briefcase. Betsy took Joe Holly's arm and began leading him toward the Oriental Cafe and Bar.

"I'm going to buy us a drink and then we can get some supper, Joe Holly. This is an important night for both of us. We are both free."

"You are not free, Mrs. Willoughby. But thanks to you, I am."

"I feel free. That's all that really matters, isn't it?"

"I don't know about that," Joe said, wondering what he had gotten himself into. He had never met a more aggressive woman than Betsy Willoughby. He puzzled about his feelings toward her and decided it must be a certain amount of fear.

As usual, the Oriental was doing a brisk business, mostly with miners, a few cowboys and merchants lining the long bar. Joe recognized the bartender by

49

his twisted, black handlebar mustache. He stood ready to serve the next customer watching for anyone who raised his hand or made eye contact for another drink.

Joe and Betsy sat at a small table near the entrance. The bar waitress, a short woman in her thirties with her hair done in ringlets hanging down in front of her ears, had just finished serving six poker players seated at a large round table in the far corner. She went quickly to take the couple's drink orders.

"I'll have a glass of your best brandy," Betsy said.

"Tequila," Joe mumbled, still wondering what he was going to do about Betsy.

Having been in the Oriental Cafe before, Joe glanced around at the customers without recognizing anyone, although some of the faces were familiar. The waitress brought their drinks. Joe turned his attention back to Betsy as she raised her glass of brandy toward him.

"Here's to our first time alone together," she toasted.

Joe lifted his tequila glass and touched hers.

"You are a very attractive woman, Mrs. . . . uh . . . Betsy. I'm sure you will someday find a man who will fit your fancy."

"I already have. His name is Joe Holly."

Joe tossed the tequila down his throat in one gulp.

"You don't know me very well, Betsy. And, I don't know much about you, except that you were good enough to get me out of that stockade."

"If it will make you feel better, I'll tell you that I was born and raised in Baltimore. My father was an army officer, turned three terms as mayor. Arnold was a friend of my father's while they were in the army. After Father came home, Arnold would come to visit. He was stationed in Washington at the time. My father was killed by some thugs hired by a scoundrel who wanted to take over the city of Baltimore."

Betsy took a swallow of her brandy.

"I missed my father very much. Arnold asked me to marry him. I guess it was both the uniform and missing my father that made me say yes. It wasn't long after we were married that Mother took sick with pneumonia and died. When Arnold was transferred to Camp Huachuca, I realized that I had made a big mistake by marrying him."

"What made you come to that conclusion?"

"Arnold turned out to be boring and abusive. I had to do everything to advance his career in the army. That meant entertaining officers I couldn't stand. I also came to hate the army, especially having to live at Camp Huachuca. It's way out in the wilderness and nothing like Baltimore. There are no plays, no concerts, no culture at all. And the food is common and tasteless. I hate it out here, and I will do anything to escape."

"Are you going back to Baltimore?"

"Heavens, no. I have no one left there. I just want to be with you, Joe Holly."

"Well, Betsy, I don't know what I'm going to do. I know horses and the army. I can't go back to Maine. As it is, my father will be furious when he hears I have been drummed out of the army. Besides, I would never go back and live with him."

The waitress brought two more drinks. They continued their conversation with Joe telling Betsy about his youth on the horse farm in Maine.

Just as they were finishing their second round, Lieutenant Connors and another named Falvey, a recent arrival to the post, came in. Connors glanced around, not searching for anything, just sizing up the bar and its customers. When his eyes landed on Betsy and Joe Holly, he walked over to the table. His left eyebrow was raised, and he had an evil-looking smirk on his face.

"Well, well, if it isn't Mr. Holly drinking with the captain's wife," Connors said. "The captain will be interested that the charges he brought against you are reinforced."

"Connors, I think you had better find another place to go," Joe said, rising to his feet.

Connors ignored Joe and turned toward Betsy.

"Mrs. Willoughby, do you realize you are sitting at a table with a man who was drummed out of the army?"

Joe could feel himself begin to tremble with anger.

"Lieutenant Connors," Betsy said as if she were talking to a child. "Why don't you be a good little boy and mind your own business."

"I am minding my own business, Mrs. Willoughby. I am loyal to your husband, as any officer in the army should be. Your friend Holly is a disgrace to the uniform."

Joe's first punch landed in the same place on Connors's stomach where he had hit Captain Willoughby. Connor gasped and bent over. Joe's next blow, an uppercut, struck Connors's jaw, and the lieutenant sprawled on the floor, lying on his back. Joe looked down at his victim and saw the blood trickling out of the side of his mouth.

The mustached bartender was quick to dash from behind the bar, but was too late to stop the fracas. Connors was unconscious.

"I don't know what is going on between you soldiers, but I don't allow fighting in here."

"The lady and I were enjoying our drinks when these two came in looking for a fight," Joe said.

The bartender turned to Falvey, who was standing with his mouth still open in surprise.

"Get your friend out of here, and don't come back until you sober up."

"We are sober," Falvey argued.

"Then don't bother to ever come back," the bartender said firmly, and he went back behind the long bar.

The conversation at the bar had temporarily hushed when Connors had hit the floor. Now it resumed as if nothing had happened. Falvey reached down and tried to lift Connors to his feet. Joe stepped over and helped Flavey drag the lieutenant out the door, where they left the unconscious form sitting on the boardwalk leaning against the board-and-batten building. Joe went back inside and rejoined Betsy at their table.

"Wow, Joe Holly, you don't fool around."

"I reckon I lost my temper. That priggish bastard had no call to talk to you like that."

"What he doesn't realize is that if he says anything to Arnold about you and me, Arnold will be embarrassed and angry with him more than anyone else."

"You know him better than I do," Joe said.

"Now that Connors is out of the way, why don't we have another round?" Betsy offered, and caught the waitress's eye.

Joe began to feel the effects of the tequila and noticed that Betsy was laughing more than usual. By the time he had finished the third tequila he had begun to relax. He also began to lose his misgivings about being with a married woman.

They went to García's cafe, where they had a supper

of carne machaca and frijoles. The dried jerky spiced with chili and tomatillos satisfied their hunger for food, but with another tequila, Joe found himself hungering for Betsy Willoughby. Sitting next to him, Betsy smiled coquettishly as she kept rubbing his leg with her knee under the table.

After entering Betsy's hotel room on the first floor of the Grand, Joe sat down on the bed as Betsy lifted the chimney from the coal-oil lamp and lit the wick. Replacing the chimney, she adjusted the flame so that the lamp gave out just enough light to see. Then she went to the window and closed the shades.

Suddenly Joe felt the fear surge through him. "I don't think this is a good idea," he said.

Betsy glanced at him and smiled. Joe watched from the bed as she unbuttoned her dress, slipped it over her shoulders, and let it fall to the floor. When she had cast off her undergarments Joe couldn't take his eyes away from her naked body.

"I think we should wait until you're no longer a married woman."

Betsy ignored him. "You have been saying all evening that you want to get rid of your uniform. May I help you with the buttons?"

With the shades still closed, the room was almost dark when Joe opened his eyes the next morning. He looked over at the sleeping Betsy next to him, and marveled at the ecstasy they had experienced with one another. She opened her eyes, put her arms around him and pulled him closer toward her.

"Joe Holly, you are some man," she said, and closed her eyes again.

Feeling her lithe body next to him again made Joe's passion return. The thought of breakfast didn't occur to either Joe or Betsy, and both lapsed back into sleep after making love again.

Awakened by hard knocking at the door to the room, Joe bolted out of bed in a groggy half sleep. Betsy sat up quickly. The rapping of knuckles on the door sounded again.

"Betsy, I know you're in there. I must talk to you!" Arnold exclaimed.

Joe had already jumped into his uniform trousers and was buttoning his tunic.

"I have nothing to say to you, Arnold," Betsy answered. "Please go away and leave me alone."

With his tunic buttoned up, Joe pulled on his boots.

"Betsy, I rode all the way into Tombstone to talk to you, so please open the door."

Joe grabbed his warbag, opened the window quietly, and tossed it out to the ground. He darted over to Betsy, and gave her a quick kiss on the lips.

"Bye," he whispered.

"Come back when he's gone," Betsy whispered in return.

"Betsy, please be reasonable," Willoughby pleaded. "Open the door and we can sit down to talk this all out."

Joe jumped from the window to the ground outside, a distance of three feet. He tossed his warbag onto his shoulder, and hustled down the side of the building to the boardwalk.

"Arnold, you'll have to wait until I get some clothes on."

"All right, but hurry, Betsy."

She went to the window and gently shut it. After

dressing, she went to the door, unlocked it and sat down on the bed.

"The door's unlocked, Arnold. You may come in now."

Arnold opened the door at once. He walked in and closed the door behind him.

"My God, Betsy, we need to work this out somehow. Everyone at Camp Huachuca seems to know that you brought that goddamn Holly into town with you."

"Arnold, can't you understand that I'm tired of you and our marriage?"

"You're being stubborn, Betsy. Think about my career!"

"You and your career have always come first with you, Arnold. I'm somewhere down your list of considerations. I was a good-looking woman to have on your arm at the commandant's parties. No more," Betsy barked.

For the first time since he entered the room, Arnold looked at the very disheveled bed, blankets and sheets nearly pulled off the mattress.

"You must have had someone in bed with you. Who was it, that goddamn Holly?"

"Why don't you just leave, Arnold. You're boring me, as usual."

Arnold's face turned crimson with rage. He swung his clenched fist at Betsy's face and struck her on the left cheek. Betsy fell back on the bed and curled up, sobbing.

"You're nothing but a goddamn whore, Betsy. I'm going to find that scum Holly and teach him a lesson!" Arnold said, and left the room, slamming the door behind him.

Betsy got up from the bed, went to the dresser, and

poured some water from the pitcher into the ceramic basin. She took a washcloth, and splashed her face. After drying it with a towel, she looked in the mirror over the dresser to inspect her bruised cheek.

"That bastard," she mumbled.

As soon as she had combed her hair, powdered her cheeks and straightened her dress, she left the hotel to try to find Joe and warn him that Arnold was looking for him. She hoped she would find him before Arnold did. It was not that she was afraid Joe would be hurt. She wanted to keep him from getting into any more trouble.

Separately, Arnold and Betsy looked in the various saloons along Allen Street. Joe had gone directly to a dry goods store to buy some civilian clothes. He chose a pair of heavy denim trousers and a sturdy denim work shirt, and went into the back room of the store to change out of his uniform. After looking at the various beaver felt hats, he removed the gold braided band from his army hat, deciding to wear it instead of spending any more money than he had to.

With his warbag on his shoulder and his Colt .44 six-shooter in its holster on his right hip, Joe left the store after telling the proprietor that he no longer needed his uniform and had left it in the back room. As he walked along the boardwalk on the east side of Allen Street he thought about his taking up with a married woman and decided to find a hotel room of his own.

Before finding a hotel, he spotted Arnold Willoughby leaving the Oriental Cafe. Joe tried to duck down a side street to avoid any trouble with the captain, but, in spite of his different clothes, Willoughby recognized Joe Holly.

"Holly, I've been looking for you!" Willoughby exclaimed.

"Looks like you found me, captain. So what?"

"I'm going to teach the lesson you didn't learn from your court-martial."

Joe let the warbag fall to the ground as he watched Willoughby reach for his revolver. Quickly, Joe had his .44 in hand and before Willoughby could get off a shot, he sent a slug into the captain's shoulder. Willoughby spun around and fell, dropping his revolver as he hit the ground. Joe reholstered his weapon, picked up his warbag, and crossed the street, making his way to the Crystal Palace.

Just as he was entering the saloon, Sheriff Behan confronted him.

"Mister, I'm going to have to put you under arrest for not only wearing a firearm in Tombstone, but using it as well."

"I was only defending myself against Captain Willoughby. He was pulling down on me."

Willoughby had gotten himself off the ground and came up, scuffing the dusty street with his boots and holding his shoulder with his neckerchief over his wound. Dirt splotched his uniform.

"I want this bastard arrested and charged with attempted murder, Sheriff."

"Captain, I am arresting this man, but not for attempted murder. He only disobeyed our firearms ordinance. I saw what happened."

"The captain disobeyed the ordinance, too," Joe said.

"The ordinance doesn't pertain to army personnel," Behan stated. "But I can order you to leave town. So, Captain, you get back to Camp Huachuca before you cause any more trouble here in my town."

Attracted by the crowd, Betsy pushed her way through and stood next to Sheriff Behan. Having heard the conversation between Behan and Joe, she edged her way closer toward the sheriff. "I'd like to put up bail for Mr. Holly, Sheriff."

"You'll have to do that over at the jail."

"Betsy, you fool," Arnold blurted out. "Let the sonofabitch rot. He shot me."

"You're lucky he didn't kill you, Arnold," Betsy replied.

Joe surrendered his .44 to the sheriff. Behan took Joe by the arm, and led him away from the small crowd, which was dispersing. Betsy followed alongside Joe.

When they were inside the sheriff's office, Behan returned Joe's .44.

"Look, I saw what happened out there. I'm not really arresting you, but keep your firearms in your warbag when you're in Tombstone. That captain comes to town and thinks he owns it. Why did that fight start?"

"The captain is my husband, Sheriff," Betsy said. "He's very jealous of Mr. Holly and me being friends."

She pointed to her cheek.

"See that bruise? The captain struck me in my hotel room a short while ago."

"Where's your uniform, Mr. Holly?"

"I left it back at the dry goods store."

"Got out of the army?"

"Drummed out for hitting that captain in his stomach."

"Well, you probably ought to stay clear of him."

"I tried, but he saw me before I could get away. If that's all, I reckon I'll head back to the Crystal Palace where I was going to have a drink," Holly said.

"That sounds like a good idea, Joe," Betsy said.

"I'd be careful as long as that captain's in town. I can't take his weapon away," Behan commented.

"Well, Sheriff, I'm not worried. He'd have quite a time shooting with my slug in his shoulder. I'd bet a drink that he's already on his way back to the post surgeon."

Joe and Betsy left the sheriff's office and went to the Crystal Palace. Joe put his warbag next to his chair at the table they found near the rear of the saloon. Joe ordered a brandy for Betsy and a tequila for himself.

"Betsy, I think I'll have to keep an eye out for that husband of yours. He's bound to come back looking for me."

"I wouldn't worry about Arnold. He's really a coward, basically. I don't know how he made it as far as captain in the army."

"Coward or not, I've seen men backed into a corner before."

"Let's forget about Arnold and talk about us, Joe."

"What about us? You're a married woman and like I said, I want no trouble from your husband."

"I'm planning to divorce Arnold Willoughby."

"When?"

"We have a sort of business arrangement. I must wait until I have more money."

"What kind of business are you and Arnold running?"

"I really can't tell you about it. Just be patient. I'll have enough money to buy us a horse ranch complete with horses."

"I'm not sure I want that arrangement," Joe said. "All

I know is that during that court-martial something inside me snapped. I can't explain it except that I suddenly felt a deep anger. I still haven't resolved these feelings. For example, I almost aimed to kill your husband instead of wounding his shoulder."

"Who are you angry at?"

"Betsy, I'm angry at a lot of things, but most of all I find myself hating the army. That trial was a mockery I can't forget. I'm happy to be away from all that, but I would have preferred to have left the army my own way."

"I feel responsible for all your troubles, but I just had to kiss you."

"You're not responsible for any of my troubles because I don't have troubles. All I have is anger toward the army. I can't bear boot-lickers like Connors or pompous asses like your husband. I was almost in a rage when I knocked Connors out. I was never like that before the court-martial."

"Time is a great healer, Joe. I'll make you feel better back in our room."

"Betsy, it's your room. I'll be in another hotel."

"Which one?"

"I don't know yet."

"What about us, Joe Holly?"

"You must remember that you're a married woman."

"Joe, I intend to get a divorce as soon as our business is finished."

Joe found himself in a dilemma. On one hand he wanted Betsy Willoughby in bed. On the other, he had no desire to make any long-term commitment to her. He had also begun to wonder what type of business the Willoughbys carried on.

John Duncklee

After two more shots of tequila, he accompanied Betsy to her room in the Grand Hotel. The idea of making love to her was too much for him to resist, despite his puritanical New England upbringing.

Chapter Six

The next morning, after Betsy left Tombstone to drive her buggy back to the camp, Joe headed to García's café for breakfast. Surprised and pleased to see Frog Eyes and Mose Handley sitting at a table, he greeted them warmly. "It's good to see you two. What brings you to Tombstone?"

Mose rose from his chair when Joe approached. Frog Eyes remained seated. "We is done free from the army, Lieutenant," Mose said, and grinned. "My enlistment is done with an' Froggy, he done quit scoutin'. Sit down and have some coffee."

Joe enjoyed chatting with his friends. Mose had no idea what he wanted to do, but had thought about being a cowboy again. Frog Eyes said that he needed money to buy ten horses for his girlfriend's father. It was the price he had to pay before he could marry the old man's daughter. "Something is bound to turn up," Joe said. "If I had the money, I would get into the horse business." But not with Betsy, he thought.

The three friends continued to meet each day at García's cafe for breakfast until Betsy returned to Tombstone three days later. She arrived at sunset. By the time she had left her buggy at the livery stable, darkness had flooded the town. The gaslights flickering in the gentle breeze gave the many pedestrians plenty of light as they made the rounds of the many saloons. Joe was surprised to see her at the door of his room at the Grand Hotel. "What are doing back here so soon, Betsy?" he asked, wishing he had followed his original plan to find a room in a different hotel.

"Actually, I have an errand to run in the morning, but I wanted to spend the night with you."

"Suppose your husband decides to ride into town looking for you again?"

"He won't. He's too busy with all his paperwork. Arnold won't even miss me. Anyway, he thinks I'm here to buy a new dress for the commandant's party next week."

"What's the errand you came all the way into town for?"

"Strictly business."

"I'm very curious as to this business of yours."

"Joe, I'm sorry, but I can't tell you. Please stop asking questions. Besides, I'm hungry. Have you had supper yet?"

"I was thinking about it when you knocked on my door. Where would you like to eat?"

"Anywhere is fine with me. I'm starved."

As they entered the restaurant and saloon next to the hotel, Joe glanced around to see if any familiar cavalry officers might be there. Sitting at a table toward the rear, Joe remarked, "I haven't seen many men from the camp in town lately."

"You probably won't see them for a month. Arnold said that the payroll wagon is delayed again because it was robbed north of Tucson."

"This is no country for a paymaster. If the Apaches don't raid, the bandits do."

"Arnold said that the troopers aren't happy with the pay situation."

"I imagine the officers aren't too joyful either."

They finished supper, including several drinks. Back in the hotel room, Betsy quickly undressed and watched from the bed as Joe took off his clothes. He slid in next to her, lustfully took her into his arms and mashed his lips against hers. Betsy's passion hovered as she gave herself to him completely. All thought vanished from Joe's mind as he felt himself explode ecstatically inside her. She moaned out of control as she joined him.

Awakening at dawn, Betsy had dressed before Joe opened his eyes. He watched as she combed out her hair in front of the mirror on the wall. "You beat me out of bed," he said.

"I didn't want to disturb you."

"Aren't you planning on going somewhere this early?"

"I have my errand to run."

"Are you coming back after your errand?"

"I might as well go back to the post. My errand is on the way."

"Why does your husband let you drive into town alone? There are bandits all over the territory."

"I'm not afraid of bandits, and Arnold got tired of

arguing with me about me not wanting an escort every time I drive to Tombstone."

"You seem like you can pretty well take care of yourself. Wait until I get dressed, and we can go for some breakfast," Joe suggested.

"I suppose that would be best. I want to get back around noontime."

Joe heaved himself out of bed and was quickly ready to escort Betsy to García's for breakfast. Except for three miners, the place was empty of clientele. Watching Betsy devour the chorizo and eggs, Joe knew she was in a hurry. He continued wondering about this important errand she had and the nature of the business she, and probably Arnold Willoughby, carried on. He had finished half his meal when Betsy took a last sip of coffee. "Joe, I hope you'll excuse me rushing off, but I must be going."

"When will I see you again?" Joe asked as he rose from his chair.

"I'm not sure, but I'll find you."

"Aren't you forgetting to buy the dress that Arnold thinks you came to town for?"

"He never pays any attention to what I wear."

"Well, good luck with your errand, and have a safe trip back to Camp Huachuca."

"Thank you, Joe; for breakfast, for everything."

He stood up, leaned over and kissed her, and she left the restaurant. While finishing eating the chorizo and eggs, Joe pondered a question: If the Willoughbys had a business together, why did she have to come to town under the false pretense of buying a new dress for the commandant's party?

After paying the bill at García's, Joe made his way to the livery stable. As he trudged through an alley, he

spotted Betsy heading toward the road leading south-
west from town. He quickened his pace, arrived at the
stable and went about saddling the sorrel gelding as
quickly as possible. After stopping at the hotel momentarily to get his Colt .44 from his room, he once again
mounted and proceeded in the direction Betsy had
gone.

For a mile, the road headed straight toward the
Tombstone Hills. As he trotted the sorrel out of town
he saw the tracks made by the buggy, but it was nowhere in sight. Following the tracks, Joe kept the gelding at a trot wondering why he couldn't see the buggy
ahead. When he came to a side road turning off to the
north, he discovered why he had not caught up to the
buggy. The wheel tracks told him that Betsy had turned
off. Realizing that this road led to the Clanton ranch,
he reined in the sorrel and pondered the situation.
"What kind of business could Betsy possibly have with
those outlaws?" he mumbled to himself.

He urged the sorrel back to a trot. The road curved
around some low hills, then crossed a wash. Judging
that he might be close to the ranch headquarters, Joe
slowed the horse to a walk. Spotting the buggy a quar-
ter mile away heading for the ranch buildings, he reined
the sorrel into the trees bordering the wash. When he
arrived parallel to the buildings and one hundred yards
distant, he dismounted and tied the sorrel to a mesquite
tree. Glad that enough bushes grew there to offer him
plenty of cover, he crouched as he walked carefully toward the Clanton ranch headquarters.

The house and cook shack had been built on a mesa.
Joe crept closer, thankful he was downwind. He hoped
that the inevitable ranch dogs would not pick up his
scent. Betsy had just pulled into the yard when he hid

himself in a small cluster of mesquite. A man stepped out of the door as Betsy stopped the buggy. "Ya got some news for us, Mrs. Willoughby?" the man asked.

Being downwind from them, Joe could easily hear the conversation.

"The news is not good, Mr. Clanton. The payroll wagon has been delayed for a month."

"What's the matter, the 'paches given 'em hell?"

"My husband said it was robbed north of Tucson. That's all I know. I will be back as soon as I find out when it's scheduled and what road they intend to take."

"We'll be here, Mrs. Willoughby."

Without any more conversation, Betsy reined the buggy horse around and left the ranch headquarters. Joe waited until the man went inside again before he began his crouching walk back to the sorrel. All the way, he found it difficult to believe that Betsy and Arnold Willoughby were in cahoots with some of the worst outlaws in the Arizona Territory.

Untying his horse from the mesquite tree, Joe waited to be sure Betsy had gone far ahead. After mounting, he rode the sorrel across country, away from the ranch road. At the main road to the camp, he saw the buggy wheel tracks leave the ranch road and and head for Camp Huachuca. Joe rode back to Tombstone still amazed at what he had learned. "Too bad they drummed me out," he muttered. "I've solved the mystery of who's giving the outlaws their information about the payroll wagons, and they will never find out; at least not from me."

All the way back to Tombstone, Joe pondered the situation. Should the army discover that the Willoughbys were involved with the payroll robbers, Betsy would find herself in a federal prison along with her husband. On the other hand, the only way the army would ever get wise to their involvement would be if the army captured the outlaws and learned the details from them. But that possibility seemed remote since the gunmen always ambushed the payroll wagons with no evidence left behind.

Leaving the sorrel gelding at the livery stable, Joe decided to satisfy his hunger at García's cafe. Frog Eyes and Mose had just finished their meals when he arrived and joined his two friends.

"What have you two been doing today?" Joe asked.

"I got me a job cowboyin'," Mose answered.

"That sounds like progress," Joe said.

"I got to go to the ranch tomorrow," Mose continued.

"Where's the ranch?"

"Mistah Gray's ranch out in the Chiricahuas."

"I hope the job works out well for you, Mose. You are damn good with horses."

"I knows cows a bit too. Ol' Mose will do anything what keeps him from choppin' cotton."

Frog Eyes did not enter the conversation, but Joe could tell by the smile that crept onto his face that he was happy for Mose.

After finishing supper at García's, Joe wished Mose luck with his new occupation. "We'll probably see you once in a while. Tombstone is still the nearest town with girls."

"I don't knows when I'll get to town, but I hope you is here," Mose said.

Frog Eyes agreed and said good night to his two friends.

Deep in thought, Joe ambled over to the Crystal Palace. Standing at the bar with a shot of tequila, mulling the situation over in his mind, he still found it difficult to believe that Betsy and Arnold Willoughby worked together giving information about payroll wagons to a bunch of outlaws. In some ways he believed that Arnold might be capable of such criminal activity. But the thought of him sending Betsy into the robber's ranch made his hatred for the chicken captain increase.

Joe found it difficult to get to sleep because his mind still concentrated on the payroll wagon situation. As he sat on the edge of the bed, he began thinking about a plan and decided to approach Frog Eyes with it after breakfast.

Rising early, Joe rubbed the sleep from his eyes, splashed some water on his face and dressed while pondering the intricacies of the idea he wanted to present to Frog Eyes. He felt that his plan could work if everything went smoothly. Of course, some parts might prove difficult and maybe make the procedure impossible to manage.

Waiting for Frog Eyes at a table in García's, Joe sipped at the hot, black coffee thinking about solutions to the weak part of his plan. His Apache friend joined him, and they ordered breakfast. "I have an idea to talk over with you after we eat," Joe said.

"What kind?" Frog Eyes asked.

"I'll tell you after breakfast when we can talk alone," Joe answered.

Sitting on a smooth cottonwood log near Boothill Cemetery, Joe began telling Frog Eyes about his plan. "I think I can find out when the army payroll wagon is due from Tucson," Joe said. "I've discovered that Betsy

Willoughby tells the Clantons about the wagon so they can go out and rob it."

"What's that got to do with us?"

"How would your people like some horses without having to steal them?"

"Arivaipas like horses. Getting hard to steal with army around."

"All right, here's the plan. I'll try to find out when the payroll wagon is due to arrive. We'll tell your people when to go to the wagon road to wait in hiding. When the Clanton gang rides out to rob the wagon, your people follow them. After the Clantons rob the wagon and are riding away, your people can surround them and take the money. This way your people do not have to worry about the army."

"No can eat money," Frog Eyes commented.

"Here is where we come in. Your people give me the money, and I'll go to Tucson to buy horses. You and I will drive the horses north next to the Catalina Mountains. At the end of the mountains, we'll drive them down to the San Pedro River where your people can take them home."

"Maybe army find out about horses."

"The army will go after the Clantons because they're the ones who will have robbed the payroll wagon."

"What you and me get for plan?"

"We'll take half the money. You can buy your ten horses to pay for your wife and have money for cattle too. I'll start a horse ranch."

"Maybe headman not like plan."

"Then we have to think of a better plan."

"Plan sound good. When we go talk with headman?"

"When you are ready," Joe said.

"Ready now," Frog Eyes said. "Three days of riding to my people."

"I'll go with you to talk to the headman."

"That good plan. Headman maybe not believe Frog Eyes."

Chapter Seven

"We should leave town separately," Joe said. "I need to check out of the hotel and buy some jerky in case we don't find any game along the way."

"Plenty game. No worry, Lieutenant."

"I'm not a lieutenant anymore, so just call me Joe."

"OK. That fine, Joe."

"You can leave first. I'll meet you beyond the hill on the road to Charleston."

Frog Eyes reined his bay gelding west toward the wagon road leading to Charleston and Camp Huachuca. Joe quickly packed his warbag and checked out of the Grand Hotel. After mounting the sorrel, he spotted Arnold Willoughby standing on the corner of Allen Street watching him. As soon as Joe looked in his direction, Willoughby quickly turned his head away. "I wonder what the chicken captain has in mind," Joe muttered to himself, and rode to a small store to buy some jerky. Although he trusted Frog Eyes's loyalty, he wanted to make sure he had something to eat in case they did not find game. Since they would follow the San Pedro River all the way to Arivaipa Canyon, he felt no need to carry a canteen for drinking water. Reaching the store, he looked back down the street to see if Willoughby continued to watch him and saw that the captain had disappeared.

Joe dismounted and entered the small adobe building.

Leaving the store with his jerky in a small flour sack, he glanced up and down the street to see if Arnold Willoughby might have reappeared. Seeing no further sign of Betsy's husband, Joe booted the sorrel into a trot to join his Apache partner.

Looking over the countryside, Joe saw the grass-covered hills turned to a straw color. Along a small arroyo, the mesquite trees still retained their small green leaflets lined up in two rows like cots in the enlisted men's barracks. He was happy that in late October the midday temperature had diminished since the intense heat of summer.

Beyond the hill, from a grove of mesquite along the arroyo, Frog Eyes rode out to meet Holly. "I saw the chicken captain watching me as I left the hotel," Joe said when Frog Eyes rode up alongside him. "We should make sure he is not following us."

"Frog Eyes watch behind. Maybe good idea Frog Eyes leave road."

Joe agreed and the former Apache scout reined the bay off the road down to the arroyo where the trees lining the banks would keep him at least partially hidden. Holly continued along the wagon road, occasionally looking back to see if anyone followed. Well past the turnoff into the Clanton ranch, Joe turned around in the saddle to take one last look back. Seeing nobody following, he reined the sorrel toward the arroyo and joined Frog Eyes. They left the arroyo riding northwest to reach the San Pedro River by the most direct route. In the distance, from a vantage point high on the *bajada* of the mountains, they saw the large north-flowing river lined with ash and cottonwood trees. The leaves on the ash trees retained their green, but the cottonwoods had begun to turn an autumn gold.

Arriving at the river, they dismounted and let their horses drink from the clear main channel. When the horses had had their fill, the two men quenched their thirst. Joe wiped his mouth on his sleeve, then turned to look back over the trail they had taken. "If the chicken captain is following us," Joe said, "he's keeping himself hidden."

"We ride in water," Frog Eyes said. "Leave no track for chicken captain."

"Good idea."

Mounting their horses, they rode into the main channel and headed north, keeping to the water that flowed slowly down the river. Joe figured they had been in the water for about two miles before Frog Eyes led the way to the west bank.

The sun was casting long shadows as it sank toward the horizon of the Huachuca Mountains when Frog Eyes reined his horse toward the river and crossed to the eastern side. There an arroyo emptied its small stream into the river. "We make camp up arroyo. Then Frog Eyes hunt for game."

After rounding a bend in the arroyo, the Apache reined in his horse in a grove of large mesquite. Dismounting, he tied his reins around a branch on one of the trees. Holly followed his companion. "You make fire. Frog Eyes hunt."

With bow, arrows and a knife slipped behind his buckskin belt, the Apache headed up the arroyo, leaving the bay tied to the mesquite tree. Holly began gathering pieces of dead wood and placing it in a pile in the middle of a small clearing. With dry sacaton grass for kindling, he added a handful of twigs and then a few larger pieces of wood. Lighting the dry grass he watched as the flames licked at the twigs. When the larger pieces caught fire, he added more wood to the blazing pile.

Dusk had begun to settle in before Frog Eyes returned carrying a small javelina that he had killed and gutted. "Plenty food for two days," the Apache said as he arrived next to the fire where Joe sat on a deadfall.

Joe watched as the Apache took the unskinned carcass to the stream and plastered it with mud. Returning to the fire he placed it on the red-hot coals. The wet mud coming in contact with the coals sizzled and a puff of steam escaped to mingle with the small amount of smoke from the fire. Frog Eyes piled more wood on top of the mud-covered carcass.

Waiting for the meat to bake, Joe unsaddled the sorrel, hobbled the forelegs and slipped the hackamore from its head. Frog Eyes untied the blanket on the bay and hobbled it. Removing the hackamore, he took his blanket to a smooth patch of ground near the fire. Holly took the blanket from his warbag and spread it on another smooth area.

Returning to the warbag, he grabbed a pint bottle of mescal and carried it to the deadfall where Frog Eyes sat gazing into the fire. Uncorking the bottle, Joe handed it to his friend and sat down next him. The

Apache took a pull on the bottle, grimaced as the fiery liquid passed down his throat and handed it back to Joe. He lifted the bottle to his mouth and took a swallow. "That tastes good after a long day," Joe said.

"Tastes good anytime," Frog Eyes replied.

Holly contemplated the possibility of Arnold Willoughby following them, hoping that they had thrown him off their trail by riding through the river. But he knew that, despite all the captain's shortcomings, he was good at tracking. Shrugging off the thought that the officer might have followed them, he passed the bottle back to Frog Eyes. The chances were, he surmised, that when he saw him on the street corner, Willoughby had been in Tombstone doing errands. And, after all, why should he want to follow?

Darkness had invaded the valley before Frog Eyes decided the meat was ready to eat. Stabbing the carcass through its coating of hard-baked mud with his knife, he removed it from the coals and put it on a nearby flat rock and began prying off the mud shell and hide at the same time. With the meat free of its shell, he began carving to separate the hams from the rest.

Handing one of the hams to Holly, the Apache took the other and began slicing off juicy morsels, devouring them quickly. Joe took his own knife and soon began to savor the wild taste of the young javelina meat.

Their hunger satisfied, they drank another swallow of mescal and rolled up in their blankets for the night.

The next morning they had covered five miles before the sun rose and filled the San Pedro Valley with a golden hue. By midafternoon they reined in their horses at the river's edge and let them drink. Continuing, they saw the few buildings in Benson but kept riding through the cottonwoods along the river. By this time,

Holly had put the thought of Willoughby following them out of his mind.

Frog Eyes did not share Joe's confidence and kept glancing back to the trail at intervals. That evening Frog Eyes chose a campsite up an arroyo that was out of sight from the main trail along the river. Finishing the remainder of the javelina, they also drank the few swallows left in the bottle of mescal as they discussed the plan to steal from the robbers of the army payroll.

The next afternoon, they reached the mouth of Arivaipa Canyon. Frog Eyes told Joe that he would ride up the canyon in the morning to meet with the headman. He would then return for Joe if the situation proved to be all right.

Holly made a campfire while Frog Eyes went off on foot to hunt down river. Just as the sun sank below the Catalina Mountains, the Apache returned to camp carrying a young mule deer he had killed as the animal drank from the river channel. "Plenty for us to eat," Frog Eyes said. "Also plenty left to bring to headman tomorrow."

The Apache put the heart and liver on the coals of the fire and began removing the forequarters of the carcass, leaving the hide on the rest. "Frog Eyes take this part to headman," he said, patting the unskinned hindquarters. "Maybe make headman happy."

He proceeded to slice strips of the meat from the forelegs and shoulders and laid the meat on the coals to broil. After sharing the heart and liver, Joe and his companion ate a few of the strips, wrapping what remained in an old flour sack to keep the flies away.

Shortly before sunrise, Frog Eyes mounted the bay carrying the hindquarters of the deer carcass in front of him on the horse's withers. Holly stayed in camp to wait for the Apache's return. The sorrel gelding grazed nearby, nibbling at the leaves on the mesquite trees and occasionally lowering its head to take a mouthful of dried grass.

Joe had asked Frog Eyes when he might return, but the Apache had shrugged his shoulders.

Sitting in the shade of a large mesquite tree, Holly's thoughts turned to his plan and his hopes that the Arivaipas would agree to robbing the Clanton gang. He also thought about Betsy, and her part in giving information about the arrival of the payroll wagon to the Clantons. In order to glean the information for his own plan, he knew he would have to depend on Betsy to reveal the arrival date. He wondered if he could somehow trick her into telling him or if he would have to trail her into the Clanton ranch again. The latter method would mean keeping a close watch on Betsy's movements. That meant he would have to wait near the road to Camp Huachuca because she might drive in to deliver her message to the gang before going to Tombstone.

By the time the sun had reached its zenith, Joe began to feel drowsy. Rolling his blanket into a pillow, he reclined under the tree, put his hat over his eyes and soon fell sound asleep.

Awakened suddenly by someone kicking his right boot, Holly thought that Frog Eyes had returned from talking with the Arivaipa headman. Lifting his hat from his face, he was startled to see Captain Arnold Willoughby glaring down at him with his Remington pointed at his heart. "Well, Mr. Holly, it looks like your carelessness is my good fortune," Willoughby snarled in anger. "I would have killed you in Tombstone, but you left town."

"Why didn't you just wait for me to return?" Holly asked.

"I decided to follow you and kill you where nobody would find your body until the buzzards and coyotes had cleaned your bones."

"What do you expect to accomplish by killing me, Willoughby?"

"Dead, you will not be sleeping with my wife, Holly. You have made me the laughingstock of the post. I overheard someone referring to me as 'The Cuckhold Captain,' and I decided to end all that by doing away with you, the one who has caused all this misery in my life."

"Willoughby," Joe said. "I am not the cause of your misery. Your wife, Betsy, is to blame for that."

"So you maintained at your court-martial. I did not believe you then, and nobody else did either. I still do not believe you. Betsy is a young woman who you took advantage of, and that is the truth of it."

Joe looked at the muzzle of the Remington pointed at him and hoped he could keep Willoughby talking until Frog Eyes returned. "Consider this, Willoughby. If you kill me, Betsy will find someone else. She's not happy being married to you. Why not accept that? You have grounds for divorce."

"The problem with your suggestion, Holly, is that I love my wife and I do not believe in divorce."

Joe wished Frog Eyes would hurry up and get back from his mission. He wondered how long he could maintain a conversation with an angry man who was aiming a revolver at his chest. "Have you considered that obtaining a divorce would free you from wondering about Betsy's transgressions?"

"You are not very clever, Holly. You would enjoy

seeing me divorce Betsy so you could have a free hand with her. I am no fool."

"You may not believe me, Willoughby, but I decided to avoid your wife some time ago. I haven't been comfortable with her advances."

"Do you really expect me to believe that? Holly, you have proven yourself unfit to be an army officer. You've lied about your relationship with my wife. If I don't kill you, you'll go back to Tombstone and jump into bed with Betsy as soon as you see her."

"I can say only that you are wrong. By the way, how can you be away from the camp for so long?"

"The major and I are good friends. I told him I had business to take care of."

"Like the business you and Betsy are engaged in?"

"What are you are referring to, Holly?"

"I can't blame you for not admitting to it."

"Holly, you are making no sense at all."

Out of the corner of his eye, Joe saw Frog Eyes approaching through the tall sacaton grass. He hoped he could keep Willoughby talking just a few minutes longer until the Apache could jump the Remington-wielding captain and disarm him.

"Killing me will make you something that you are not. Willoughby, you are not a murderer. Think about that before you decide to pull the trigger. I'm planning to leave Tombstone, anyway. Since I was drummed out of the army, I've given a lot of thought about what I want to do for a living. I've decided to get into the horse business. I know horses better than anything else."

"The best market for horses is the cavalry, and you've burned that bridge before you've even start. No commander will buy horses from a drummed-out officer."

Without moving, Joe saw the Apache rise slowly and

quietly until he gained a position to jump Willoughby from behind. As Frog Eyes slipped his knife from his buckskins, Joe continued to draw Willoughby's attention. "Camp Huachuca is not the only post in Arizona Territory."

Willoughby, about to reply, gagged as Frog Eyes jumped, grabbed him around the throat with his left arm, knocked the Remington from Willoughby's hand and forced him to the ground with his knife ready to plunge into the officer's heart.

Joe sprang up, took the revolver in his right hand, and directed it toward Willoughby. "You can turn him loose," Holly said to Frog Eyes. "Nice work! You saved my hide!"

"Frog Eyes kill chicken captain."

"He's not worth killing, my friend. Let him go."

Reluctantly, the Apache removed his arm from around Willoughby's neck and stood up, his knife still in hand and ready for action. Willoughby rubbed his throat. As he sat up, Joe said, "Stay right where you are. The tables seem to have turned."

"If you intend to kill me, do it now," Willoughby said.

"If I intended to kill you, I would have given that pleasure to my friend."

"What are you doing up here with an Apache, Holly?"

"I believe that comes under the heading of my business, Willoughby. You may have caused me to get drummed out of the army, but now I answer to no one, least of all to you."

"I think there's something strange about you and a former Apache scout in this part of the country. I thought I was tracking two horses."

"Lucky for us you did not heed your thoughts."

"What do you have planned for me, Holly?"

"I really haven't given that much thought. How does staking you out over an ant hill sound?"

"Good Lord, Holly, you're no better than the savages."

"You've been a real pain in the ass, Willoughby. I think it might do you some good to think things over while you walk along the river."

"Suppose the Apaches find me?"

"You might find that a challenge. You should be glad that I didn't have my friend run his knife into your miserable heart."

Willoughby fell silent. Joe took Frog Eyes aside and asked him if all was ready to visit the headman. The Apache told him that the headman would receive them whenever they arrived at the canyon settlement. "We need to get him away from here before we go to see your headman," Holly said.

They returned to Willoughby, who had not moved from his sitting position. "Where did you leave your horse?" Joe asked.

"I tied him to a mesquite about a hundred yards up river when I saw your horse grazing."

"Get your horse," he said to Frog Eyes. "The chicken captain and I will wait here for you."

The Apache trotted back up the canyon and returned in a few minutes riding his bay gelding. Holly handed the Remington to him. "Keep our friend covered while I saddle my horse. If he decides to leave, just shoot him in the leg."

Joe took his hackamore out to where the sorrel grazed and slipped it over the horse's head. Removing the hobbles, he led the sorrel to where he had left his saddle. Holly took his time saddling his horse. After tightening the cinch, he mounted and rode over to join the Apache and the worried captain.

"All right, Willoughby, get up and start walking to your horse. Just remember that you are covered by your own Remington and my Peacemaker."

Quickly, Willoughby picked up his hat from where it had fallen when Frog Eyes had jumped him, knocked it against his right leg and put it back on his head. Getting to his feet, he brushed the dirt from his dark blue pants, and began trudging along the trail. Holly and Frog Eyes rode behind the captain with their weapons covering him.

Arriving at the tree where he had tethered his horse, Willoughby untied the reins, tightened the cinch and prepared to mount. "Before you get aboard your horse, hand me the reins," Holly ordered, slipping his .44 Colt into its holster.

The captain looked at Holly with his left eyebrow arched and surrendered the reins. When he had put his left foot in the stirrup and swung his right leg over the horse, Holly remarked, "I don't want you to think about trying to escape."

With Joe in front, leading the mounted, chagrined Willoughby and Frog Eyes taking up the rear with the Remington aimed at the captain's back, the trio rode in silence south along the river toward Tombstone and Camp Huachuca. When they had covered about three miles, Holly reined in the sorrel and told Willoughby to dismount. "Now, what are you going to do with me?" the captain asked fearfully.

"You are going for a walk," Joe replied. "You should be able to make Benson in a couple of days if you keep going."

"How will I explain all this?" Willoughby asked in a pleading tone of voice.

"You'll have plenty of time to figure that out, Willoughby. Maybe they'll believe you if you tell them that your horse farted you off and ran away."

"Suppose the Apache find me?"

"As I have said, you have always referred to them as savages. Perhaps you will experience their savagery."

"I have jerky in my saddle bags. Will you allow me to at least take that with me?"

"I suppose I could be magnanimous. Open your saddlebag slowly. If by chance you have a weapon concealed in it and think you might have a chance to escape you will be a dead man before you get it out."

Willoughby turned toward his horse, unbuckled the left saddlebag, reached in and withdrew a small bundle containing some jerky. Placing it under his left arm, he rebuckled the straps.

"You might think about tossing that flour sack away before you enter Benson or they might not believe that your horse ran away. Have a nice walk, Willoughby, and give my best regards to Betsy."

Seething with anger, the captain turned and began walking. Joe and Frog Eyes sat on their horses for a few minutes, watching, before reining around to head back to Arivaipa Canyon.

The Apache took the lead with Joe leading Willoughby's horse, following the canyon that bisected the foothills in front of the mountains to the east. By late afternoon Joe saw Frog Eyes wave at something. Looking closely, Joe noticed the Apache guards hidden on both sides of the canyon. Shortly after, they arrived at the foot of a trail that led to a low mesa overlooking the stream. On top of the mesa, they came to the clusters of wickiups that comprised the Arivaipa settlement. Joe looked straight ahead, but from the corner of his eye saw people coming out of the dwellings made from sticks and grass to gawk at the visitors.

Frog Eyes reined in the bay at a large fire circle in the middle of the settlement. Mesquite logs, nearly completely burned, smoldered, sending off whisps of gray smoke into the gentle, intermittent breeze wafting down the canyon.

While Joe and his Apache companion remained on their horses, Joe glanced casually around to see at least a hundred pairs of eyes staring at him. As if he were making a grand entrance onto a stage, a middle-aged man with long black hair streaked with gray, held back by a beaded buckskin headband, left one of the largest dome-shaped dwellings and approached the visitors. Frog Eyes and the headman conversed in Apache for a moment until Frog Eyes turned to Joe. "Headman say get off horses. You welcome to village."

They dismounted. The headman beckoned to a group of young boys who came trotting up to take the reins. "We go with headman to talk," Frog Eyes said, and followed the headman into the wickiup.

In spite of the small fire burning in the center of the circular structure, it took Joe a few moments before his eyes became accustomed to the dark interior. In the Apache language, Frog Eyes introduced Joe to the headman. "Headman name Etazin. He say he happy to meet friend of Man With Eyes of Eagle."

Joe smiled and nodded. Etazin's expression did not change. The two Apaches conversed for a few minutes as Joe waited patiently, looking around at the sleeping hides rolled up and placed next to the wall. Several woven baskets containing various grains and seeds lined another part of the wall. Finally, Frog Eyes turned to speak to Joe. "I tell headman about chicken captain. He wonder why you no let me kill chicken captain."

"Tell him that chicken captain is the man who gets information about the payroll wagon."

Frog Eyes gave Joe's explanation to the headman. "Headman want to know more about plan."

Repeating the plan to his Apache friend, Joe glanced at Etazin from time to time and saw that the headman listened intently to his words. He wondered if the man understood any English.

After Frog Eyes had spoken at length to the headman, he turned once again to Joe. "Etazin ask how he know you no take money and no bring horses."

"Tell him that you will be with me all the time."

After Frog Eyes interpreted Joe's statement, the headman spoke. When he had finished, Frog Eyes told Joe that Etazin had agreed to the plan but wanted to know if thirty warriors would be enough to stop the Clanton gang. "What kinds of weapons will they use?" Joe asked.

"They have rifles, pistols, and bows and arrows," the Apache replied.

"How many rifles and pistols?"

Frog Eyes posed Joe's question to the headman. "Headman say have ten rifles, six pistols and plenty ammunition."

"That should be enough if they take the gang by surprise," Joe said. "Tell Etazin that I have brought the chicken captain's horse to him as a gift."

Frog Eyes repeated what Joe had said in Apache and for the first time since they had entered the wickiup Joe saw a faint smile from the headman. "Etazin say he have gift for you after eat."

A woman entered the wickiup and handed a pint bottle filled with a cloudy, yellowish-brown liquid to the headman and left. Etazin lifted the bottle to his lips, took a swallow and passed the bottle to Frog Eyes, who also took a drink. "What is this?" Joe asked.

"Tiswin. Apache make drink from corn," Frog Eyes replied, and handed the bottle to Joe.

He took a small swallow and passed the bottle back to the headman. "Tiswin is strong," he said.

"Get drunk easy," Frog Eyes said.

After they had passed the bottle another time, the same woman came in carrying a basketry plate loaded with chunks of roasted meat. The headman took some and passed the plate to Frog Eyes, who helped himself and gave the plate to Joe. "This deer I bring," Frog Eyes said.

I am glad you brought him a deer and not a horse," Joe replied.

"Why white eyes no like eat horse?"

"We think horses are too beautiful to eat."

"Apache like horse better than cow."

"Why does the Apache raid for cows?"

"Not plenty horse. Have to eat something. That why headman like plan."

The bottle of tiswin made another round. After they finished with their meal, the headman spoke to the woman. She took the empty plate, leaving the men to their drink.

"You lucky, Joe. I know gift from headman."

"What is it?" Joe asked.

"Short time you see."

Noting the impish grin on Frog Eyes's face, he wondered what the gift would be. The woman returned shortly, leading a young woman with raven-black hair done in two braids and clothed in buckskin. Holly looked up into her soft, dark brown eyes and beautiful copper-colored face. The tight-fitting blouse revealed her symmetrical female body. The woman released the girl and exited the wickiup, leaving her to stand by the entrance. The headman spoke to Frog Eyes.

"Etazin say this girl for you."

"Tell the headman that I thank him, but tell me who she is. She does not look Apache."

Frog Eyes relayed Joe's thanks to the headman and turned again toward his friend. "Girl Mexicana. Etazin capture in raid six year ago. All people killed. She only live. He take back here. Etazin make raid to help pay back white eyes and Papago for killing many Apache women and children before."

"What does this gift mean?"

"Is gift. You give headman chicken captain horse. Headman give you girl. You lucky, Joe. Girl better than horse."

"I do not understand," Joe said. "Is this girl a gift for tonight or what?"

"Girl yours. You take where want to take. Etazin like you. Give you good gift. You go now. Girl take you to wickiup."

Joe suddenly felt strange. He knew that to refuse the headman's gift would be an insult, but the thought of being alone with the girl made him uncomfortable. "I thought we were finished with our business with Etazin and we can start riding back to Tombstone," Joe said confused.

"Talk finished. We stay night here. You with girl. Frog Eyes go see father of someday wife."

"What about our horses?"

"Horses in corral. You go with girl now. No be 'fraid, Joe."

Frog Eyes said something to the headman, got to his feet and beckoned Joe to follow. Holly rose and watched Frog Eyes leave through the entrance. The girl turned and stepped back for Joe to leave and then followed him. Outside she touched Joe's arm to get his attention. "Follow me, señor. I will take you to my *casa.*"

Her English spoken with a Spanish accent surprised Joe. He followed the girl across the central clearing and into a small wickiup. He stood inside the entrance watching the girl take firewood from a pile and place it on the fire. Glancing around, he saw the sleeping hides rolled up by the wall, but those seemed to be her only possessions.

Leaving the fire, she unrolled the sleeping hides. "Sit down, señor. I am Lucía. I am happy that you are here and will take me to my home in Tumacacori."

"My name is Joe Holly. I did not come here to take you anywhere."

"Please, *por favor,* take me home. I have family there."

"They told me the Apache killed your family when they raided your ranch."

Lucía looked down to the floor and said, "That is true. They killed my parents and my two older brothers. I hid under my bed, but they found me and brought me here. That was six years ago. The raid was for revenge because of what the people from Tucson did here."

"What did they do to you?"

"I belonged to Etazin until he gave me to you. He treated me like a daughter. I was only twelve years old when they made their raid. There have been warriors who have asked Etazin to sell me to them, but he has always refused. I am very thankful for that kindness he showed me."

"What do you do here?"

"I work. I help the woman who brought me to Etazin's wickiup this evening. She is his first wife. He has two others, but she is still his favorite. She bore him two sons who are now warriors. I help prepare food and sew clothes."

"You sound as if your life here is not too unhappy."

"I am lucky to belong to Etazin. He is kind to me. As I said, he treats me like a daughter. I do not want to marry an Apache. They killed my family, and I cannot forget that."

"But you said you have family in Tumacacori."

"I have my *tío* and *tía* and four cousins. They have a farm near the river. The Apaches did not raid them because they wanted my father's horses. When they brought me here, I watched them butcher the one we called Manchado because he had a white spot on his belly. I cried for days after that."

"Frog Eyes and I are riding back to Tombstone. How will you get to Tumacacori?"

"I will find a way, Señor Joe. Please take me with you. I will do anything you want me to do. Look."

Stripping her buckskin blouse over her head, she stood, naked from the waist up. Joe saw her coppery skin and her beautiful breasts. He became aroused in spite of his embarrassment. "Sit down, Lucía. Put your blouse back on. You are very beautiful, but I feel strange at the thought of you giving yourself to me when I don't really know you. You are not a whore, and I don't want to take advantage of this situation where you seem so desperate to have me take you away from here."

He watched as she put the buckskin back on, noting the grace with which she moved. "I think you are a good man, Joe. Please promise to take me with you."

Joe hesitated a moment before replying. His desire for her grew every minute as they talked, but he felt strongly that to take advantage of such a beautiful woman would be something he might regret later. "All right, beautiful Lucía. I will take you with me to Tombstone and try to get you back with your uncle, aunt and cousins in Tumacacori. But it's a long way to walk. Can you get a horse from Etazin?"

She threw her arms around Joe and kissed him. "I will ask him for a horse. I am sorry if I surprised you just now, but I am very grateful to you, Joe. You really are a very good man. Will you tell me all about yourself, or would you rather sleep now?"

Joe told Lucía about his life. From time to time she rose to put more wood on the fire, but as he spoke, her soft eyes looking at him almost made him tremble. He did not mention the plan for robbing the Clanton gang, but he did tell her about the trouble he'd had with the army. He noticed that mentioning another woman did not diminish her look of gratitude toward him.

"What are you planning to do now, Joe?" she asked when he had finished.

"I know horses. I want to find a ranch and raise good horses. There is always a market for good horses."

"If the Apaches do not come and steal them," she said.

"I will have to take my chances. The Apaches are not the only ones who steal horses."

She unrolled another hide and put it next to the first. "Are you ready to sleep?" she asked.

"I guess I'm more tired than I thought," he replied, and crawled onto the hide.

Lucía slid down next to him, put her arms around him and kissed him again tenderly. Joe took her in his arms and returned the kiss. "You are a beautiful girl," he said as he released her.

"I have never kissed a man before. I must tell you it feels good to kiss you, Joe. You are a very good man."

Fully clothed, they went to sleep with their arms around each other.

The sun had just begun to seep through the small spaces in the walls of the wickiup, dotting the dirt floor and bringing enough light so that when Joe opened his eyes, he saw that Lucía had not moved during the night. He gently touched her cheek with his hand and she opened her eyes turning to smile up at him. He smiled at her, marveling at her innocence and beauty. She closed her eyes again and snuggled close to him. In spite of their clothing, he felt her firm breasts on his chest and remembered how beautiful she had looked the night before when she stood in front of him naked from the waist up.

"We had better be going, Lucía. Frog Eyes is probably waiting for us."

"I will get us some food before our ride. Are you hungry?"

"I probably am, but I haven't thought about being hungry."

"I will be back with some food," she said, and got to her feet.

Rubbing the sleep from her eyes, she pushed back the hide flap from the entrance and left. Joe reached for his hat and put it on as he waited for her return. His thoughts flew back to the way he felt when she had kissed him. Raising his head with his eyes closed, he wondered if this beautiful Mexican woman had cast some sort of spell on him.

It seemed like a long time before Lucía returned with some tortillalike bread made from corn meal and several pieces of venison. "I asked Etazin to lend me a horse. He agreed and gave me a small pinto. He also said he would miss me, but he was happy to see me happy. I will probably miss him, too."

When they had finished eating, Lucía rolled up the sleeping hides and put them under her arm before glancing around and leaving the wickiup. "This has been my home for a long time," she said.

Arriving at the corral, they found Frog Eyes with his bay and Joe's sorrel saddled and ready. The pinto stood outside the corral, bridled and blanketed. Joe watched Lucía jump up to mount the pinto at almost a vault. He marveled at her lithe and graceful movement. After handing her the bundle of sleeping hides, he swung himself onto the sorrel, and with Frog Eyes in the lead, the three rode out of the village through the clusters of people who had gathered to watch. Lucía waved at them.

They rode single file down the canyon until reaching the river where they watered the horses. The well-traveled trail south allowed Joe to ride next to Lucía. "I'm curious," Joe said. "Apache women generally walk, but you ride a horse as well as a man."

Lucía looked over and smiled. "I am not an Apache woman. I learned to ride horses long before they raided the rancho. My brothers and I would help my father work the cattle. You must remember I was twelve when they took me away."

"Where did you learn to speak English?"

"Our neighbors were Americanos. We used to ride over to their place and play with their children. They have a daughter, Martha, who became my best friend. My brothers and I learned English from the Bards, and they learned Spanish from us."

"So you can speak three languages."

"Yes."

"In all the time you spent with the Apache, did you ever attempt to escape and go home?"

"I wanted to, especially when they first took me away, but there was always one of Etazin's wives watching me. When I grew up, I knew I could never get away. You saw the guards in the canyon. There are others you did not see."

"What if I had not come to the village and given Etazin the horse?"

"I do not know, but I am very glad that you arrived and gave Etazin that horse."

They continued to converse as they rode behind Frog Eyes, who looked at the trail for tracks.

Reaching the point where Willoughby began his travels on foot, the former scout easily picked up the captain's trail. After several more hours, Frog Eyes reined in the bay to wait for the others to catch up. "Tracks easy," the Apache said. "He drink from river two times and make water two times."

"Tell me when we might be getting close to him," Holly said. "I don't want him to see us."

"Tracks still from day before. Maybe he no sleep."

Reaching the arroyo where they had spent the night

95

before arriving at Arivaipa Canyon, Joe decided to make camp for the night. After watering their horses in the river, they rode up the arroyo and reined in at the familiar spot.

The hobbled horses nibbled at the seed heads of the tall sacaton while Joe and Lucía gathered wood for a fire. Frog Eyes, as before, had gone up the arroyo to hunt.

With the fire blazing, Joe took his bedroll out of the warbag and rolled it out under the large mesquite where he had slept before. After putting her sleeping hides next to Joe's bedroll, Lucía looked up at him and smiled.

As they stood watching the fire, she turned toward him. "I want to kiss you, Joe. That makes me tingle all over and feels good."

The thought of embracing Lucía had been going through his mind all afternoon. He took her into his arms, teased her lips with his, then, pulling her even closer, kissed her fervently.

His passion rising, Joe released her and with his hands cupping her face, looked into her soft, brown eyes. "You are so innocent, Lucía. And so absolutely pure and beautiful. I think we should gather more wood for the fire."

"I am not totally innocent," she said. "I know what men and women do. When I was little I peeked in my parents' bedroom. I have also seen Apache people love each other. When you and I are kissing, all of me wants to know how that feels."

Joe felt like telling her she was close to discovering that mystery, but decided that gathering firewood might be the best thing they could do at the moment.

He realized that he had made a wise decision when

Frog Eyes suddenly appeared carrying two cottontail rabbits. Joe felt somewhat embarrassed knowing that the Apache had most likely seen him kissing Lucía.

Lucía and Frog Eyes conversed in Apache for a moment. Handing the rabbits to her, he took his knife from his leggings and gave it to her. Proceeding to the small stream in the arroyo, Lucía began cleaning and skinning the rabbits. Holly watched from a distance, admiring her swiftness and skill at the task. After separating the carcasses into quarters, she took them to the fire circle and placed them on one of the rocks. From the mesquite tree, she cut two small, green branches, trimmed the twigs and leaves, sharpened one end of each skewer and shoved the points through the quarters, four on each skewer. Taking a piece of the firewood, she scraped the red-hot coals into a mound away from the flames. She then put the skewered quarters of rabbit meat on the coals. In a moment the meat began to sizzle, and as it cooked, Lucía kept turning the skewers until the meat became a golden brown.

Holly sat next to Frog Eyes, watching. His thoughts went to Betsy, trying to picture her in the same situation and found himself thinking that Betsy would be no more than a burden in many ways.

Dismissing his thoughts about Betsy Willoughby, he watched Lucía take the skewers from the coals, remove the quarters with the knife and pile them all on one of the flat rocks in the fire circle. Handing the knife to Frog Eyes she said, "There is the meal. I hope you enjoy it."

"You're not joining us?" Joe asked.

"The Apache way is for the women to wait for their men to finish. I have things to do."

She turned and started up the arroyo. Frog Eyes had

already speared one of the quarters with his knife and intently chewed the meat away from the bones. "Mexican girl make good wife for you, Joe," he said between bites. "Mexican girl like Joe."

"How long have you known Lucía?" Holly asked.

"Frog Eyes with others when we take girl to Arivaipa."

"Did you kill any of her family?"

"Frog Eyes too young to be warrior. Frog Eyes help drive cattle and horses."

"Why didn't some Apache warrior take Lucía for a wife?"

"Etazin not allow. She like daughter to Etazin. Him put too high price for Mexican girl. Anyway, Mexican girl too skinny for Apache warrior."

Holly found the rabbit delicious but he made sure that Lucía would have plenty when she returned. Returning from the stream after rinsing his hands, he saw her ambling down the arroyo. She went to the fire and began eating.

Dusk settled over the valley as she finished. Frog Eyes had put his blanket under another mesquite tree about fifty yards away and sat sharpening his knife with a smooth stone from the stream.

Lucía returned from washing her hands in the stream and sat down next to Holly on her sleeping hides. "Did you have enought to eat, Joe?"

"I'm stuffed."

"That is good."

"Lucía," he said. "You do not have to wait for men to eat anymore. You are not an Apache."

"It is what I have been used to for six years. Besides your friend, Man With Eyes of Eagle, is Apache. He would be offended by me eating at the same time with the men."

"Frog Eyes has been a scout for the Army. He would understand."

"Why do you call him Frog Eyes? He is Man With Eyes of Eagle."

"When he scouted for the army, the troopers gave him that nickname because of his large eyes."

"He does have large eyes. We Mexicans have nicknames also. Someone who is short is called Chapo. A thin man is called Flaco."

"I think everybody has nicknames. Maybe I should call you Soft Eyes."

"Why would you call me that?"

"Because when you look at a man with those soft, brown eyes you can melt the man's heart."

"Do I melt your heart, Joe?"

"I haven't figured that out yet, Soft Eyes. Right now, I think we should get some sleep."

He reached over, put his arm around her shoulders and kissed her lips. Soon after they laid down, he listened to her slow breathing as she fell asleep. In the light of an almost full moon, Joe stared at Lucía in her peaceful sleep. He could not believe what had happened. The entire essence of this beautiful, innocent woman made him yearn for her love. Yet, he felt afraid of his own feelings. In some ways he found himself thinking that he wanted her forever. It was the first time he had thought about living his life with one woman. It was obvious that Lucía was a loving woman and there was a definite attraction between them despite the manner in which they met. His thoughts jumped to his brother Edward's doughty wife compared to the almost wild beauty of Lucía. Then, pondering his uncertain future gave him doubts about the situation. He closed his eyes, shut out the moonlight and fell into a deep sleep.

Riding by Benson the next morning, Frog Eyes reined in the bay and dismounted. Studying the ground squatting on his legs, he waved Joe over. "Chicken captain," he said, pointing at the tracks. "Him tired. Tracks maybe three hours old."

"He's probably still in the town resting and trying to find a horse," Joe said. "He might take the morning stage, but it won't leave for a while. We should be careful and ride on the other side of the river in case the stage catches up to us."

The Apache jumped up on the bay and reined him off the wagon road through the giant cottonwood trees and across the San Pedro River. Joe and Lucía followed. They had traveled for two hours when they heard the grinding wheels of the stagecoach in the distance. Joe looked through the trees and across the river. "If we stop here, they will never see us from the road."

The dust from the horses' hooves and the iron-tired wheels of the Concord coach billowed into a brown cloud that hovered in the air in a forced suspension, taking its time to settle back down to the road and surrounding vegetation. From behind the cover of the cottonwood trees, the trio watched until the stagecoach rumbled off in the distance. Satisfied that they were once again alone, they booted their horses and continued to Tombstone, arriving in late afternoon.

After paying for a room in the Grand Hotel, Joe and Lucía rode to the livery stable two blocks away. Frog Eyes had already made his way to China Mary's establishment after making sure that Joe knew where to find him.

Hungry from the long ride, Joe and Lucía stopped at García's cafe. Sitting down at a table, Lucía said, "It seems strange to sit in a chair again."

"I expect you will find many things strange after six years with the Apache people," Joe said.

They ordered a hearty meal of beefsteak smothered with green chile sauce. Lucía conversed with García in Spanish, enjoying the opportunity to speak her native tongue. As they finished their meal, Lucía turned pensive but finally asked Joe if he could arrange for a bath back at the hotel.

"I probably have an inch of trail dust on me, too," Joe replied. "I will ask about a bath as soon as we get back."

"I will wash your back, if you will wash mine," she said, her eyes twinkling and her mouth giving him an impish smile.

"I've never had anyone wash my back," he said.

"I never have either, but I think it would feel good."

"I'm sure it will feel good."

Returning to the hotel, Holly inquired about the bath at the hotel desk. The clerk said it would take an hour for the maid to prepare the hot water. "A bath is two bits," the clerk said, brushing back the few hairs left on his balding head.

"We'll need two bathrobes," Joe said.

"That will cost you another two bits."

"Put the charges on my bill," Joe said, eager to get things settled.

"The bathroom is at the end of the hallway," the clerk said, not looking up, but pointing over his shoulder down the dark corridor.

"Thank you," Joe replied in a tone of voice that mimicked the almost surly attitude of the self-important clerk.

Back in their room, Joe found Lucía sitting in the wicker-bottomed chair, smiling at him. "Do we have a bath?" she asked.

"In an hour," he answered. "According to the clerk it takes that long to heat the water. I see you are enjoying another chair."

"I am enjoying everything, Joe."

A while later, a knock on the door and a voice announcing that the bath was ready brought them to their feet. Entering the bathroom, they saw the tarnished copper tub in the middle of the floor with steam coming from the surface of the hot water. Next to the tub they found a pail of cold water to add in case the water proved too hot for them. On top of a wooden wash stand a cake of soap, washcloths and towels had been placed alongside the two bathrobes Joe had asked for. "You go first," Joe said. "This tub isn't big enough for both of us."

"If I go first, you will get the dirty water."

"I'll just add more trail dust to it. Besides, you said you haven't had a nice hot bath in a tub for six years."

"There are some pools in the rocks up the canyon where we would take baths. In the summer the sun heats the water. In winter I did not go there."

Lucía put her hand in the hot water to test its temperature. "That is going to feel good," she said, and began taking off her buckskins.

Joe could not take his eyes from her. He watched as she bent her head back into the water to wet her long black hair. Taking the soap, she stroked the bar through her hair until it became completely lathered.

With hanks in both hands, she scrubbed away and Joe noticed the suds had turned brown.

Satisfied that her hair was clean, she rinsed it in the clear hot water until all the soap had been washed away. "Look, Joe," she said. "The dirt from my hair has made the water muddy."

"Wait until you see the water after I'm finished."

Stepping into the tub, she gingerly let herself down into the water. Joe tossed her a washcloth, which she dunked into the water before filling it with soap. "Take off your shirt, Joe, and wash my back, please."

Unbuttoning his shirt and pulling it off by the sleeves, he revealed a chest covered with reddish-brown, curly hair. She looked at him, but did not say anything. He took the washcloth and began scrubbing her smooth, copper-colored back. As if it were all part of his role as a back-washer, he guided the soapy cloth around her neck and over her firm breasts. Losing his inhibitions to desire, he dropped the cloth into the water and began caressing the soapy breasts with his bare hands, feeling her brown nipples harden at his touch.

"That feels so good, Joe."

He sloshed water over her chest and back to rinse off the soap. With a graceful exit from the tub, Lucía grabbed a towel and began rubbing her hair. Joe stripped, stepped into the water, kneeled and ducked his head to lather his hair with the soap. With her body still glistening wet, Lucía grabbed the pail of cold water from the floor to rinse the soap from his hair. Without realizing that the cold water might surprise him, she poured the water from the pail over his head.

"Ee yi!" Joe exclaimed.

"Too cold?" she inquired.

"Cold enough to freeze my hair," he said, and laughed.

She soaped the washcloth and began scrubbing his back. Moving around to his chest she filled his chest hair with suds, dropped the washcloth into the water, and ran her fingers over his chest. "I have never seen so much hair on a chest," she remarked. "It feels good. Does this feel as good to you as it did to me when you rubbed my chest?"

"I cannot answer that," he said. "All I can say is that I've never felt anything more beautiful than your chest."

"Good. Now stand up and I will wash the rest of you."

"I think you had better leave that to me or we will not get out of this bathroom for a long while," Joe said, and grinned broadly.

Standing up in the tub, he proceeded to wash his privates and legs. Dropping back into the water, he rinsed off the soap.

"Do you want me to rinse you with the clean water?"

"No thanks. I will be fine with a good toweling off."

Once dry, they donned the bathrobes, picked up their clothes and returned to the room. Lucía had brought her towel to finish drying her hair. Opening the window, she placed the wicker chair in front of it and fluffed out her hair in the breeze coming into the room.

Sitting on the bed, Joe smiled as he enjoyed watching her. "Tomorrow morning I will take you to the dressmaker and get you some new clothes," Joe said.

She stopped drying her hair, tossed the towel over the back of the chair, and stood up so quickly the bathrobe flew open. Rushing over to the bed, she sat down next to him, and kissed him. "Joe, you are such a good man. I am having such strong, happy feelings that I cannot keep from kissing you."

He grabbed her shoulders with both hands. Instead of fearing Lucía like he feared Betsy, Holly was afraid of himself. He wanted the young Mexican girl, but he felt that he would be taking advantage of her were he to make love to her. In the short time that he had known Lucía, he found himself becoming very fond of her, and with those feelings came protectiveness. With Betsy, he was dealing with a lustful married woman. With Lucía, he held innocence in his arms. For Lucía, he felt responsibility as well as the need to control himself until such time that he might consider marriage. As things stood, the last thing on his mind was marriage since he had no idea how he would be able to make a living outside the army.

Releasing her shoulders and cupping her face in his hands, he said, "Lucía, I think we had better put our clothes back on, or we might end up where we shouldn't be."

"Is there something wrong with me?"

"There is absolutely nothing wrong with you. I just think we should wait until we are both sure of each other. We really haven't known one another very long."

"Maybe you are right. But, Etazin gave me to you."

"I'm glad he did. Now I can make sure you get home to your people."

"But I told you I have no family. They were all killed."

"You have your uncle and aunt and cousins."

"They have enough mouths to feed without taking me in. I want to stay with you, Joe."

"You don't know me very well."

"I know you enough to want to be with you."

"We'd best wait and see how the plan works out before we make any decisions along that line."

"The plan will work fine. You are very smart."

"Time will tell. Now, let's get some sleep. You sleep in the bed, and I will roll my blankets out on the floor."

"There is room on the bed for both of us. I will put my buckskins back on."

The next morning Joe opened his eyes to see Lucía in peaceful slumber. Gazing at her face, his thoughts focused on his feelings toward her. Trying to decide exactly what he felt, finally he tenderly put his right hand on her cheek. Her clean, long hair had a sheen with a tinge of blue with the raven black. Opening her eyes, she reached out, pulling him to her. "Good morning," she whispered, and put her head on his shoulder, kissing his neck.

"I've been awake for a little while thinking about you and thinking about us."

"What are you thinking right this minute? Maybe I think the same things."

"I wish I could offer you a home, but I don't know where I'm going."

"As long as I can be with you, I do not care where or how we live. I promise that I will follow you to wherever you want to go or whatever you want to do."

"I know you mean that, but all I have right now is a plan to get enough money to buy some horses. If the plan doesn't work, I have no idea how I can start my horse business."

"If your plan does not work, I am sure you will think of another way. I feel very safe with you. You have made me feel more wonderful than I have ever felt in my life. I will do whatever you want me to, Joe. I am your woman."

"I'm warning you that life with me may not be easy," he said.

"My life has not been easy so far. I will take my chances with you. You are a good man, Joe Holly. Etazin told me about your plan with him. He looks forward to paying back the white eyes for the killing they did with the Papago."

"I have heard you mention that before. I'm curious, especially since you told me that Etazin likes my plan to seek revenge. If you know about my plan, then you know that it's the army payroll that we will take from the Clantons after they've finished their robbery."

"Etazin understands all that. He has always felt that if the army had protected his people as they had promised, the massacre would not have happened. So, by getting horses from the army money, Etazin feels happy."

"Do you know all the details of the so-called massacre?"

"It happened three months before the raid of revenge when I was captured. The story of the massacre is told over and over at the village, and I have heard it many times."

Lucía looked away, cringing at the thought of what she had heard about the massacre. "Most of the people from Tucson were Papagos. There were around fifty Mexicans and six gringos. According to the story that is told, there were around one hundred fifty men with weapons. The Papago were the worst. They hate Apaches. After sneaking up on the village, they began slaughtering people, mostly women and children. Then the others joined in. Eight warriors were killed, and over a hundred women and children. The Papago stole thirty children."

"Where were all the warriors?"

"They were up the canyon hunting. Etazin was at the settlement at the beginning, but he escaped with his wives. He went to find the warriors, but he was too late. When they returned to the settlement, they found the corpses. Most of the women had been stripped of their clothes and killed after the Papago had used them."

"After all that, I wonder why Etazin trusts me," Joe said.

"He probably does not trust you but sees another chance for revenge. Before I was captured, they had been over in Papago country and raided several ranchos there. Etazin is very smart. The gringos do not know it is the Arivaipans who are doing these raids. Now you know the story."

Joe thought about what Lucía had told him. He found it odd that the army had not intervened to stop what amounted to vigilantism.

After a late breakfast at García's, they went to a dressmaker's shop on Fifth Street. Wide-eyed looking at the samples, Lucía had difficulty making up her mind. At last she focused on an emerald green dress with a lace collar and cuffs. "This is very pretty," she said. "But I could not ride wearing it."

"You can ride in your buckskins," Joe suggested.

"May I try on this one?" she asked the proprietor.

"It is a sample, but if it fits I will let you buy it. The dressing room is right there," the woman said, looking at Lucía's buckskins with a slight scowl. "The dressing room is right there," she repeated, pointing over her shoulder.

When she came out of the little cubicle, her face was aglow with happiness. "It fits perfectly," she said.

"You make that dress look beautiful, Lucía," Joe said. "Keep it on and we'll find you some shoes."

As Joe paid for the dress, Lucía got her buckskins from the dressing cubicle, and they left the shop to find another where they could purchase a pair of shoes. "I wonder if I still can wear shoes," she said, as they walked toward the store the woman in the dress shop had recommended.

"Try them out and make sure they're comfortable," he replied. "By the way, my dear lady, you look very elegant in your new dress."

After purchasing her shoes, they returned to the hotel room where Joe told her that he needed to check the livery stable to see if Betsy had come to town. "If I do not come back soon, do not worry about me. Here is some money to buy your supper," he said, handing her some coins.

"I shall go to García's if you are not back by supper time. I enjoy speaking Spanish with him."

After kissing each other, Joe left her in the room, wishing he could either stay with her or bring her along.

Leaving the hotel, he walked toward the livery stable. Having gone a half block, he was surprised when Betsy drove her buggy up next to him and reined in the horse. "Get in," she said.

Joe ambled over, stepped up into the buggy and sat down next to Betsy. She leaned toward him for a kiss. "Not here, Betsy. Someone will see us, and I don't want your husband to come after me again."

"Where have you been, Joe? Arnold went on a scouting mission last week, so I came to town looking for you. The clerk at the Grand said you had checked out."

"I had some mares to look at," he lied. "But I didn't buy them."

"Where did you have to go?"

"The mares are at a ranch over by Sonoita Creek. They were too old. Some so parrot-mouthed I wondered if they'd last through another foal. I need young mares and a good stallion to breed to them. I'll need to borrow money, and I figure it will be easier to talk to a banker with young mares as collateral than the old Nellies I looked at."

"Joe, you won't have to borrow any money to buy your mares and stallion. I'll have plenty of money in ten days, and we can go off to New Mexico or some place where Arnold cannot find us."

"Where are you going to get the money? Did you find a silver mine?"

"I told you I have a business. I can't tell you any more than that. My business will pay off in ten days. Just think, Joe Holly, in ten days we can be together forever."

"I appreciate your thinking of me, Betsy, but I like southern Arizona. There is good horse country here."

"Joe Holly," she said angrily. "I drove into town today to find you. Now that I have, I'm planning to spend the night with you and take care of my business in the morning. You should be able to understand that I can't live in southern Arizona with you as long as Arnold is stationed at Camp Huachuca."

"Betsy, I can't spend the night with you tonight or any other night."

"Why not? You know I love you, and I know you want me as much as I want you."

"I'll try to explain everything to you someday. Right

now it's like the business about which you say you cannot tell me."

"Are you seeing another woman, Joe Holly?"

"I told you that I've been looking for mares."

"Please meet me at the Grand tonight," she pleaded.

Joe became exasperated. Suddenly he decided that since he had the information about the payroll wagon's arrival from Betsy, he would speak directly to her. "Betsy, I can't meet you, and you'll have to accept that," he said, stepping out of the parked buggy.

"You are a bastard, Joe Holly," she said, and swung the buggy whip at his head.

He blocked the whip with his arm, grabbed it and jerked it out of her hand. "Now, listen to me. You'd better get a hold of yourself."

He tossed the whip in back of the buggy seat, turned away and headed toward Allen Street. Hearing the buggy grind away, he looked to see where Betsy might be going. Disappointment loomed when he saw her drive into the livery stable. That meant that she would spend the night and most likely stop in at the Clanton ranch on her way back to Camp Huachuca in the morning.

Had Betsy left town immediately he could take Lucía to the Oriental for supper without risking a confrontation with the wife of Arnold Willoughby.

Before returning to the Grand, he needed to find Frog Eyes to give him the information he had discovered by chance. First he poked his head into García's, but only a few miners occupied tables. Next, he stopped by China Mary's.

Joe had never frequented the parlors or cribs of Tombstone, but he had learned about them from his troopers. One time, Frog Eyes had mentioned that he always patronized China Mary's because many of the others, including the "fallen doves" who plied their profession in the cribs, seemed indifferent to the Apache scouts from Camp Huachuca.

Entering the brothel, Joe saw a huge Chinese woman sitting in a large overstuffed chair behind a small table that held nothing more than a flowery patterned teapot and a matching cup. Other furniture in the reception room consisted of two well-worn sofas. The woman gave Joe a heavily jowled smile and asked if he would care to see some of her girls.

"No thanks," Joe said. "I'm looking for an Apache by the name of Frog Eyes. Is he here?"

"No Apache by name of Frog Eyes here," she said with her broken English.

"I forgot, he probably goes by Man With Eyes of Eagle."

"Ah yes, Eyes of Eagle spend night with Lai Ming. Still in room. You sit down. I go see if busy."

"Thank you," Joe said, and took a seat on one of the sofas.

The large woman struggled to her feet and waddled slowly down a hallway, shuffling her feet as she went. A few minutes later, Frog Eyes appeared followed by China Mary. The latter, with an obvious attempt to look important, enthroned herself again in the overstuffed chair.

"I need to talk to you alone," Joe said to the Apache.

The two men left the Chinese brothel and stopped in a vacant alley. "The payroll wagon is due at the camp in ten days. That means the Clanton gang will attempt to rob it at least the day before. If you leave for Arivaipa now, Etazin will have plenty of time to get his warriors in position to learn where the Clantons will attempt their robbery."

"Frog Eyes get things from room. Then go Arivaipa."

"Good. I'll meet you in Davidson Canyon. Don't forget."

"Frog Eyes no forget. Need money for ten horses. You more lucky. Get wife for only one horse. Etazin like white eye."

Joe smiled at his friend and gave him a pat on the shoulder.

Back with Lucía in their hotel room, Joe explained what had happened with Betsy and Frog Eyes. "I had hoped that after our talk, Betsy would have gone back to the camp. She went to the livery stable so she will spend the night here in Tombstone, probably right here in the Grand Hotel."

"Now that you have your information from this Betsy, what difference does it make where she spends the night?" Lucía asked.

"I want to take you out for supper in your new dress, but I don't want to see Betsy Willoughby again."

"I would enjoy supper with you. I do not worry about Betsy Willoughby. She can do nothing to me."

"All right. You may be right. We will go out to the Oriental tonight."

She put her arms around his neck and kissed him. "I have one question. Are you planning to take me with you when the Apache warriors rob the Clanton gang?"

"I think you should stay here until I know that everything has worked according to my plan. It will be too dangerous out there, and I don't want anything to happen to you."

"I would like to be with you. I am not afraid of danger. I can help you, Joe. I will not like staying in this hotel wondering."

"Let's wait and see what happens with all this business."

"You are such a good man, Joe. Do not worry about the plan. Everything will go well."

"I sure hope so," Joe said. "Are you hungry?"

"I will be ready in a minute," she said.

Captivated as she put on her new dress, Joe watched with appreciation of her beauty and grace. As she combed out her long, black tresses, he put on a clean shirt from his warbag.

As they left the hotel for the Oriental Cafe and Bar, all thoughts of Betsy had vanished from his mind. However, approaching the corner of Allen Street, Joe cringed as Betsy came straight toward them from the intersection. He couldn't think of any way to escape the confrontation. Stopping in front of them on the board sidewalk, Betsy radiated anger. "Well, Joe Holly, I thought you said you had been looking at some mares."

"Good evening, Betsy. I'd like you to meet Lucía." Turning to Lucía he said, "This is Betsy Willoughby."

Betsy squinted and stuck out her chin. "Why are you insulting me by introducing me to this Mexican whore?"

Lucía started for her, but Joe grabbed her arm. Seething with anger, Joe controlled himself with great effort. "That is uncalled for, Mrs. Willoughby. Lucía is my wife."

Lucía glanced quickly up to him. Betsy stood with a look of complete bafflement on her face. Finally, she said, "Joe Holly, you are a real bastard. Now, get out of my way."

Double Vengeance

Betsy stomped with angry determination on the wooden boardwalk, brushing past Joe and Lucía who continued to the corner. When they were on Allen Street and out of Betsy's sight, they stopped and faced each other. "Don't let her ruin our supper," Joe said. "I didn't think we would meet her like that."

"You told her I am your wife, Joe. What did you mean by that?"

"I had to say something after she called you a whore. It's a good thing I was able to get hold of you, or there would have been blood on the sidewalk."

"I liked being called your wife, Joe."

"Well, you aren't my wife yet, so remember I said that to get away from Betsy Willoughby."

After the meal of beefsteak, beans and rice, Joe ordered brandy for both of them. As she sipped at the snifter, she looked at Joe starry-eyed and smiling.

A breeze had sprung up while they dined. As they left the Oriental, Joe reached for his hat to keep it from blowing off his head before taking Lucía's arm to escort her back to the hotel. Once in their room they chatted for a few minutes before retiring for the night.

Suddenly, the sound of people yelling "Fire!" made Joe jump quickly out of the bed and over to the window. Looking out over the roofs, he saw people running in the streets and an orange glow in the middle of town. Lucía joined him at the window.

"Quick!" he exclaimed. "We'd better get out of here. The whole town might go up in smoke."

Lucía quickly put on her moccasins while Joe pulled on his boots. "Roll up your dress and put it and your shoes in my warbag," he said.

She moved quickly, putting the dress and shoes into the bag and snatching her rolled sleeping hides from

115

the floor where she had left them. Joe shouldered the warbag, opened the door, followed her into the hall and down the stairs. With a look of terror on his face, the clerk stood behind his desk immobile. "You'd better get out of this tinderbox," Joe yelled at him and the terrified man seemed to snap back from his near trance.

Leaving the hotel, they crossed the street to observe what they could. "Hurry, we have to get our horses from the livery," Joe said. "It looks like the fire's heading this way."

At the livery stable, they caught the sorrel and the pinto and led them from the corral. Joe quickly saddled his horse as Lucía tied her riding blanket onto the pinto. The livery boy was nowhere in sight.

"We have to get out of the path of the fire," Joe said. "I think the best way is out the Charleston Road."

They booted their horses into a lope, riding west until they had safely left the inferno behind. Circling south to get behind the fire, they reached the edge of town where a few board-and-batten buildings had been spared by being upwind from the fire. "You stay here with the horses, Lucía," Joe said as he dismounted and handed her his reins. "I'm going down there to see if I can help in some way. If the horses spook at the smoke, ride farther south and wait for me."

"Be careful, Joe."

"Don't worry, beautiful lady."

He trotted down Allen Street toward the center of town, where the flames threw showers of sparks into the sky. Whiskey bottles sounded like gunshots as they exploded from the intense heat.

Joe arrived at a crowd that stood helpless, gazing at the flames as they engulfed one wooden building after another. He watched as three men gave up a fire hose that had a mere trickle coming from its nozzle. "It was a great time while it lasted," remarked a man in miner's clothes standing next to him.

Joe did not reply. He watched a cluster of fallen doves chattering excitedly to one another. He wondered if there had been anybody caught inside any of the burning buildings. He left the forlorn crowd and returned to Lucía and the horses. "I guess we might as well find a place to camp," he said.

Mounting the sorrel, Joe led the way to a grove of mesquite trees by the arroyo east of town.

Chapter Eight

Furious after her confrontation with Joe and Lucía, Betsy left Tombstone, despite the late hour. The sunset had turned the western sky over the mountains into an array of orange and red as she drove into the Clanton ranch.

Delivering her message, she drove back to the Charleston road to head for Camp Huachuca. All the while, she contemplated what she might do to get Joe Holly back from the girl she thought was his Mexican wife. She wondered if, when she got her share of the robbery, the money would convince Holly to rejoin her. If the money did not impress Joe, she would continue selling information to the Clantons and making more money than Arnold would ever earn in the army. She would figure out how to leave later.

At almost ten o'clock that night, the guard at the camp's entrance waved her through the gate. She left the horse and buggy at the stables for the night man to take care of and carried her overnight bag to the house. Her entrance awakened Arnold who had just fallen asleep. "Is that you, Betsy?"

"Yes, Arnold," she replied curtly.

Willoughby came out of the bedroom.

"I thought you planned to spend the night in Tombstone."

"I decided not to."

"Did you get your new dress?"

"I didn't like it, so I wouldn't buy it until she had resewn the sleeves," she lied. "Go back to bed, Arnold. I'm going to stay up for a while and relax after the long drive. Is there any whiskey left?"

"There is a full quart in the cupboard," he answered. "I think I'll have one with you."

"For God's sake, Arnold. Why can't you leave me alone and go back to bed."

But Willoughby poured whiskey into two glasses, came back to the living room and put one glass on the coffee table in front of where Betsy sat in the middle of the sofa. Carrying his glass to the end table next to his favorite stuffed chair, he sat down with a sigh. "There's something troubling you, Betsy. What is it?"

"Nothing," she huffed, and took a swallow of the whiskey.

"You've not been yourself for some time, and it seems to me you are becoming more and more out of sorts lately."

"Arnold, for God's sake, why are you doing this to me? Leave me alone."

"Is it that sonofabitch Holly? Have you been seeing him again?"

"Arnold, you're being absurd. Please go to bed and leave me alone."

They sat in silence for a few minutes. Betsy filled her glass with more whiskey.

"I'm thinking about requesting a transfer to Fort Lowell," Arnold said. "I think you'll be happier in Tucson than isolated out here at Camp Huachuca."

"Do they pay you more regularly at Fort Lowell than they do at Huachuca?"

"One cannot count on being paid on time out here on the frontier. You know that. However, the payroll wagon should arrive in a few days. Once I am paid, you can spend a few days in Tucson to see how you like it."

Betsy filled her glass again. She had begun to feel the effects of the whiskey, and it became obvious to Willoughby that his wife would soon become drunk.

"I think you've had enough to drink tonight, Betsy. It's way past time for bed and I have a lot to do in the morning."

"Then go to bed, Arnold," she said, slurring her words. "I'm not ready for bed, and I have nothing to do tomorrow. I never have anything to do in this hellhole."

"Well, I'm going to bed. Please join me."

"Sweet dreams, Arnold," she said, and filled her glass yet another time.

Willoughby rose wearily from the stuffed chair and retired to the bedroom. Betsy continued to drink until she found herself getting dizzy. Finally she curled up on the sofa and went to sleep.

After a fitfull sleep, Willoughby awakend early and, as usual, brewed a pot of coffee while he dressed. Grabbing his coffee from the kitchen, he sought the overstuffed chair in the living room. He sat down, looked at his disheveled wife asleep on the couch and shook his head in dismay. Examining the less than half-bottle of whiskey on the table, he picked it up and carried it to the cupboard. Rejecting the idea of breakfast, he finished his coffee and left for the commandant's office, hoping to find Major Armbruster at his desk.

Willoughby returned the trooper's salute and knocked on the door. Hearing permission to enter, he turned the knob and stepped into the office. The commandant looked up from the papers on top of his desk. "Good morning, Major," Willoughby said.

"Good morning, Arnold. What brings you here so early?"

"I need a favor, a big favor."

"What kind of a favor?"

"I need to request a transfer to Fort Lowell as soon as possible," Willoughby said.

"Sit down, Arnold. I detect some urgency in your tone of voice."

Willoughby sat stiffly in the leather upholstered chair in front of the major.

"It's a personal matter, Major. I'm worried about Betsy. I think she is still seeing Holly in Tombstone. I can't talk to her anymore because she clams up when I ask her what's bothering her. I think a change of scene would do her good."

"Perhaps you're right, but a transfer based on your marital problems might be difficult to sell to Colonel Haynes. However, I have also noticed that you are having some sort of problems and was going to ask you about your situation. You are not concentrating on your command."

"It's difficult to concentrate on a command when my wife spends too many nights in Tombstone. At least in Tucson, she would have no excuse to remain in town because Fort Lowell is nearby. Tucson might offer her

121

a more pleasant environment. She constantly refers to Camp Huachuca as a hellhole."

"Military life on isolated posts can be a serious problem for our wives, Arnold. Have you thought about sending her back to Philadelphia?"

"That would probably end our marriage, too."

"Can you encourage her to mix more with the other women on post? I've noticed she seems to shun the activities that the others enjoy."

"I think her attitude toward the other women stems from her view of army life in general. In Tucson there are many more respectable women than in Tombstone. She might be inclined to find women friends there."

"I'll see what I can do, Arnold. It will take awhile, I'm sure, but I'll start your request with my approval and recommendation today."

"I cannot thank you enough, Major Armbruster."

"I hope your transfer will patch up your marriage. By the way, Arnold, I hope you stop seeking revenge against Mr. Holly. I am sure you know that I am aware of the shoulder wound he gave you in Tombstone."

Surprised that the major had gotten wind of the ill-fated attempt to settle his anger against Joe Holly, Willoughby's face colored with embarrassment. "How did you find out about that?"

"Arnold, you came back from your time off without your mount, saddle or weapon. I have to investigate these things. I just put two and two together."

"Once I am at Fort Lowell, Holly will be out of my hair."

"Maybe, maybe not, but I would stay clear of him if I were you, Arnold."

"Thank you for your understanding, Major."

Willoughby left the commandant's office feeling satisfied that he had accomplished what he had wanted. Tucson would be the solution to Betsy's contentment.

His spirits bouyed by the prospects of the transfer to Fort Lowell, Willoughby went about his duties with a smile throughout the day. His subordinates wondered what had happened to erase the captain's recent grouchy demeanor. He dismissed the troop a half hour early.

Returning to his house on Officers' Row, Arnold found Betsy sitting on the sofa with a drink of whiskey in her hand. Her hair hung loose and uncombed, and she had not changed from the clothes she had slept in. "For Christ's sake, Betsy! What are you trying to do to yourself?"

She sat looking into her glass without replying.

"I have good news for us, dear. This morning I requested a transfer to Fort Lowell. Major Armbruster approved it and started the paperwork. I think you will much happier in Tucson, my dear."

"All right, Arnold, Captain Arnold Willoughby," she said, obviously drunk. "You can transfer to hell for all I care."

"Betsy, be reasonable. There's a lot to do in Tucson. You'll be able to make friends with respectable women there."

"Respectable women? Arnold, I cannot bear to be around respectable women. All they talk about is clothes, babies, and how rich their husbands are."

"Tucson will certainly offer more than that horrid Tombstone."

"Maybe you should go to Tucson, and I'll move into Tombstone and become a fallen dove. I'll bet a year of your army pay that I would make more money as a lady of the night than you do as a captain in the goddamn cavalry."

"You're talking nonsense, my dear. You'll feel differently when you are sober."

"I don't feel like being sober, Arnold. In fact, I'd appreciate it if you'd get another bottle of whiskey. This one's nearly empty."

"You have had enough whiskey, Betsy."

"Then I'll go and get myself another bottle."

Willoughby succumbed to her threat, not wanting her to wander outside in her present condition. If Armbruster saw her, it might jeopardize his request for transfer. "All right, I'll get you a bottle. I will be back shortly."

He left Betsy on the sofa and strode over to the sutler's store, hoping it would be closed. His smile had turned back to the usual scowl. All the way across the parade ground, he contemplated the situation with Betsy and hoped his transfer would not be delayed somewhere along the line.

Disappointed that the sutler's store had not closed, he purchased a bottle of whiskey and returned to his house. Without speaking to his wife, Willoughby put the unopened bottle on the table and removed the empty one. Then, he went about making himself some supper of cold beef and cold beans.

He ate standing up in the small kitchen and when finished, went to the bedroom to read.

Chapter Nine

Joe and Lucía had established a comfortable camp in Davidson Canyon to await the arrival of Frog Eyes and his kinsmen. Three days before the expected arrival of the payroll wagon at Camp Huachuca, Frog Eyes and Etazin suddenly and silently appeared at the camp. Joe and Lucía greeted them warmly, and Lucía began roasting venison on the coals of their fire.

"Where are the others?" Joe asked.

"Others in hills. Nobody see," Frog Eyes said.

"How many warriors are there?"

"Thirty warriors."

"Good. I have thought about the best way to do this," Joe said. "We need to know two things: where the Clantons plan to rob the payroll wagon and which road the payroll wagon is traveling on."

Frog Eyes translated what Joe had said to Etazin.

"Etazin say he send scouts to Clanton Ranch. Scouts follow Clantons to place where stop to rob wagon.

125

Send other scouts to follow wagon. When sure of road, scouts come back."

"Does Etazin know where the Clanton Ranch is located?"

"Him know. No worry, Joe. Apache know all ranch everywhere."

The venison ready, they ate their fill, and the two warriors mounted their horses. "Etazin say you stay. When scouts come back, he send for you."

"Tell him we will wait right here."

The headman stood up, cupped his hands around his mouth and made a sound like a screech owl. He repeated this in several directions toward the surrounding hills of the canyon. Joe had stood up after the first signal, watching the hills. Warrior after warrior suddenly appeared and began descending onto the floor of the canyon. Impressed by their ability to remain so effectively hidden, Joe found himself more confident that the plan would be successful.

At last the entire raiding party arrived, riding their horses down the canyon to the camp. Assembled in front of Etazin, they listened to their headman explain how they would carry out the raid on the Clanton gang. Finished with the details of the plan, the headman and Frog Eyes mounted their horses and left with the others, leaving Joe and Lucía at the camp.

"What did Etazin say?" Joe asked.

"He told them everything that he expected would happen. Instead of sending two scouts to wait for the Clantons to leave their ranch, he is sending three. He thinks he knows the place where the gang will rob the payroll wagon and where they will attempt their escape."

"It sounds like he is trying to put himself into the minds of the Clantons," Joe said.

"Etazin is a wise leader and has led the warriors on many successful raids by avoiding pursuit by your army."

"I hope he has time to send for us prior to the raid on the Clanton gang."

"He said he will send a messenger," she assured.

"I wish we could have gone with them right now," Joe said, excitement showing in his voice.

"His plan is based on the Apache skill at hiding. They are used to these tactics, and Etazin wants to be able to take the Clantons completely by surprise. He thinks that you might not be able to hide and you might be seen."

"That makes sense to me," Joe said. "Watching them come down from the hills from their hiding spots makes me believe in their skill. While we talked here, the hills looked the same as they have all day. After Etazin gave his signal, I saw warriors suddenly appear as if the rocks had come to life."

"I have heard warriors talk about how they hid from your soldiers as they chased them. Sometimes they would laugh when they told their stories of a raid at the village in Arivaipa. The soldiers never learned that the Apache did not want to attack them. They just wanted to raid farms and ranches for cattle, horses and weapons."

"Maybe Arnold Willoughby is not so much a cowardly chicken captain, but wiser than most by not trying to pursue an enemy one cannot see," Joe said. "When he trailed Frog Eyes and me to Arivaipa Canyon, he certainly showed either courage or stupidity to ride off alone to search me out."

"I do not know your chicken captain, but I do not like his wife. If you had not held me back when she called me a whore, I would have strangled her right there on the street."

The next morning, Joe and Lucía had finished their breakfast of venison when the messenger arrived. He informed Lucía that the scouts had determined the payroll wagon's route and that the Clanton gang had left their ranch.

Refusing anything to eat, he told Lucía that she and Joe should go with him to where Etazin waited.

They gathered their things quickly and rode off with the messenger to meet the headman. Eager to see the plan executed without any major difficulty, Joe expressed his concern to Lucía. "I'm worried the troopers might drive off the Clantons," he said.

"From what the messenger said, the Clantons outnumber the troopers guarding the payroll wagon."

"Then they'll have the advantage of numbers and surprise. I never thought I'd be wishing a gang of robbers success in holding up an army payroll wagon."

Etazin had established what Joe recognized as a command post away from the trail they figured the Clantons would use to get away after robbing the wagon. He had chosen a hill from which he could observe the gang's movements and be in a good position to give his signal to the warriors hidden in the rocks and vegetation surrounding the canyon.

He explained that his warriors, using the element of surprise, would attack the Clantons swiftly before they knew what was happening. He had also positioned scouts to observe the outcome of the Clantons' success or failure in holding up the payroll wagon. When the results became obvious, one of the scouts would return and report to Etazin. The other would stay observing the soldiers.

Joe listened carefully as Lucía translated the Apache plan into English. "Your Etazin is an excellent tactician," Joe said.

"What do you mean, tactician?"

"Tactics are what a commander uses to plan a battle and execute it."

"Etazin is like a general to the Arivaipas."

"I am surprised that the Apache haven't been able to outfight the army."

"They have never tried to outfight the army because they know there are too many soldiers."

From far up the canyon came the muffled sound of gunfire. "Sounds like the Clantons might be attacking the payroll wagon," Joe said. "I hope they don't kill any of the troopers."

"Why do you worry about the troopers? It is not you who is robbing the wagon," Lucía asked.

"I'm aware of that, but I hate to see soldiers killed for any reason."

"Why did you become a soldier?"

"That was my father's idea. I never gave any thought to it except that he wanted me to follow in his footsteps. I just accepted it. But I soon began to hate being in the army."

Interrupting their conversation, a scout appeared and spoke with Etazin. The headman, obviously giving orders to the scout, pointed in one direction and then to the narrow defile in the canyon where he planned to take the Clantons by surprise. The scout left the command post and disappeared from view.

Etazin spoke to Lucía without turning away from the canyon. Lucía translated what he had said to Joe. "He said that the Clantons attacked the troopers escorting the wagon and made them surrender. The Clantons are now heading this way. They tied up the troopers and put all their weapons in the wagon. The scout also told Etazin that the gang ran off all the horses."

"I wonder how long it will take for the commandant of Camp Huachuca to go after the Clanton gang."

"The scout said that the Clantons all wore masks," Lucía said.

Etazin, looking down at the canyon from between two boulders, reached out with his left arm and held his hand in a signal to Joe and Lucía to stop talking. The sound of a crow came up the hill from below. The headman returned the crow's cry twice. Then he turned to Lucía and spoke quietly.

"Etazin says for us to come up on the boulders where we can see what will happen," Lucía said.

They edged their way up until they came to a place where they kneeled behind the boulders. Two shots rang out, echoing in the canyon, then three more. The Apache war cries sounded like members of an orchestra tuning their instruments. Joe spotted four riders gallop away from the battle and down the canyon. Two more followed, spurring their horses through the sandy floor of the canyon. The gunfire stopped and, seemingly out of nowhere, Frog Eyes appeared. He spoke quickly to Etazin, then turned to Joe. "Clanton gang surprised. Warriors jump on them from sides of canyon. Six run away. Two dead. Three have knife wound. All tied up. Good fight for Apache, get horses and guns. Warriors drive wagon to arroyo beyond hill. You look down. See."

They turned to look down the hill and saw the wagon being driven by two warriors with the others walking behind obliterating the tracks with sweeping branches.

Etazin spoke to Lucía. Then she told Joe that the warriors would drive the wagon up the side arroyo that eventually led to a trail that would take them around the main canyon through which the trail went.

Joe and Lucía were to follow Etazin to where they had left their horses so that they could ride to meet the others. Dusk began to invade the landscape.

At the meeting point, Joe inspected the contents of the wagon and found four pack saddles, a dozen rifles from the troopers and the strongbox containing the payroll money. Breaking the lock on the iron hasp, he opened the top and saw that the money had been separated into canvas bags. He hefted the bags to judge how much they weighed. "Tell Etazin that we will need two horses. Make them Clanton horses just in case we run into a cavalry patrol on the way to Tucson. We can put the pack saddles on the horses and leave the wagon here. Also, ask him if he wants to count the money."

Lucía spoke to the headman and returned to Joe to translate what he had said. "Etazin says that since Man With Eyes of Eagle is going with us, he sees no need to count the money now. He agrees that two Clanton horses will be safer to pack than the troopers' horses. He says that his men will bring them in shortly."

"To avoid any suspicion, I think we should go around the Santa Rita Mountains and enter Tucson from the south," Joe said.

"Then we can stop in Tumacacori to visit my relatives."

"We can do that. I don't want to get to Tucson until the news of this payroll wagon holdup dies down, and the army tries to figure out who the masked robbers were. Did I hear Etazin mention Geronimo?"

"The warriors referred to one of their people as Geronimo to make the Clantons think they were Chiricahuas instead of Arivaipas. That was Etazin's idea."

"I think there will be much confusion when all is said and done. And the more the army is confused, the safer we will be until we spend the money for horses, ours and those for Etazin."

Two warriors rode in, leading two of the Clanton horses. Joe unsaddled them, tossing the heavy stock saddles into the wagon. Replacing them with the wooden-framed pack saddles, he transferred the canvas bags from the strongbox into the panniers, dividing the load between the two horses. He spoke to Etazin as Lucía translated. "We will go south and then north to Tucson. It may take some time to buy your horses, but when I have yours driven to the San Pedro north of Tucson, we will send Man With Eyes of Eagle to Arivaipa. In the meantime, you have the army and Clanton horses that you captured. I will put these two pack horses in with the rest as extras."

Etazin nodded his head in agreement and said something to Lucía. "He says that you had a good plan and now he is counting on you to finish the business."

"Tell him we wish him and his warriors a safe ride back to Arivaipa."

Lucía translated Joe's words. Etazin gave Joe one of his rare smiles, mounted his horse and followed by his warriors, rode away.

Frog Eyes took the lead shank of one of the pack horses. Joe, with the lead shank of the other horse in his right hand, mounted the sorrel. Lucía jumped onto the pinto and the trio left the wagon. The Apaches had unharnessed the army mules and divided the weapons among themselves. There was nothing left in the payroll wagon but the empty strongbox, two pack saddles and two stock saddles belonging to the Clantons. Joe hoped the army would find the wagons before the Clantons came back for their dead companions.

They had decided to ride as far as they could toward the Santa Ritas. The almost full moon gave Frog Eyes enough light to find his way to the trail he knew that led through the Salero Hills and on down into the Santa Cruz River Valley. The trail wandered uphill for several miles. They stopped occasionally to rest the horses. At one point, the trail crossed a narrow stream that provided enough water for all.

The first glow of early morning light seeped in just as the trail steepened to surmount a bluff. Once on top, they rode through rolling hills of grassland with a few scattered oak trees along the small arroyos between the hills. Frog Eyes reined in the bay gelding next to a small grove of oak. "Frog Eyes hunt," he said. "Good wood for fire."

"We are far enough away," Joe said. "The horses will enjoy this good grass."

Frog Eyes hobbled the bay and went off on foot. After unsaddling the sorrel and the two pack horses, Joe hobbled them and turned them loose to graze. Lucía had begun to gather firewood from the dead branches on the lower part of the scrubby-looking oak trees. Clearing a circle of the straw-colored grass, she bunched some in the middle and piled small pieces of oak on top of the grass. Lighting the fire she piled on larger pieces until the flames burned vigorously.

After taking care of the horses, Joe helped gather wood and when they had a pile that would last several hours, he suggested to Lucía that they try to sleep.

Spreading her sleeping hides beneath an oak that

provided shade from the morning sun, she invited Joe to share her bed.

They fell asleep next to each other on the sleeping hides. When they opened their eyes they looked up to see Frog Eyes busily cutting steaks from an antelope's hindquarters.

The wood had burned down to coals. Lucía blew the covering of gray ashes away and laid the steaks on the coals to broil. The three were soon feasting, satisfying their hunger after the long night's ride.

To avoid encountering any cavalry patrols from Camp Buchanan, they slept until late afternoon. Darkness had covered the foothills of the Santa Rita Mountains by the time they approached the Salero Hills. Slowed by the rugged terrain, they finally reached Josephine Canyon with its cool, clear stream flowing through huge boulders.

After watering the horses and themselves, they continued winding their way down the long *bajada* toward the Santa Cruz River. Lucía became excited because she knew she would soon see her remaining relatives on the small farm outside Tumacacori. Reaching the floodplain, Joe reined in the sorrel. "I am concerned about one thing," he said. "The money is in bags that have U.S. Army printed on them. We need to find some other kind of container."

"I am sure Tía Alma will have some old flour sacks," Lucía said.

"That will do, but she must not be told why we need them."

"Leave that up to me, Joe. I will think of something that will not arouse any suspicion."

"Is there a place where we can hide the money?"

"There is a cave in Tinaja Canyon. It is not far from the farm."

"Will it be a safe place?"

"I think so."

"I think it might be a good idea if Frog Eyes stayed with the money."

"The cave is plenty large enough, and there is a lot of grass for the horses on the surrounding hills. We used to run our cattle on those hills before the Apache raid."

Lucía led them across the river and up Tinaja Canyon for two miles where the stream passed through a narrow canyon bounded by large rock formations. She reined up under the entrance to the cave. "There it is," she announced, pointing up. "I will climb up into the cave and you can hand up the sacks of money."

Dismounting from the pinto, she climbed a narrow fracture in the boulder below the mouth of the cave and gained entrance as Joe and Frog Eyes untied the tarps covering the pack saddles.

Mounted on the sorrel next to the boulder, Joe took the sacks one by one from Frog Eyes and handed them up to Lucía. When all the sacks were in the cave, the two men unsaddled the pack horses and lifted the wooden frames and their trappings up to her. The last thing to go up was the remainder of the antelope, enough food for Frog Eyes for several days. "We'll be back as soon as we find some flour sacks and Lucía has a chance to visit with her relatives," Joe said.

Chapter Ten

When the troopers had managed to cut themselves free from the bonds the Clanton gang had tied them up with, they walked to Camp Huachuca. News of the payroll robbery spread rapidly. Disappointed that they would not receive their two months' pay, the soldiers grumbled among themselves.

After learning about the robbery, Arnold Willoughby informed Betsy, admonishing her to be careful of her expenditures. "But, Arnold," she said, "I have to pick up my two dresses in Tombstone tomorrow."

"Why are you buying more dresses?"

"You want me to look nice at the post parties, don't you?"

"Yes, of course, but this is not a time to spend money for dresses. There's no telling when another payroll wagon will get through."

"I ordered the dresses, Arnold. Reneging would be very embarrassing."

"Well, all right, but see if you can come back tomorrow without spending more money on a hotel room."

"I'll start early."

The next morning, Betsy drove her buggy out through the main gate of Camp Huachuca at sunrise. The morning air had a winter chill to it as she kept the horse at a trot. Betsy had felt a great excitement since learning about the robbery. Driving down the road toward what she thought would be a rich reward for her efforts only heightened her anticipation.

Letting out a sigh as she spotted the road into the Clanton Ranch, she slowed the horse to a walk. Five mongrel dogs ran out barking to meet her. She stayed in the buggy until Old Man Clanton appeared on the porch and called off the dogs.

"If you came for your money," the old man said, "there isn't any."

"What do you mean, Mr. Clanton? News of the robbery is all over the camp."

"They only know half of the story."

"Half?"

"After we got the escort tied up and left with the wagon, we got jumped by a band of Apache raiders. I not only lost the payroll, but the devils killed two of my men. They took the horses, the wagon with the payroll and our weapons."

"Where did the Apaches come from?"

"The men heard a couple of them refer to Geronimo. I guess he must have crossed the border again. I suppose we were lucky not to have lost more men."

Her spirits shattered by the bad news, Betsy slumped on the seat of the buggy. "I'll let you know about the next payroll wagon, Mr. Clanton."

"All right, but I'm not sure if my men will be enthusiastic about the chance of getting attacked by those devil Apache again."

Turning the buggy around in the spacious barnyard, Betsy left the ranch headquarters and returned slowly to the road to Tombstone. She felt angry and disappointed, and hunger pains stabbed at her stomach, for she had left the post without breakfast.

Leaving the buggy at the livery stable, she went to the newly rebuilt Oriental. Trying to quell the anger she felt, she ordered a whiskey. "Make it a double, and I would like a beefsteak."

Before her meal arrived, she had tossed down two double shots of the strong, rank-tasting whiskey. Her stomach pains increased until suddenly she no longer felt them. She ordered another double shot when the waiter brought her steak. Eating ravenously, she devoured the meal quickly. Her head felt light from the whiskey, and she thought about the Clantons being attacked by the Indians. She laughed. Now she would have to postpone all her plans, the major one being her strong desire to leave Arnold and return to Philadelphia. Ever since her confrontation with Joe Holly and Lucía, she had decided to stop pursuing the former lieutenant and go back to what she always referred to as the "civilized" part of the country.

After another drink, she bought a bottle of whiskey, paid her bill and weaved out of the Oriental. Going straight to the newly rebuilt Grand Hotel, she took the last vacant room and sat on the bed with her whiskey on the bedside table.

Remembering the times she had enjoyed with Holly, she felt a fierce jealousy toward Lucía, and vowed in her drunkeness to rip her hair out if she ever saw the woman alone. She could not understand why Joe had chosen a Mexican whore instead of her. Drowning all mental processes with the whiskey, Betsy crumpled under the covers with her clothes still on.

Late the next morning, she awoke with a splitting headache and a stomach that felt like everything inside it had somehow caught fire. From the pitcher on the washstand, she poured water into the basin and washed her face. Then, taking her brush and comb from her bag, she began working on getting her hair in enough order to go out on the street to get some breakfast. Before leaving the hotel, she tilted the whiskey bottle up to her lips and took two swallows. The fire in her stomach diminished and she slipped the bottle into her bag.

After a breakfast that she could not finish for fear of vomiting, she went to the livery stable. The stable man harnessed her horse and hitched him to the buggy. With her headache still pounding inside her skull, Betsy drove the buggy to the road leading to the post. She could not shake the disappointment from her mind.

Arriving at the stabling area of Camp Huachuca, she reined in and left the buggy for the troopers to unhitch and to take care of. Inside her house, she felt glad that Arnold had not come in from the field. She took the bottle of whiskey out of her bag and poured a glass.

The whiskey felt good in her stomach, but she continued to brood about the unsuccessful robbery. An hour later, Arnold arrived. When he saw Betsy, a deep scowl furrowed his brow. "Dammit, Betsy, I thought I asked you to come right back from Tombstone to save money."

"Well," she said, a slight slur to her words, "I chose to spend the night."

"I suppose you met up with Holly."

"Arnold, I never saw Joe Holly. Besides, he's married to some Mexican whore."

She poured more whiskey into her glass. "You don't have to worry about Joe Holly."

"Whatever is bothering you, the whiskey is not the remedy. Is the reason you spent the night in Tombstone because you were drunk?"

"So I was drunk. What difference does that make?"

"It makes a lot of difference. You are not attractive when you're drunk, Betsy. I can't understand why you've been drinking so much lately."

"I like to drink. When I'm drinking I don't have to think about this godforsaken Camp Huachuca out in the middle of nowhere."

"You won't have to think about it much longer. I told you that I've requested a transfer to Fort Lowell in Tucson. You should be happier there."

"Suppose I don't want to go to Tucson?"

"I'm sure you'll enjoy life in Tucson more than here. You have complained constantly about Camp Huachuca. Fort Lowell is within easy reach of town, and there are many things going on there."

"When is all this going to happen?"

"The major sent off the request a week ago. He personally recommended my transfer, so it should come through shortly."

"I wish you had told me about this before you put in for the transfer," she said, worrying about how she would be able to get word to the Clantons about the next payroll wagon's arrival. Then she realized, in spite of her drunkeness, that if Arnold was no longer the payroll officer at Camp Huachuca, and they were in Tucson, she would not know about payroll schedules. She would be doomed to living with Arnold until she found another way to make her own money.

"I'm sure you'll be far happier in Tucson," he said, and went to the kitchen to prepare supper.

Betsy poured more whiskey into her glass. "Oh shit," she said.

Chapter Eleven

With Frog Eyes settled in the cave, Joe and Lucía left for her uncle's farm near Tumacacori. Riding north when they reached the mouth of Tinaja Canyon, Lucía explained that they were on the Camino Real, the road that connected Tucson with Mexico. "Do you see the big church ahead?"

"Yes. What's it doing way out here?"

"That is San Cayetano de Tumacacori. It's an old Spanish mission. Since the United States took over this part of the country, it has not been used much. People around here go to church in Tubac, which is three miles north of Tumacacori."

"What's in Tubac?"

"It started as a *presidio,* a garrisoned town, when the Spaniards were here. Now, there is not much there except for a few houses and the small church."

Lucía reined the pinto onto a narrow side road. "My uncle's farm is across the river."

Double Vengeance

The Santa Cruz main channel held a twenty-foot-wide stream of clear water. Before crossing, they let their horses drink. The other side of the tree-lined road went straight to the bottom of the foothills. Halfway, Lucía pointed to an old adobe house with an adobe barn and a small corral next to it. "There is my uncle's house. The farmland around here is mostly his. I wonder if they will remember me."

"In another hundred yards you will know," Joe said.

Three dogs of mixed breed ran barking toward them as they approached the house, which had a porch on front extending along the entire length. An apron-clad middle-aged woman stood in the open doorway. Her right hand shaded her eyes, even though the porch shielded her completely from the sun. After a furtive glance out to the fields, she continued to look at the visitors without calling off the dogs. Lucía and Joe reined up a short way from the house. "Tía Alma, it is me, Lucía."

The woman looked intently, her forehead etched with a wrinkled scowl. *"Dios mío!"* she exclaimed. "I did not recognize you. We thought you were dead. Where have you been all these years?"

Lucía dismounted and hurried over to embrace her aunt. "It is a long story," she said. "I will explain it all later. Where is Tío Manuel?"

"He is out in the field as usual. I will call him in."

She went to the end of the porch where an iron triangle hung from a rafter. Picking up an iron rod, she banged on the triangle, sending the signal that Manuel should come back to the house.

Joe dismounted. "This is Alma, Joe. Tía, this is Joe Holly."

"Aye, *Dios mío!* It is a pleasure to meet you, Señor Holly."

"The pleasure is mine, señora," Joe said touching his hat brim.

Surprise and happiness radiated from Manuel's face when he recognized Lucía. "We had given up on ever seeing you again years ago. What a blessing that you are alive and well. Come in and tell us everything that has happened."

Manuel ushered Lucía and Joe into the kitchen and told them to sit down while Alma made a fesh pot of coffee. "Where are my cousins, Alfredo, Rosalia and Elisa?"

"Alfredo works for the Americanos as a cowboy. Rosalia and Elisa are married. Elisa lives in Tubac with her husband and two children. Rosalia lives in Tucson. She has one son. Now it is time for your story."

"I hid under my bed when the Apache came and killed everyone. They found me and took me away. I screamed and cried, but they would not let me go."

Lucía continued with the story of her capture and the years she grew up as the daughter of Etazin, the Arivaipa headman.

Her uncle and aunt sat in rapt attention, listening to her tell about her years away with the Indians. Finally, Alma, remaining within earshot, rose from her chair and began preparing supper.

Returning to the table with bowls of *bírria* made from goat, chile and other spices, Alma sat down again as Lucía continued. Joe picked out a few of the words in Spanish as he listened to the familiar tale.

Joe and Lucía spent the night after putting their horses in the corral. Lucía told him that they would have to sleep in separate rooms. She did not want to upset her uncle and aunt.

After breakfast the next morning, Joe and Lucía walked along the river. When he was sure nobody had followed, he asked her if she wanted to remain in Tumacacori with her uncle and aunt while he and Frog Eyes went to Tucson to buy horses for Etazin.

"I will go with you and help you drive the horses to the San Pedro River. Besides, I want to be with you more than I want to be with my uncle and aunt. You might need me more than you think you will."

"Then we should get back to the cave after you get some old flour sacks from your aunt."

"That will be easy. When we get back to the house, you can be saddling your sorrel while I get the flour sacks from Tía Alma. I also want to find out where my cousin Rosalia lives in Tucson."

On their way back to the farmhouse they met Manuel trudging out to his field. They said their good-byes, and Joe thanked him for his hospitality. As Joe saddled the sorrel, Lucía went into the house and shortly came out with an armful of old flour sacks. They were soon riding back to the cave in Tinaja Canyon. An hour after joining with Frog Eyes they had transferred the payroll money into the flour sacks, burning the marked government bags in the campfire. During the transfer they counted the money and discovered they had six thousand dollars, more than enough to buy horses for Etazin and enough mares for Joe to start his horse business. "Maybe the payroll wagon was carrying Fort Bowie's money, too." Joe said. After saddling and loading the pack horses they left Tinaja Canyon. Joe soon found himself in unfamiliar country. "How far are we from Tucson?" he asked Lucía.

"Two days."

"Is there another trail? This one looks well used."

"This is what we call El Camino Real because, as I said, it is the main road that goes from Tucson into Mexico. There is a trail on the east side of the river, but it will be slower going."

"We're not in any hurry, so let's try that. I don't want anybody getting curious about what's under the tarpaulins. Lead the way."

Pointing toward the river Lucía said, "About a mile north there is a trail leading to a river crossing. We can pick up the trail on the other side."

"Try to think about a place near Tucson where we can hide the money until I find the horses to buy."

"I do not remember Tucson very well, but to the west there are some craggy-looking mountains."

"I remember seeing them when I stayed at Fort Lowell. When we get near the city, we can ride up there and look for a good place."

Before sunset, Lucía led them to a canyon in the Santa Rita Mountains where a stream furnished them cool, clear water as it gurgled through smooth, rounded rocks of various colors. "Farther up the canyon there are pine trees, but here there is a lot of grass for the horses tonight," she said.

The three travelers dismounted, unsaddled and hobbled all the horses before proceeding to make their camp. Lucía had chosen a spot with a broad view of the long alluvial fan so that should anyone approach they would be spotted a long way downslope.

Frog Eyes meandered off to hunt as Joe and Lucía gathered wood for the campfire. "I'm glad you came along," Joe said. "It's nice to have someone who knows the country and is trail-wise."

"I am glad, too. I like being able to help you, Joe. And my memory is getting better."

Burdened with a deer carcass, Frog Eyes returned to camp. By nightfall they were all stuffed and ready to sleep, no matter how cold the December chill that slithered down the mountain slope on its way to the river's floodplain.

Before sunrise, they found the horses grazing nearby, led them to the stream and let them drink their fill. Joe marveled at the lush grassland through which they rode. It stretched from the base of the mountains to the mesquite *bosques* and cottonwoods growing along the river. This should be good horse country, he mused.

By the time the sun eased over the top of the Santa Ritas, they had crossed the river and headed toward the craggy mountains west of Tucson. Frog Eyes told Joe about a good place to hide the money. He had been there with a raiding party several years before he became an army scout. He led Joe and Lucía west of the mountains to a pass from where they could observe anyone approaching for miles on both sides of the mountains. Just below the top of the pass, he pointed out a mound of volcanic rocks that would hide the flour sacks from view. Joe put six hundred dollars in his pockets, leaving the rest of the money in the flour sacks that they hid beneath a pile of rocks. Before leaving for Tucson, they approached the hiding place from all directions to make sure that any traveler could not see the flour sacks and brushed their tracks away with the branches from a bush called desert broom.

Entering through the gate in the wall around Tucson in early evening, they first found where Rosalia lived. The men left Lucía there to stay with her cousin. Joe found a room at the Cosmopolitan Hotel, and Frog

Eyes went to the brothel he had frequented whenever he had come to Fort Lowell with the troopers. He took what was left of the venison to try and barter it for the favors of one of the doves. The plan for the following day was for Joe to inquire about the availability of horses for sale. They would all three meet at the Cimarron Cafe for supper. Joe put up the sorrel and the pack horses at J.Z. Tyler's corrals. The former soldier had been disappointed that J.Z. had gone home and left a young boy in charge of the livery end of the business.

"What time does Mr. Tyler get here in the morning?" Joe had asked the lad.

"He's here by the time I finish feeding, around six o'clock."

Joe went down Congress Street until he came to The Lucky Dollar. He heard the the noise from the crowded bar twenty yards away. *Maybe I'll meet somebody here who has horses for sale or knows about some.*

He hesitated for a moment at the door to The Lucky Dollar just long enough to look over the crowd. The bar had a few empty spots, so Joe aimed for a place between a cowboy and a miner. When the bartender finally got around to taking his order, Joe asked for a tequila. Tossing down the shot, Joe turned to the cowboy on his left. "Do you work around here?"

"Yep, I work for the Canoa Ranch south of here."

"I'm looking to buy some horses," Joe said. "You wouldn't know where I might find some, would you?"

"The Canoa raises all its own colts. They might have some fillies or old mares for sale. Most of the ranches around here raise all their own horses."

Joe began to wonder if he would find enough horses

to buy. *J.Z. Tyler should be able to find a bunch. After all, he's in the horse business.*

"Where did you come from?" Joe asked.

"Marfa, Texas. It's south a ways from Fort Davis."

"Been here long?"

"Six months."

"Do you like it here?"

"It sure beats that Marfa country. I figure to stay here a spell. How about you?"

"This country's all right. I'll probably stay if I can get into the horse business."

"The foreman at the Canoa's lookin' for a bronc buster."

"That's good to know in case I can't find any horses to buy," Joe said.

After his third tequila, Joe said good night to the cowboy and left The Lucky Dollar to go to his room in the Cosmopolitan Hotel.

Stretched out on top of the bed, he thought about Lucía. There was an innocence about her that both intrigued and attracted him. Certainly she was different from any of the girls he'd known in Maine. He enjoyed listening to her speak English with her Mexican accent, although it was not as pronounced as some he'd heard. He also found her beautiful, either in buckskins or dolled up in her new dress from Tombstone. *I wish I knew if this plan was going to work out to put me in the horse business.*

Chapter Twelve

Sitting alone, Joe enjoyed his breakfast in the Cafe El Gallo. It gave him time to think things out without distractions. Remembering not to appear eager to buy anything from a horse trader, he didn't hurry his breakfast because he did not want to arrive at the corrals before J.Z. The clock on the wall behind the scarred pine counter said seven o'clock when he finished eating and paid his bill.

Approaching the corrals, Joe saw J.Z. sitting on his bench whittling on a piece of wood as he soaked up the first of the sun's rays. With his hat pulled down to shade his eyes, the horse trader remained whittling even when Joe stopped in front of him.

"I see you're still ridin' that Steeldust sorrel, Lieutenant," J.Z. said. "He must be turnin' out awright."

Joe couldn't figure out how J.Z. had recognized him since Joe had not even seen the man look up from under his hat. "The sorrel's a good horse. I don't have any complaints at all."

"Where did you get those other two you brought in last night?" JZ.. asked.

Joe was unprepared for the question. "I bought them in Tombstone."

"Hmm . . . They've got Old Man Clanton's brand on 'em. No tellin' why he come to sell horses that young. I'll bet they ain't four years old."

Joe searched his mind for something to say to change the subject of the Clanton horses. *This might be a big country, but it's not much bigger than a village when it comes to knowing who lives where. Seems this J.Z. knows everyone in the territory right down to the brands they burn onto their horses.*

"If you've come for your stock, it'll be six bits," J.Z. said.

"I'm not ready to leave yet. I stopped by to see if you have some cheap horses for sale."

"Now, Lieutenant, I don't deal in cheap horses," J.Z. said with a tinge of pride in his voice. "You ought to know that since you bought that good Steeldust from me."

"You can just call me Joe Holly, Mr. Tyler. I'm no longer in the army."

"I was wonderin' how come you weren't wearin' that uniform. Now that it's winter, that wool oughta feel good."

"If you don't have any cheap horses, maybe you can tell me where I can find a couple hundred head."

"Hell's fire, Holly, what are you goin' to do with a couple hundred head a horses?"

"I have a buyer. Do you know where I can find any?"

"It might take a spell ta get a couple hundred head together. That's a helluva bunch a horses."

"How many can you put together in a week?" Joe asked.

"I don't rightly know until I start askin' around. First off, I need to know just what kind a horses you're wantin' to buy: geldin's, mares, youngun's or old ones, fat ones or buzzard bait."

"My buyer doesn't much care except what you call 'buzzard bait' isn't what he's looking for. They don't even have to be broke to ride, just, hmm . . . ah, inexpensive. By the way, Mr. Tyler, as you're asking around you might inquire about top-quality broodmares. I'm in the market for enough to start a breeding program with, maybe twenty head or so. And, if you can find some top stallions I'll look at them, too. Maybe you can find more Steeldust horses like my sorrel."

"This is all fine and dandy, you comin' in here and wantin' me to go out and find all these horses for you, but how do I know you'll pay for 'em once I get 'em here in my corrals?"

"That's certainly a fair question, Mr. Tyler. Suppose I give you five hundred dollars deposit as a sign of good faith?"

"That sounds good enough."

"All right, Mr. Tyler. And, suppose I give you the five hundred and you just sit here on your bench whittling without ever asking anyone if they have horses for sale?"

"Someone's got to trust someone in this deal, or there won't be a deal. I expect you could put your five hundred with a banker. Then I go out and get these horses, and if you don't pay for 'em, you forfeit the five hundred."

"That arrangement sounds reasonable to me," Joe said. "I'm staying at the Cosmopolitan. Start with the hundred head of cheap horses."

"That's another thing, Holly. Exactly what do you call a cheap horse?"

"I paid you thirty for my sorrel, so a cheap horse ought to go for somewhere around ten to fifteen I would think."

"That won't leave a lot of room for me," J.Z. said, a slight whine in the tone of his voice.

"I guess that's your challenge as a horse trader, Mr. Tyler. Shall we go to the banker?"

"We'll go see ol' Beasley at Territory Bank and Trust. I'll be there in an hour or so."

"I'll meet you at the bank, Mr. Tyler."

Chapter Thirteen

J.Z. Tyler's recognizing the two Clanton horses by their brands bothered Joe as he made his way to the Territory Bank and Trust on Congress Street. He wondered if news of the army payroll robbery had reached Tucson and if the Clanton gang was under suspicion. *I can't go around asking questions because people would wonder why I'm so curious. Tyler seems like a man who sticks to his own business. He appeared to drop the subject of the Clanton horses of his own accord. I expect I shouldn't be concerned unless something happens to make me concerned.*

Snuggled next to Zeckendorf Mercantile, across the rutted dirt street from the bank, a small restaurant provided Joe with a place to wait for J.Z. and sip a cup of inky black coffee at the same time. He shifted his thoughts from the Clanton horses to Lucía, realizing that he missed being with her. In his mind there was no comparison between Lucía and Betsy Willoughby, even though he had not experienced the Mexican woman completely. As he sat with his coffee, it was not the first time he tried to imagine what it would be like making love to her.

The image of her standing naked in front of him in the wickiup vanished immediately when he saw J.Z. drive his buggy up to the front of the bank across the street, ease himself to the ground and waddle to the hand-carved wooden door.

Joe put down his half-empty cup with a nickel on the table, left the restaurant and lost no time getting across the street to the bank. J.Z. had just settled himself in one of the two chairs in front of the banker's desk. Waving his hand back and forth, he introduced Joe to Jonathan Beasley. Standing, the banker reached across the desk to shake Joe's hand. "Please sit down, Mr. Holly. What can I do for you gentlemen?"

"We need you to hold Holly's five hundred-dollar deposit on a horse order he's given me," J.Z. said. "Once I get fifty head bought, you release the five hundred to me. Then he'll put up another deposit on another fifty head."

"That sounds much like a land deal," Beasley said, tapping his index finger on the desktop. "When you have the horses bought, J.Z., both of you come in and let me know and you'll receive the deposits."

"What in the world are you going to do with a hundred head of horses, Mr. Holly?" Beasley asked.

Joe thought quickly. "You might say I'm going into the horse business."

"Will your deposit be cash or draft, Mr. Holly?"

"Cash," Joe said, reaching into his pocket. "Here it is."

He counted out five hundred dollars onto the desktop and pushed it across for Beasley to count. The banker had watched Joe count and didn't bother to count the money again. He opened a drawer in the desk and took out a piece of paper. Dipping his pen in the inkwell, he proceeded to write out a receipt for the deposit.

Handing the document to Joe, he said, "I will look forward to seeing you gentlemen soon. You must be new in town, Mr. Holly. Where are you from?"

"Maine," Joe replied.

"Are you planning to settle here in Tucson?"

"It all depends on how the horse business goes."

Joe was not comfortable with the curiosity of the banker. He stood up from the chair and shook Beasley's hand. "I must be going now. It is nice to meet you, Mr. Beasley."

"The pleasure is mine, Mr. Holly."

Outside the bank, Joe asked J.Z., "When should I check back with you?"

"I'll leave word at the Cosmopolitan when I have the fifty in the corrals, and you can come over and look at 'em."

"That will be fine, Mr. Tyler," Joe said.

J.Z. untied his buggy horse from the hitching post and pulled himself onto the seat. Flicking the reins on the horse's rump, he drove away from the bank toward the next intersection where Congress Street crossed Main Street. There he turned right toward his corrals near the edge of town.

That evening Lucía and Frog Eyes joined Joe at the Cimarron Cafe where he told them about the current status of the horse-buying project. They enjoyed a meal and agreed to meet again in five days before they went their separate ways. Joe stopped at The Lucky Dollar before returning to his hotel. As he stood at the bar with his tequila, he again thought about Lucía. He had had trouble keeping his eyes away from her during supper.

Roaming around Tucson the following day, he discovered the land office. Out of curiosity, he entered the building and found a well-dressed man sitting behind a desk that had several stacks of important-looking, seal-covered papers on it. "Good morning," the man said, getting to his feet and reaching out to shake Joe's hand. "I'm George Phillips. What may I help you with?"

"Joe Holly. I'm thinking about getting into the horse business, and I wondered if you might know of a ranch for sale."

"There's a few for sale here and there. Are you looking for any particular area?"

"I just need water and good grass for horses is all."

"There's a place along the Cañada del Oro. The owner is tired of Apaches raiding his livestock. It's got a well at headquarters and there's water from the mountains in a couple of canyons."

"How much country are you talking about?"

"The headquarters is on eighty acres, and the rest is open range. There are very few cattle out there because of the Apache raids."

"How much money are we talking about.?"

"The owner's asking fifteen hundred. The house and corrals should be worth that much."

"When can I go out to look the place over?" Joe asked.

"I could probably get away tomorrow. Are you able to pay cash?"

"That's my intention, Mr. Phillips."

"No offense, I just need to know before I spend a lot of time showing you around."

"What time do you want to meet in the morning?"

"How about six? The trip will take a couple of days."

"How far from town is this place?"

"Pretty close to a day's ride. We can make it there by midafternoon. You'll have a few hours of daylight to look it over. We can spend the night, see more country in the morning and ride back the next day."

"All right. Sounds good. I'll meet you here in the morning at six."

Joe left the land office and continued his stroll around Tucson thinking about Lucía. *I can't seem to get that girl out of my mind. I want her and know very well that I could have her, yet something holds me back. The picture of her standing naked in front of me won't go away. I enjoy being with her no matter what we are doing, and she is a woman who would help rather than hinder.*

Joe saddled the sorrel early, ate a hearty breakfast at the Cimarron Cafe and rode over to met George Phillips at his office at six o'clock. A few minutes after Joe's arrival, Phillips drove up in a buggy. "I didn't realize you would be riding," the real estate dealer said.

"I assumed you would be horseback to show me the ranch."

"It doesn't take a saddle horse to show you eighty acres and a house."

"I guess you're right, Mr. Phillips, but I'd just as soon ride."

Joe preferred not conversing with the man. That way he wouldn't have to answer a lot of questions, the responses to which he would most likely want to keep to himself. Everyone was curious about a stranger, especially one who voiced being in the market for one thing or another.

By midmorning, the sun had warmed the desert air, and Joe shed his jacket, tying it in back of the cantle. They soon pulled up at an adobe structure that had a set of strong corrals at one side. A squeaky windmill turned lazily in the soft breeze, bringing water up from the well beneath it and filling a masonry storage tank with a small trickle of water every time the sucker-rod went up. There were several horses standing in one of the corrals.

"This is the Butterfield stop," Phillips said after they had reined in in front of the building. "It might be a good idea to get a bite to eat here, even though the ranch is only an hour away across the Canada del Oro."

"You're the leader," Joe said, even though he wasn't excited to sample the stage stop food.

Joe thought Phillips must have read his mind when the land man said, "The grub here isn't fancy, but it'll keep the sides of your stomach from stickin' together."

Joe and Phillips were the sole customers because the stage had left for Florence an hour before they had arrived. After a chunk of boiled meat and a bowl of beans, they continued on the road to their destination, Rancho Tecolote.

Upon their arrival, Phillips introduced Joe to Ben Hicks, owner of the ranch, and they went inside for coffee. Hicks never mentioned the Apache raids he had been a victim of. Instead, he described the mountain country as having strong grass and plenty of running streams. When Joe told him about his plan to raise horses, the old cowman praised the country to an even greater extent.

John Duncklee

After breakfast the following morning, Joe and George Phillips rode off to look at the foothill and mountain pasture, returning to the ranch headquarters just after noon. Joe had seen enough to know that he wanted the ranch for his planned horse operation. After the trip back to Tucson Joe asked Phillips about the fifteen hundred-dollar price tag Hicks had put on the ranch. "That seems a bit high for that old house and eighty acres of property," Joe said.

"You may be right. In fact, you're the first prospective buyer I have shown the ranch to. Most people know about the Apache situation out there and want to stear clear of that."

Joe made no mention of his acquaintance with the Arivaipa Apache. "I can see why nobody wants to try ranching in a place where the Apache like to raid. I'll tell you what I'll do, Mr. Phillips. I'll pay one thousand dollars for Rancho Tecolote and not a dime more."

"I don't know what Hicks will say to that offer, but I'll present it to him," Phillips said. "I'll need some deposit money to show you mean business."

"We can take care of all that tomorrow afternoon," Joe said, knowing it would take a while to get some of the money from the cache in the Tucson Mountains.

Joe found Frog Eyes that evening, and they agreed to meet early the following morning for the ride into the Tucson Mountains. It would have been just as easy for Joe to ride alone to get the money he needed for the ranch, but he wanted Frog Eyes to witness what he did to avoid any possible misunderstanding later with Etazin.

Phillips was sitting in his chair when Joe walked into his office at three o'clock the next afternoon. "Mr. Phil-

Join the Western Book Club
and GET 4 FREE* BOOKS NOW!
A $19.96 VALUE!

Yes! I want to subscribe to the Western Book Club.

Please send me my **4 FREE* BOOKS**. I have enclosed $2.00 for shipping/handling. Each month I'll receive the four newest Leisure Western selections to preview for 10 days. If I decide to keep them, I will pay the Special Members Only discounted price of just $3.36 each, a total of $13.44, plus $2.00 shipping/handling ($19.50 US in Canada). This is a **SAVINGS OF AT LEAST $6.00** off the bookstore price. There is no minimum number of books I must buy, and I may cancel the program at any time. In any case, the **4 FREE* BOOKS** are mine to keep.

*In Canada, add $5.00 shipping/handling per order for the first shipment. For all future shipments to Canada, the cost of membership is $16.25 US, which includes shipping and handling. (All payments must be made in US dollars.)

NAME: _____

ADDRESS: _____

CITY: _____ STATE: _____

COUNTRY: _____ ZIP: _____

TELEPHONE: _____

E-MAIL: _____

SIGNATURE: _____

If under 18, Parent or Guardian must sign. Terms, prices, and conditions subject to change. Subscription subject to acceptance. Dorchester Publishing reserves the right to reject any order or cancel any subscription.

lips, I have the deposit for Rancho Tecolote. Please write me out a receipt for two hundred dollars."

"That's fine, Mr. Holly. I'll have the receipt for you in just a moment. However, I sent word to Hicks concerning your offer of a thousand and he thinks the ranch is worth more than that. He is counteroffering twelve hundred dollars, not to include any cattle or horses."

"Mr. Phillips, I believe I told you yesterday that my offer is for one thousand dollars and not a penny more. My offer does not include any livestock. Here is the two hundred deposit. Tell Mr. Hicks that he has forty-eight hours to either accept my offer or reject it. I would appreciate a receipt now."

The land dealer wrote out the receipt for Joe's deposit, muttering, "I don't think Hicks will accept it, but I'll give it a try."

Joe left the land dealer's office thinking about Lucía, wondering if she would like living on Rancho Tecolote. Suddenly, he realized what his thoughts meant. *I reckon I'd better tend to business and see if J.Z. Tyler has any horses for me to look at.*

Arriving at the Tyler corrals, Joe found J.Z. at the far end of the main alley talking with three men on horseback. Joe waited by the bench for J.Z. to return. The riders rode out of the alley and headed for town as J.Z. stood beckoning for Joe to join him by the largest corral. As Joe approached, J.Z. looked at the horses milling around inside the corral.

"There's fifty-two head in there. I was going to go over to the Cosmopolitan and leave you a note," J.Z. said.

Joe peered over the corral at the horses. With his keen eye for horseflesh he picked out one bay that favored its left foreleg. "That bay gelding's lame, J.Z.," Joe said.

"Looks thataway, don't he? Damned if I didn't miss that when they brought the last of this bunch in just now. I must be gettin' old."

"It may have just happened," Joe said. "Mind if I go in the corral and have a better look?"

"Help yourself," J.Z. said, and opened the gate.

Joe walked into the corral and stood in the middle as the horses trotted around, avoiding him as best they could. He managed to separate the lame bay gelding and corner him. Approaching slowly, Joe talked to the animal in a slow, low voice. The horse stood still as Joe held his hand out toward his head. "There now, bay horse," Joe said as he ran his hand along the horse's neck. "Let's have a look at that left leg of yours."

Joe felt the bay's leg, looking for something out of the ordinary that might be causing the lameness. Finding nothing, he picked up the bay's hoof. "So this is what's bothering you old fellow. This stone is sure enough wedged in there tight."

Joe held the hoof in his left hand as he reached into his right hand pants pocket for his folding knife. Opening the blade, he dug around the stone that was pressing against the frog of the hoof, loosening it so that it fell out. Releasing the hoof, Joe stood up. "Let's see how that feels, old bay horse."

Joe ambled back to the gate where J.Z. waited. "Had a stone in his hoof," Joe said. "Sure is a gentle horse. I didn't even need a rope."

"How do the rest look to you?" J.Z. asked.

"I think they'll do fine, Mr. Tyler. I see no reason why we can't settle up on these. I would appreciate you keeping them here for a couple of days."

"No problem with that. I'll have to charge you a feed bill after three days, though."

"I may have a ranch to turn them out on in a couple days."

"What ranch are you talkin' about?"

"The Tecolote out by the Cañada del Oro."

"Hell's fire, you won't have any horses left if you turn 'em out on that outfit. Old man Hicks has been raided by Apaches so many times he's given up trying to run any livestock there."

"That's what I hear. I reckon he'll sell cheaper than most," Joe said.

"A feller generally get what he pays for," J.Z. said. "I'll meet you at the bank in an hour."

Chapter Fourteen

Entering the bank, Joe saw Phillips, the land man, sitting by the banker's desk engaged in conversation with Beasley. The banker glanced at Joe as he stopped by the polished wooden gate leading to the space occupied by Beasley and his secretary. Phillips turned to look at Joe after Beasley rose from his chair and motioned for Joe to join them.

"Good day, Mr. Holly," the banker said as he offered his hand. "I understand you have purchased Rancho Tecolote. Congratulations."

"I made an offer for the ranch," Joe said.

"I saw Hicks an hour ago, and he accepted your offer," Phillips interjected.

"I suppose that means I have bought Rancho Tecolote," Joe said. "When can I take possession?"

"I would say two weeks will be enough time to get the papers ready," Phillips answered. "I was just discussing the transaction with Mr. Beasley because he holds a mortgage on the property."

"You didn't tell me about any mortgage," Joe said. "Maybe I didn't buy Rancho Tecolote after all."

"The mortgage presents no problem to the sale of the ranch, Mr. Holly," Phillips said quickly. "Hicks is planning to pay it off."

Beasley cleared his throat. "Perhaps you would consider assuming the mortgage, Mr. Holly. The balance is seven hundred and fifty dollars."

"I'd have to think about that. It's something I hadn't considered," Joe replied. "I came in to meet Mr. Tyler and settle up on some horses. I guess I'll see you in two weeks, Mr. Phillips."

Phillips shook hands with Beasley and Joe before he gathered some papers from the desk. "Are you still at the Cosmopolitan, Mr. Holly?"

"I'll be away for a while. When I get back to town, I'll stop by your office."

J.Z. waddled through the door just after Phillips left the bank. He and Joe took care of their business with Beasley holding five hundred dollars for the next fifty head of horses J.Z. was to buy. The horse trader pushed himself up from his chair, bid the banker and Joe good day and left the bank. Joe stood up, but sat down again after Beasley said, "Before you go, Mr. Holly, I would like to talk to you about the mortgage on Rancho Tecolote."

"I think I'd rather pay cash for the ranch just as I've paid cash for the horses I'm buying from Mr. Tyler," Joe said.

"I must admit that the interest is a bit high on the mortgage, but that is because of the Apache raiding activity out there. You are aware of that, are you not, Mr. Holly?"

"I've been told that the Apache raiding is the reason for Hicks's selling out."

"It really has been rather fearful for him and his wife way out there. They both had such hopes when they built the house and corrals. Are you sure you want to put yourself in that same position?"

"Mr. Beasley, I'll just take my chances on the Apache raiding parties."

Beasley looked down at the papers on top of the desk and then looked up again at Joe.

"By the way, I am curious as to your arrival in Tucson. Where were you before coming here?"

"I was living temporarily in Tombstone. Before that I was stationed at Camp Huachuca."

"What was your rank, if I may ask?"

"I was a lieutenant."

"Why did you leave the army, Mr. Holly?"

"I'm wondering why you seem to be cross-examining me, Mr. Beasley. I don't think all this should be any concern of yours."

"I am truly sorry, Mr. Holly. You see, bankers are curious about the people they do business with, and I do hope we can continue to do business. You seem to be well capitalized, and I certainly hope you will seek the bank's services whenever you care to."

"Thanks, Mr. Beasley. I hope I don't have to borrow any money because I'm counting on my horse business to provide for me. If that's all, I have other matters to attend to."

As he walked back to the Cosmopolitan Hotel, Joe concluded that doing any more business than having Beasley hold the cash for the horses he was buying from

J.Z. would be too much. The next thing the banker would want to know was where all his money came from. As far as Joe was concerned, the loss of the payroll was a small price for the injustice the army had dealt him.

Joe spent the rest of the day getting supplies for the trail drive to Arivaipa and informing Frog Eyes and Lucía that they would start early the following morning. He was happy to see Lucía again and looked forward to being with her on the ride to deliver the horses to Etazin.

The sun made its first faint light as Joe opened J.Z. Tyler's big corral gate to let out the fifty-two head of horses. Frog Eyes rode the point to keep them from running off wild through the desert. Joe and Lucía rode the drag to keep the bunch moving. The two Clanton horses had pack saddles on them with the provisions, cooking gear and bedrolls. Joe thought it best to include the two with the rest so that he wouldn't be asked to prove ownership of them. The herd soon strung out following each other as if they had been taught to do so. By the time they crossed the Rillito, the sun had been up over the Rincon Mountains for almost an hour. About midday, Joe rode ahead to tell Frog Eyes to head away from the Tecolote Ranch so that he might avoid any questions from Hicks at a later date. The least number of people who knew about the trail drive, the better.

Well past the ranch headquarters, Joe told Frog Eyes to choose the way north since the former army scout knew practically every boulder, tree and arroyo in the valley. Frog Eyes headed toward the Cañada del Oro, to take advantage of the cover as well as the water. The stream ran along the base of the foothills until it turned sharply into a deep canyon that divided the mountain from a long, high ridge. Frog Eyes told Joe that his people had used the canyon to hide stolen livestock until they had enough to take back to Arivaipa Canyon. Mesquite, catclaw and other desert trees and shrubs began to be replaced by several varieties of oak, manzanita and some juniper as the elevation increased. The day had begun to wane when they reached the canyon, so Joe called a halt to the drive and the threesome once again began making camp for the night. Joe felt good that the next day's drive would be downhill most of the way to the San Pedro River.

Their saddle horses hobbled, the three went about making camp for the night. Frog Eyes headed up the canyon to see if there was game to hunt. Lucía soon had a fire going and the coffeepot heating water. Joe sat on his bedroll and watched her at work, getting things ready to cook once the wood had burned down to coals. He had enjoyed riding with her all day. With the sun showering the western sky with a last good-bye of red, yellow and purple, the temperature in the canyon fell as the cold air drained from the higher elevations. He rose from his seat to move closer to the campfire.

"The coffee should be ready shortly," Lucía said.

"That will taste good and warm us up at the same time," Joe remarked. "Have you ever been to the top of this mountain?"

"No. I spent most of my time in the canyon with the other women and children."

"I'm told that there are tall pine and fir trees on top. I'd like to ride up there some day."

"Man With Eyes of Eagle could tell you the best way."

Joe wanted to say that he hoped she would join him

on the ride up the mountain, but he kept those thoughts
and others to himself. He realized that during the time
they had been apart in Tucson he had missed her very
much.

"When we get all this trail driving done and the rest
of the horses delivered to Etazin, we can ride to the top
of the mountain from Rancho Tecolote," Joe said.

"I am anxious to see the ranch after hearing you talk
about it."

"By the time we get the next bunch of horses delivered, we should be able to go out there."

The coffeepot boiled over and the dark brew sizzled
as it hit the coals. Lucía grabbed a rag, saved for the
purpose of protecting her hand as she lifted the pot
from the fire. "I guess I was thinking more about the
ranch than the coffee," she said, laughing.

They gathered the horses by early morning light. Joe
counted them as they followed Frog Eyes out of the
canyon along a narrow game trail leading to a broad
mesa covered by straw-colored grasses with a few scattered oak trees by the arroyos. The sun had poked over
the Galiuro Mountains and Joe felt happy to have the
chill of early morning gone. They were riding through
a landscape strewn with large granite boulders heaped
upon each other. Then the long bajada leading to the
river below began. Joe trotted ahead to ask Frog Eyes
if a particular crack in the stretch of mountains he saw
was the canyon of their destination. The Apache con-
firmed that the canyon with the green trees at its mouth
was Arivaipa and that it would take them the rest of
the day to get there. Joe reined up the sorrel and waited
for the horse herd to pass.

When they reached the river, Joe noticed that there
was a greater stream flow than when he and Frog Eyes

had left for Tombstone with Lucía after his first meeting with Etazin. He smiled as he remembered watching Arnold Willoughby begin his walk to Benson after Frog Eyes had jumped and disarmed him. Joe also had a fleeting thought about Betsy Willoughby, and wondered if she still drove her buggy to the Clanton ranch with information about the payroll gleaned from her husband.

Watching Lucía as he rode along behind the horseherd, Joe thought about her innocence and youthful beauty. *She isn't much younger than I am. Maybe she seems young because of the way she enjoys laughing.*

The horses followed Frog Eyes across the river and then along the same trail Joe remembered riding along previously. It was late afternoon when they reached Arivaipa Canyon. Lucía reined up to wait for Joe. "I am looking forward to seeing my friends," she said. "How long will we stay?"

"I am hoping to start back to Tucson in the morning," Joe replied.

"Suppose Etazin wants a feast?"

"I wouldn't want to disappoint him."

Joe saw the lookouts as Lucía waved to them on their way up the canyon. When they arrived at the village on the mesa, they drove the horses into a small pasture that was fenced with brush woven tightly together. The threesome put their horses and the two Clanton packhorses into a corral after unsaddling them.

Etazin greeted them at the fire circle and Joe explained that there would be more horses as soon as he could find more to buy. Lucía interpreted for them. Joe felt happy that Etazin liked the horses and that he understood about the difficulty in finding so many at one time.

After Lucía translated that Joe had bought Rancho Tecolote, Etazin offered to send word to other bands not to raid the ranch anymore, but he could not guarantee that Geronimo would stay away because he was in Mexico with his warriors.

In spite of their trail weariness, Joe and Lucía joined in the feasting to celebrate the arrival of the horses. When it came time for them to retire to the wickiup they had shared the night Etazin had given Lucía to Joe, they entered the structure and Lucía arranged their bedding.

"I talked to my *tía* in Tucson," she said, smoothing out her sleeping skins.

"What about?" Joe asked.

"About us being together. She said that the church law forbids a man and woman to do love before they are married."

"I know that."

"But I don't know what I am," she said. "Before I went with Etazin to live here, our family went to the church in Tubac when a padre came there, but I don't remember much of that. When I came here all that changed and they taught me the Apache way. Now that I live away from here, I am confused."

"I can understand that," Joe said. "I'm a little confused myself. I think about what it would be like to be with you completely. I also wonder if I am in love with you."

"I think about that, too. I know I am in love with you, Joe. It is a feeling I have never had before. I tingle all the time I am near you and when I am away from you, I want to tingle."

She stood up from smoothing the bedding and Joe put his arms around her, pulling her into his embrace.

171

He felt her tenseness vanish as their lips met and his hands stroked her neck and back. Passion took over any doubts either had before, and they sank to the floor of the wickiup.

Chapter Fifteen

Arnold Willoughby grasped the transfer orders and shook them happily as he hastened to his house on Officers' Row at Camp Huachuca. Reaching the adobe dwelling, he flung open the door and tossed the official-looking papers onto the low table in front of Betsy, who was sitting on the sofa with a glass of whiskey in her hand. "Our transfer to Fort Lowell came through," he announced. "I'll join you with a drink to celebrate, even though it's only ten o'clock in the morning."

He went to the cupboard and poured himself a small glass of whiskey. Betsy kept looking at her glass. Slurring her words she said, "Arnold, it's your transfer, not mine. Please don't say *our* transfer."

Arnold carried his drink over to his favorite chair and sat down. "Betsy, dear. You will enjoy Fort Lowell and Tucson much more than this godforsaken place. You'll be able to make friends there instead of being stuck way out here in the wilderness."

173

She took a sip from her glass and turned her head toward her husband. "Arnold, you don't seem to realize that I don't care a damn about making new friends. I don't have any friends here in this dump, so why should I want to make friends in another army wasteland?"

"Fort Lowell is closer to Tucson than Camp Huachuca is to Tombstone. I'm sure you'll find Tucson far more to your liking than Tombstone."

"You really like trying to second guess me, don't you, Arnold? Can't you possibly understand that I hate the West. I'm from Philadelphia. I don't like all this dry, barren country that townspeople call cities when they don't even have cobblestone streets. If I have to stay out here, I'd just as soon be near Tombstone as Tucson."

"I think I know why, Betsy, and that is the major reason for my applying for the transfer."

"For heaven's sake, Arnold, are you still worried about Lieutenant Holly?"

"You know he has caused us plenty of trouble."

"I haven't seen hide nor hair of Joe Holly, so quit worrying about him. The last I heard he was with some Mexican woman."

"Well, we have two weeks to report to the commandant of Fort Lowell. That should give us plenty of time to pack and get to Tucson."

"Whatever you say, Arnold. Get me another drink, please."

By late afternoon, the Willoughbys were both drunk. Arnold tried to get Betsy into bed, but she pushed him away and finally passed out on the sofa. He staggered into the bedroom and fell asleep fully clothed in his uniform.

* * *

174

Double Vengeance

In spite of a painful hangover the following day, Arnold began packing for the transfer while Betsy slept on the couch in the living room. He wanted to leave Camp Huachuca as soon as possible now that his transfer orders had arrived. Word about Holly setting him afoot from Arivaipa to Benson had filtered through the troops, embarrassing him. Betsy's drunken behavior was another thing he hoped would change at the new assignment near Tucson.

Snoring occasionally, Betsy slept until late morning. Arnold had finished his packing and was making arrangements to have Betsy's buggy readied for the trip to Tucson. When he returned to the house off the perimeter of the parade ground he found his wife sitting on the couch with her head in her hands. "Your buggy will be ready in the morning, Betsy. I think you should get packed as soon as possible."

"For Christ's sake, Arnold, we have two weeks to get to Tucson. What's your hurry?"

"I want to get out of here, that's all, and there's a detail leaving tomorrow."

"I'll bet that's not your real reason. I'll get packed shortly, but right now all I want to do is sit here and have a drink."

"There's nothing left to drink. We finished it yesterday afternoon."

"Then go get some more, Arnold. I feel terrible, and a drink will get me ready to pack."

"Betsy, I think it's time you stopped the drinking."

"Well, dear Arnold, if you won't get me a drink, I'll go to the sutler's store and buy a bottle myself. Would you like that?"

"I want to get an early start for Tucson. If you start drinking now we won't get out of here in time to make it to Posta Quemada. You don't want to sleep on the ground, do you?"

"Arnold, I really don't care where I sleep tomorrow night. I just want a drink right now. Can't you possibly understand that I have a very bad hangover?"

She pushed herself up from the sofa, wavered somewhat unsteadily and stepped over to the table in the foyer to grab her purse.

"All right, Betsy, go back and sit down. I won't have you going outside looking like you just got out of bed."

She returned her purse to the table, smirked at her husband and went into the bedroom. With his head bent toward the ground, a grim look on his face, Arnold walked to the sutler's store to buy a bottle of whiskey.

The temperature had dropped in Tucson during the night they stayed at the Posta Quemada stage stop. Arnold welcomed the cool fall weather because Tucson, at a lower elevation than Camp Huachuca, experienced hotter summers. The detail arrived at Fort Lowell, near the arroyo named Rillito, the following afternoon. Since he had more than a week before he was to report to the commandant, Arnold decided to leave his saddle horse at the stables and drive the buggy into Tucson for a few days' stay in a hotel, hoping that Betsy would be happier than if she were forced to move immediately into another house on an army post.

Arnold stopped the buggy outside the Cosmopolitan Hotel and registered for a room. He smiled when Betsy seemed happy with the prospect of staying away from their new assignment for a few days. But he became instantly dismayed when she asked for a bottle of whiskey. "Betsy, why don't we try to make a fresh start together without the whiskey?"

"Oh Arnold dear, a little whiskey won't hurt us. We should celebrate getting out of that godforsaken hole."

"I'll be back shortly. We can talk about it more after I have seen to the horse and buggy."

"On your way back, be a nice husband and buy some whiskey, will you, dear Arnold?"

After leaving the horse and buggy at J.Z. Tyler's corrals, he began walking back to the hotel. He had covered half the distance back to the hotel when he was surprised to see Joe Holly riding toward him. Holly was busy in conversation with an Apache whom Arnold recognized as Frog Eyes. He was able to duck into an alley before either saw him. Once in the alley, Arnold hurried to a vacant lot, hiding behind a building until he was sure that the two had passed. Then he made his way to the hotel by way of another alley. Before entering the hotel, he remembered he was supposed to buy a bottle of whiskey for Betsy. The Lucky Dollar saloon was two doors from the hotel. Arnold looked down the street to make sure Holly had not ridden back again and went into the saloon for the whiskey. In addition to the whiskey, he purchased a bottle of mescal for himself.

Back in the hotel room, Arnold poured Betsy a drink from the whiskey bottle and a mescal for himself. He didn't mention seeing Joe Holly to Betsy. He just sat in a chair watching his wife get drunk and thinking about his bad luck to get transferred in order to be rid of Holly and then seeing him first thing riding down the street in Tucson. He wondered if the former lieutenant had moved to Tucson or was just passing through. He hoped it was the latter.

* * *

The following morning, Arnold had to shake Betsy to awaken her. "It's time to get out of bed and pack, Betsy. I've decided that it will be best to report in today after all, rather than wait."

"Arnold," Betsy groaned. "Go away and leave me alone. I need more sleep."

"I'll let you sleep for another hour, and then we must be going to the fort. I'm going to the livery to get the horse and buggy ready for the drive out there."

Betsy grunted without opening her eyes. Arnold left the hotel for J.Z.'s corrals, stopping at a small restaurant for a cup of coffee. He hoped that he wouldn't see Joe Holly again. Parking the buggy in front of the hotel, Arnold went to his room to get Betsy and their luggage. His wife didn't stir until he shook her awake. "Arnold, for God's sake leave me alone," she grumbled.

"I have the buggy parked out in front of the hotel. We need to get going to the fort."

"Why do we have to report all of a sudden? You said we had a week before we had to be there."

"I decided I want to get settled before I have to report to the commandant," he said, and grabbed one of his valises.

"I'd rather stay here. I'm sick and tired of army forts and the army in general. Why don't you go out to the fort, report in to your commander and then come back here for the night."

"You know very well that wouldn't work. Come now and get out of bed so we can leave."

"Arnold, I don't feel well. I think I have a fever or something. I'll stay here while you go out to the fort."

"Goddammit, Betsy, why can't you cooperate?"

"You seem in such a hurry to report to the fort today.

Yesterday, you said we could spend a week here and begin again."

"Well, I've changed my mind. I think it's best for both of us if we report now instead of in a week."

"You don't even care that I am sick."

"Oh for God's sakes, Betsy. All you have is a hangover and you know it."

"Well, dear Arnold, you may go to the fort and report in to your dear commandant, but I am staying right here in bed. Good-bye."

Arnold Willoughby sighed wearily and carried his two valises to the buggy, loaded them into the back and took his seat. Loosening the lines from the brake handle, he slapped them on the horse's rump and began the drive out to Fort Lowell. As he pulled away from the Cosmopolitan Hotel, he hoped that Betsy would stay in bed all day and not venture out on the street where she might meet up with Joe Holly.

As he drove the buggy along the Rillito, a major tributary to the Santa Cruz River, Arnold thought about Betsy and the marriage that seemed shattered by her attraction to young officers and whiskey. He remembered how much he had once loved her and the fun they'd experienced back in Philadelphia during his courtship of her. He wondered whether they could recoup that happiness if they were to live once again in the city where she felt life began and should also end. How thoughtless he had been to insist on seeking a post in the West, where advancements were easier to come by than if one stayed in the luxury of the eastern cities. He'd been correct about the advancements because his captaincy had only taken a year and a half after his transfer to Arizona Territory.

Spotting Joe Holly riding along the street in Tucson

gave him reason to worry that Betsy might also see him if she managed to get out of bed. His thoughts about his marriage had gone so far into the negative aspects of it that he wondered suddenly if he really cared what happened with his wife and Holly except for the further embarrassment it would cause him. When at noon he saw Fort Lowell's adobe buildings, his thoughts jumped forward to his new assignment and his curiosity about what he would be called on to accomplish under Colonel Haynes, a commandant who'd earned much respect from every officer in Arizona Territory.

Familiar with the layout of the fort, he went first to the stables to leave his saddle horse in the care of the sergeant on duty. Willoughby then drove to the headquarters building, parked the buggy in the shade of a large mesquite tree and strode across the street to report for duty in his new billette. Returning the sentry's salute, he opened the door and entered. The sergeant at the reception desk took his name and rose to enter the commandant's office. Arnold stood at attention in case Colonel Haynes came out of his office to greet him. The sergeant reappeared. "The commandant will see you now, Captain Willoughby."

"Thank you, Sergeant," Arnold said, and moved toward the open door to Haynes's office, ready for his new assignment.

"Good afternoon, Colonel," Arnold said upon entering.

"I have been expecting you, Captain Willoughby. Ned Armbruster sent me a letter about your request for transfer. Sit down. I'd like to talk to you."

"I am grateful for the transfer, Colonel," Arnold said. "Did Major Armbruster explain about my wife?"

"Actually, Ned told me at great length about the trouble you had with Lieutenant Holly. I was very disappointed to learn about Holly's dismissal. I knew his father at Gettysburg. Fine officer. Lost an arm from a rebel bullet."

"I saw Holly in Tucson," Arnold said.

"I am aware that he seems to have settled here. I have word that he has purchased a ranch north of Cañada del Oro. He has also bought a large number of horses."

"I don't know anything about that. I'm not happy that he has chosen Tucson as a home."

"There's nothing I can do to help you there. The man is a civilian now and beyond my jurisdiction unless he does something that concerns the army."

"Colonel Haynes, I am not asking for help. Neither am I asking for help with my wife. These are matters that concern only me, and I must deal with them in my own way."

"I have a surprise for you, Captain. I hope it is a pleasant one. I know it will be challenging. I am assigning you to investigate Holly."

"I don't understand."

"Well, when I learned about Holly's purchase of Rancho Tecolote and all the horses he has bought from J.Z. Tyler, I began to wonder where he got all the money. His father raises horses in Maine, and I know his income is not enough to send his wayward son enough money for all this activity. Then I began thinking about the payroll robbery that happened close to Tombstone when Holly was still there."

"Are you thinking that Holly robbed the payroll wagon?"

"Putting together the amount of money Holly is spending and the time of the robbery, it gives reason to ponder the circumstances."

"Other than striking me, his superior officer, and kissing my wife, I find it difficult to believe that Holly would rob the payroll wagon," Arnold said.

"He might have had enough resentment built up against the army to cause him to attempt retaliation."

"That's a possibility, Colonel, but Holly didn't seem the type to go to such extremes."

"Well, let me explain something. I sent Lieutenant Holly to Camp Huachuca with secret orders. You are aware, of course, of the numerous payroll robberies by the bandits, so I had thoughts that the bandits might be getting information about the payroll shipments from someone inside the post. Holly was to investigate the situation and report his findings back to me personally."

Arnold thought about what Haynes had told him. "Was I under suspicion, Colonel?"

"I had nobody under suspicion. I merely thought it a good idea to have the situation investigated in case my feelings could be correct. Holly has never contacted me since he left for Camp Huachuca."

"I am not surprised at that," Willoughby said. "After he was drummed out, he gave everyone the impression that he hated the army. Your theory about his possible desire for retaliation may be close to fact."

"I suppose that at times I'm trying to compare him favorably with his father."

"I'm not sure if I am the best one to investigate Holly."

"On the surface, given the fact that you have had considerable trouble with Holly, you may be right. But it is for that very reason that I think you are better suited for the assignment than anyone else I can think of."

"Now I'm really confused," Willoughby said, nervously scratching his chin.

"All right, Captain, I'll try to explain my thinking. I am aware of your pursuit of Holly and your subsequent walk back to Benson from Arivaipa Canyon without your mount. He was a civilian then, right after his drumming out. Incidentally, what did you expect to accomplish by that manuever?"

"When I look back at that, I'm afraid I must conclude that I was foolish from anger at the man for fooling around with my wife."

"Are you aware that had you killed Holly, you would probably spend your remaining days on earth in a stockade?"

"The rage swept away all my logic, Colonel. All I wanted to do was to force Holly away from my wife. The entire matter was very embarrassing."

"This is why I am choosing you to investigate Holly in this matter of the payroll robbery."

"Colonel, I am completely confused. Why does my past foolishness make me a candidate to look into this matter?"

"You are perfect for the job. Holly will never suspect you are investigating him because of what has happened between the two of you. You must attempt to gain his confidence by pretending to forgive him for his familiarity with your wife. Once you have convinced him that you would like to forget the past, you might be able to discover where he is getting all the money he is spending on a ranch and mares."

"When do you want me to start the investigation, Colonel Haynes?" Willoughby asked, still wondering why he was perfect for the job and how he would win Joe Holly's confidence.

"As soon as you are settled. Did you bring your wife out here to the fort?"

"She's still in Tucson. I thought it best that she rest from the trip. I will drive her here tomorrow and be ready to begin the Holly business the next day."

"Good luck, Captain. Keep me posted."

The late April afternoon sun cast long shadows from the adobe buildings of Tucson as Willoughby arrived driving the buggy toward the Cosmopolitan Hotel. All the way from Fort Lowell he had mulled over what the commandant had said, and he still couldn't understand why the colonel thought he was perfect for the job of discovering whether or not Joe Holly was behind the most recent payroll robbery. Remembering the rumors that had flown around Tombstone after the escort detail had made its way to Camp Huachuca, Arnold had assumed Geronimo had made away with the money.

The thought of having to deal with Holly did not appeal to him at all. As he considered the assignment in depth, he wondered if the colonel had given him the orders as punishment more than any suspicion of Joe Holly's part in the payroll robbery.

Entering the hotel room, Willoughby saw Betsy sitting on the bed with a drink in her hand. "How did you spend your day, dear?" he asked.

"I slept until this afternoon. Then I went out and had a nice lunch and came back here an hour ago."

"How do you like Tucson?"

"Oh, Arnold, I don't know. I'll let you know once I have spent a few more days here."

"Well, we have to get to Fort Lowell tomorrow. Colonel Haynes has already given me an assignment that I'm not sure I can do."

"Why in the world did you go out there, Arnold?" Betsy complained. "You had a week before you had to report. Didn't you realize that the colonel would give you something to do as soon as you arrived? Sometimes I wonder if you ever think."

"I only did what I needed to do, Betsy. I'm glad that I got that over with. By the way, please don't drink too much tonight because I want to get an early start in the morning."

"Why not leave me here so I can get to know Tucson? When you finish your assignment, you can take me out to the fort."

"I have no idea when I'll complete my assignment. In fact, I may never finish it. We certainly can't afford to pay for a hotel room for what might be a couple of months."

"For heaven's sake, Arnold. What in the world is going to take you a couple of months to finish?"

"The colonel has ordered me to investigate that robbery of the Camp Huachuca payroll."

"That shouldn't take you two months. Everyone in Tombstone knows it was Geronimo," Betsy answered quickly.

"I heard all those rumors, too," Arnold said, averting his eyes from his wife. "I'm supposed to substantiate the rumors."

"Knowing you, it will take more than two months even to get started."

"I'll do what I'm ordered to do, Betsy. I think it's about time you began to understand the army way."

"Arnold, I understand the army way, and frankly, I can't bear the army way. That's why I'd rather stay in this hotel than move into one of those drab adobe houses at Fort Lowell. They all have leaky roofs and bugs. I didn't come out here to get bitten by a scorpion or black widow."

They dined early at the Cafe Ronquillo, a block away from the hotel. Returning to the Cosmopolitan, Betsy stayed up drinking after Arnold had gone to bed. At six o'clock the following morning, Arnold shook his wife awake. She immediately began complaining about having to rise so early to go out to live in a mud house with a leaky roof and spend her days and nights searching for bugs. Arnold listened until his patience waned.

"All right, I've heard enough complaining. Get your things together and let's get going," he said.

Reluctantly, Betsy packed her things for Arnold to carry out to the waiting buggy in front of the Cosmopolitan Hotel. Just as she was gathering her skirts to step up into the conveyance, Joe Holly and Frog Eyes rode by on their way to J.Z. Tyler's corrals. Suddenly Betsy stopped and stood in front of the buggy's seat with her skirt still gathered in her hands. Arnold looked to see what his wife was staring at and saw the two riders jogging their horses along the rutted Tucson street.

Arnold thought to himself that it was too bad that he had to go to Fort Lowell when here was an opportunity to follow Joe Holly to find out what he was up to. But he felt a sudden twinge of regret that Betsy had seen the former lieutenant.

With her eyes directed to the step on the buggy, Betsy sat down as Arnold climbed aboard and took the lines in his hands. They arrived at Fort Lowell in the middle of the afternoon.

*   *   *

Double Vengeance

The house assigned to the Willoughbys at Fort Lowell was smaller than the one they had lived in at Camp Huachuca. Betsy grumbled about its size, but went about getting settled as best she could while enduring the sick feeling of her hangover. Arnold put his clothes in the armoire and in the wooden chest of drawers before leaving for the stables to see about his horse. He wanted to get away from Betsy and begin his investigation of the former lieutenant who had caused him too much trouble.

Before riding to Tucson the following morning, Arnold stopped in at Colonel Haynes's office to report that he was beginning the investigation. Haynes suggested that Arnold might visit Jonathan Beasley at the Territory Bank and Trust. "Be sure to mention that you are under my command and that you are investigating the robbery," Haynes said.

"What information can I expect from this banker, Colonel?"

"Beasley is a friend of mine. He knows about everything that goes on in Tucson. By the way, Captain, why didn't you file charges against Holly for stealing government property when he took your mount?"

Willoughby felt the heat of embarrassment rush to his face. "It was my personal horse, Colonel."

As he rode away from Fort Lowell, Arnold welcomed the assignment to investigate Holly because it would mean he would not have to deal with Betsy and her drinking. As he rode along the well-traveled thoroughfare, he thought about how he had once been enthusiastic about his army career. Many of his colleagues had mentioned that he was destined for command, but now with a drunken wife, Arnold lost interest in something that would never happen as long as Betsy was in her cups most of the time. He wondered how long he could put up with her.

As he entered the stage road and headed south for Tucson, Arnold began an attempt to organize the investigation. He puzzled over the commandant's suggestion to inquire about Holly with Beasley. Bankers were supposed to be close-mouthed concerning what they knew about people. Part of their business tactic was to inquire about everything and put all the information in some sort of mosaic of thought that might give them advantages in their dealings.

Once Beasley knew that Arnold came on orders from his friend, the commandant of Fort Lowell, he told Arnold about the Joe Holly transactions he was familiar with. "Where is this ranch he bought?" Arnold asked.

"It's north of town about fifteen miles. The Cañada del Oro separates the bottom country from the foothills. The Butterfield stage route is just west of the ranch headquarters."

"Did Joe Holly tell you what he intends to do with the ranch?"

"From what I can gather, he is buying some mares and a stud from J.Z. Tyler. I would see what Tyler can tell you if I were you, Captain."

"Thank you Mr. Beasley. You have been a great help," Arnold said, and left for the Tyler corrals.

As usual, J.Z. sat whittling on a piece of cottonwood when Arnold arrived and dismounted. "Mornin', Cap'n," the horse trader said without looking up.

"Good morning, Mr. Tyler," Arnold replied. "I wonder if you would be good enough to answer a few questions."

"Depends on the questions, I reckon."

"I would like to know how many mares Mr. Holly has purchased from you."

"Now, Cap'n, I think that comes under the headin' of Mr. Holly's and my business and is sure no concern to anybody else."

"I have also heard that he has bought an unusual number of other horses and driven them off to his ranch. Could you give me verification of this?"

"Now, Cap'n, that comes under the exact same headin'. These are questions you should ought to be askin' Mr. Holly, don't you reckon?"

"Can you tell me where I might find Mr. Holly?"

"I haven't the foggiest idea where you might find Mr. Holly, and if I did, it would come under that same headin'. Mr. Holly is a customer of mine, and I hold that what he does with the horses he buys from me is his and only his business. That goes for where he is and what he's doing, wherever that is. If you were as good a customer as Mr. Holly, I would give you the exact same loyalty. What you military fellers don't understand is that business comes first with us that's in business 'cause there ain't nobody but our customers to put them double eagles in our hands. Now, Cap'n, if you'll excuse me, I've got a heap of whittlin' to do on this here chunk of cottonwood."

Without another word, Arnold pursed his lips, spun around and strutted angrily to his saddle horse. It was late morning as he rode away from Tyler's corrals, pondering what he had learned during his investigation. At least he had found out that Holly had bought a ranch north of the mountains near the Cañada del Oro where it crossed the Butterfield route. Crossing the Rillito, he had but one fleeting thought about Betsy back at Fort Lowell. He hoped that she wouldn't cause any trouble at the post by leaving the house when she was drunk.

Just beyond the Rillito, the foothills at the southern slope of the mountains began. The Butterfield stage route, that eventually led north to the town of Florence, had been gouged out of a butte cut by river flooding. At the top of the trail the *bajada* began and sloped up to an east/west ridge that formed the west end of the mountains. Looking ahead along the trail as he neared the ridge, Arnold saw that to the north, the trail went downhill to another floodplain. According to the directions he had been given, he would be near the Cañada del Oro once he reached the bottom of the trail. As the sun left the western sky aglow with clouds turned red, pink and purple, he spotted the stage station at Steam Pump Ranch. Spending the night at the stage stop might give him an opportunity to glean information from the horse handlers about their new neighbor, Joe Holly.

After supper, the two stage company men and Arnold sat on the rough wooden benches smoking pipes by the stone-faced fireplace. "Do either of you know Joe Holly, who bought the old Hicks place by Cañada del Oro?" Arnold asked.

"He stopped by once a while back," one of the men replied. "He went by yesterday driving a big bunch of horses with another man. I recognized the sorrel he was riding."

"Which direction was he heading?" Arnold asked, trying to be calm in stating his question.

"I'd say he was going to his ranch."

Arnold rolled out his bedroll on a cot in one of the

small rooms often used by stage passengers spending the night.

In the morning, eager to proceed with his investigation, he saddled up right after a breakfast of beef and beans. The sun poked its way over the high mountains to the east just as Arnold rode up a hill overlooking Holly's ranch headquarters. From behind a community of cholla cactus he looked below to the corrals where Joe and Frog Eyes were finishing getting their horses saddled. Beyond the corrals in a large pen, fenced with ocotillo stalks wired together, Arnold saw what looked to be around a hundred head of horses of all colors and descriptions. His eyes followed the two men as Joe opened the gate to the pen and Frog Eyes rode in to the far end getting the herd moving while Joe remained outside the pen waiting. As soon as the horse herd began trotting through the gate, Joe began riding the point position along the trail leading from the ranch headquarters to the stage road beyond. By leading the bunch, he kept them together and prevented them from scattering every which way.

As the horse herd trotted alongside the ranch house, Arnold watched a Mexican woman wave to Holly. Before returning to the house, she waved to Frog Eyes as he brought up the rear of the bunch.

Arnold reined around his brown gelding in order to keep the *cholla* between him and the two horse drovers as he watched them get the herd started. When they had covered the distance from the ranch headquarters to the stage road, Arnold glanced around to see if he could spot a trail from which to follow Holly and Frog Eyes without being seen. Above all, he didn't want to give them another chance to put him afoot. He hoped they wouldn't spot his blue woolen uniform

John Duncklee

through the vegetation. Reining his horse to avoid the *cholla,* he headed toward a small arroyo that separated the low hills from the broad floodplain of the Cañada del Oro.

He allowed the brown gelding to nibble on a mesquite as he waited for Holly and Frog Eyes to distance the herd from the ranch. Arnold's thoughts returned to Betsy and the dilemma he found himself in with her. Whiskey had taken control of her, and she had become an embarrassment to him as a cavalry officer. He felt helpless to find a way to get her to stop drinking to so much excess. Then there was Joe Holly.

On one hand, he held Joe Holly in contempt, not only for making a play for his wife, but for taking his horse and forcing him to arrive in Benson walking with nearly worn-out boots. On the other hand, he admired him for starting a new life away from the economic security of the army. In one way, he welcomed the opportunity given him to investigate the former lieutenant. In another way, Arnold wondered if he would be able to prove Holly guilty and have him sent to a federal prison where he could no longer make advances toward Betsy. But who was the Mexican woman at Holly's headquarters? Was she a maid, a housekeeper, a woman of the night to whom Holly had given full-time employment? When he judged that the drovers had advanced far enough ahead of him so that they could not see him following, Arnold rode to the stage road so he would be able to see their tracks plainly. He wished he knew where they were going with a hundred head of horses so that he wouldn't have to spend time on the trail. Ahead he saw the cloud of dust hovering and then settling on the ground. At least with no wind, the dust from the four hundred hooves would help keep him hidden from view.

The grassland became lusher as the herd plodded higher. Soon, Arnold found himself riding through small oak trees that dotted the grassland. There were also sotol and manzanita on some of the low hills that seemed to beckon him toward the mountain.

By midafternoon, they had rounded the northern end of the mountain and were heading downslope to the San Pedro River. Arnold stayed behind a large grove of oak until he was sure that Holly and Frog Eyes couldn't see him. In the far distance he thought he could see the familiar mouth of the Arivaipa Canyon. Was Holly in the business of selling horses to the Apache band in the canyon? Arnold Willoughby became more confused than ever about Joe Holly's activities since he was drummed out of the army.

After dry-camping a far distance upslope from the floodplain of the river, Arnold slept until a bunch of coyotes began yipping at each other as they paused on their way home after an early morning hunt. Saddling the brown, he rode to a high point from which he could observe where Holly and Frog Eyes might be going. The sun bathed the river floodplain landscape first. Searching with his glass, Arnold finally saw the dust from the horse herd down along the river. Directing it north, he saw the horses plodding their way over the stage road on the east side of the stream. He urged the brown gelding with his spurs and they began the last of the long descent to the bottom of the valley. Arnold no longer worried about being seen by the two drovers. They were far ahead of him.

As he suspected, the tracks of the hundred horses

veered east from the stage road at the mouth of Arivaipa Canyon. Arnold stopped momentarily, then reined the brown around and headed back in the direction he had come.

Chapter Sixteen

Joe and Frog Eyes were both tired from the drive when they reached the village in Arivaipa Canyon. Before turning the herd over to Etazin, Joe told his companion to cut out the ten horses he wanted to present to his future father-in-law. Frog Eyes trotted over to a wick-iup, hailed those inside and then conversed a few moments after they came outside. The man went to a small corral and caught a horse. Jumping on the horse's back, the man rode with Frog Eyes to the herd where he rode through them looking the horses over. Joe watched, not knowing if the Apache was looking at horses to use for riding or for eating.

Several other Apache men arrived and drove the horses farther up the canyon from the settlement. Joe unsaddled his sorrel gelding and put it in the corral behind Etazin's wickiup. Etazin welcomed him and invited him to talk inside the dwelling with Frog Eyes present to interpret. The headman expressed his satisfaction with the horses Joe had bought and considered the dealing complete. However, Joe explained that there was still money coming to Etazin from the amount they had taken from the Clantons. Etazin told Joe that he was in no hurry for the rest of the horses and that he appreciated Joe's honesty, especially when compared to other white men he had known.

After spending half the night feasting with his friends, Joe slept until the sun had flooded the canyon with morning. He arose, saddled the sorrel and said his good-byes. "You know where the ranch is," he said to Frog Eyes. "My door is always open to you, and your people, Etazin."

As he rode westward out of the canyon, Joe had good, warm feelings about his friendship with the Arivaipa Apache people and wondered what his father would say if he knew about it all.

Heading upstream toward the trail up the long *bajada* from Catalina Mountain, he thought about Lucía and how he had come to love her deeply. A winter rainstorm slipped in and Joe reined up long enough to put on his slicker. By the time he reached the oak country, the rain had turned to large flakes of snow. A soft breeze tossed the flakes every which way until he rode down into Cañada del Oro after it debauched from the mountain to head southward toward his ranch. The snow had changed back to rain.

The day before, while Joe was talking with Etazin, Arnold Willoughby had ridden into Joe's ranch. He had in mind to ask the Mexican woman a few questions before returning to Tucson and reporting in to the Fort Lowell commandant with his findings.

Lucía saw Arnold ride up to the ranch house as she

was filling the water trough in the corral. She wondered what an army officer could want, especially one riding alone a long way from the nearest fort. Arnold dismounted, tied his horse to the hitchrack and started to walk to the front of the house. As he started for the front door, Lucía left the corral at a trot to see what he wanted. Arnold turned around quickly when he heard two dogs barking as they ran to meet him. Lucía yelled at them to stop barking, but the two mongrels kept circling Arnold, growling. Arnold noticed her beauty and wondered how old she might be. And other wonderings came to his mind as well, especially about whether she and Joe Holly were lovers.

"What can I do for you?" she asked, partially out of breath.

"Is this the Joe Holly ranch?" Arnold asked, knowing full well it was.

"Yes. Mr. Holly is not here right now, but he should be here shortly," she said.

"Perhaps you can answer a few questions for me," Arnold said, extending his hand toward the dogs to try and make friends with them.

"I do not know until you ask them."

"I am Captain Arnold Willoughby from Fort Lowell. I would like to know where Mr. Holly was going with a large bunch of horses the other day. The army might be interested in acquiring some."

Lucía hesitated before answering what she thought was a strange question from the officer whose name she recognized as the man married to Betsy. "I am sorry, Capitán, but I have no idea about Mr. Holly's business. All I know is that he deals in horses."

"Do you work for Mr. Holly?" Arnold asked.

"No, señor. Please come in the house. I have coffee on the stove ready to drink."

"Thank you for your hospitality, uh . . ."

"I am Lucía."

She showed him into the kitchen. After he sat down, she filled two cups with coffee and brought them to the table.

Arnold wondered if this was the same woman Betsy had mentioned in connection with Joe Holly.

Lucía knew that Arnold Willoughby had caused Joe to leave the army. Joe had told her everything about him. With determination, she refused to answer his questions about Joe, the horses he drove to Arivaipa and where he got the money for the horses and the ranch.

They had nearly finished their coffee when the dogs began barking in earnest, sounding the warning that someone or something had invaded their territory. Lucía rose quickly from her chair and stepped to the window, where she saw the reason for the canine commotion. "Capitán, we have Apache visitors you may not want to meet. I will go out and find out what they want. You had best stay here in the house out of sight."

"You might consider letting me handle this situation," Arnold said, unholstering his Navy Colt.

"Put your pistola away, Capitán. These people did not come here to raid, or they would have done so already."

"How can you be sure of that?" Arnold asked nervously.

"I know Apache ways, Capitán. I spent many years with them. Just keep out of sight, and I will go out and talk with them."

Double Vengeance

She opened the door and stepped out of the house, speaking the Apache language. With the door ajar, Arnold heard the conversation, wondering what it was all about. Lucía and the one who seemed to be the leader talked for ten minutes. She came back into the house, but the Apache group stayed mounted on their horses.

"They have noticed your horse tied to the hitchrack, Capitán. They are going to take it. I asked them to leave your saddle. They said they would leave the saddle, but they want the carbine."

"They don't give me much choice," Arnold said.

"You are lucky that they are not insisting you accompany them as a prisoner."

"I am sure you are correct in that assumption. Are you sure they will leave once they have what they want?"

"I have listened and believe what they say. As I told you, I spent many years with Apache people. This group and I have mutual friends. That is why, at my request, they are leaving without harming you or taking you prisoner."

"I guess I am indebted to you."

"No, Capitán, you are just lucky that it is me you are visiting and not someone else. I must go back outside and finish the conversation."

Arnold watched her leave through the door and walk back toward the Indians. His mind raced in curiosity. How long had this woman lived with the Apache and why? What was Joe Holly doing with a Mexican woman who was obvious friends with the enemy?

He watched through the window as one of the men dismounted, strode over to his mount and removed the carbine, saddle and bridle, replacing the latter with a braided rawhide reata. "Goddammit, every time I follow Joe Holly I get my horse stolen out from under me," Arnold mumbled as he watched the Indians rein their horses around and leave.

Lucía came back inside showing no nervousness or sign that she might be upset by the encounter. "You are lucky, Capitán. That horse and carbine of yours is a small price to pay for your life."

"I must agree with you. Those Apaches looked like they are capable of most anything."

"Let me tell you something about those people, Capitán. They were here before the Spaniards came and certainly before you Americanos arrived. I have listened to their reasons for raiding ranches and farms. I watched as they raided my family's ranch and killed my mother, father and brother. I was lucky to be spared. I was scared almost to death that they would kill me later, but that did not happen. They brought me to their settlement and raised me as one of their own."

"How did you escape?"

"I did not escape. I left with their blessing."

"You certainly have an interesting story to tell. Not many have been captured by Apache and lived to tell about it."

"Have you heard of Mickey Free? He was a captive raised by Apache and when given the chance to return to the Americans, he refused. He had stayed too long with his band."

"You don't seem angry with them even though they murdered your family. I don't understand," Arnold said after she filled the coffee cups and sat down again.

"I cannot explain that myself. I was terrified when it all happened and for a long time after. But they were good to me and cared for me. After I learned their language I came to understand their point of view. They did not kill my family because they hated them. If they had not killed him, my father would have tried to kill them."

Arnold sat with his coffee cup to his lips as he considered what Lucía had told him. He decided on one more attempt to get information about Joe Holly from her.

"I am charged with investigating a payroll robbery that happened a while back," he said. "Some say that it was bandits from Tombstone and some say it was Geronimo. I know that Geronimo and his band are up in the Sierra Madres in Sonora, so it couldn't have been him who robbed the payroll."

"Capitán, are you sure Geronimo is in Sonora?"

"From all reports he is. He hasn't been seen coming across the border, and we have lookouts everywhere."

"Perhaps your lookouts cannot see at night, Capitán, because the man who took your horse and carbine just now was Geronimo."

"How do you know that?"

"I have known Geronimo for several years, ever since he came out to the settlement the first time after I was captured."

Arnold scratched his head in amazement. Then he suddenly realized he had a long walk back to Fort Lowell. "Thank you for your hospitality and saving me from what fate I don't know. It is a long walk back to the fort."

"I have a spare horse you may borrow. You can leave it at J.Z. Tyler's corrals when you get to Tucson. I am sure we will be going into town for supplies in a few days."

"You are very kind, Lucía."

Lucía had decided it was better to treat the captain

with kindness rather than hostility since he was obviously trying to get information about Joe from her. She brought a black gelding to the house from the corral. Willoughby put his saddle on, mounted and rode off south to Tucson. Lucía watched him leave and returned to the corral when she saw that he was on the stage road away from the ranch headquarters. The captain seemed nice enough, but she found herself not trusting him because of remembering what he had done to the man she loved.

Arnold Willoughby envied Joe Holly having a beautiful woman like Lucía. He also realized that his worries about Betsy taking up with Holly were over. However, he had not changed his mind about Holly being connected to the payroll robbery. Arnold decided to report his findings to Colonel Haynes and recommend that Holly be charged with the robbery. All the circumstantial evidence pointed toward the man he had been responsible for getting drummed out of the army. Now, he would be the one to have him charged with armed robbery of an army payroll. As he rode toward Tucson, he hoped he could get back to the fort without anyone learning about him losing his mount to Geronimo. Hopefully, Colonel Haynes would keep the incident confidential.

Joe arrived at the ranch just before noon the following day. Excitedly, Lucía ran to the corrals when she saw him ride up and dismount. After greeting him with a long hug and kisses, she told him about Arnold Willoughby's visit.

"I wondered if he was following us to Arivaipa," Joe said. "On the way back I saw tracks from someone who had ridden over the tracks of the horse herd. So you think he's investigating me about the payroll robbery?"

"He said he was investigating the robbery, and he came to the ranch. He must think you did it. Oh, I forgot to tell you about Geronimo visiting here while the Capitán hid inside. I had to lend Willoughby the black gelding."

Joe listened intently while Lucía told him the details of Geronimo's visit and how nervous Willoughby had been. "He seemed very grateful that I lent him the black."

"He damn sure should have been. The poor devil can't seem to keep a saddle horse between his legs," Joe said, and laughed. He wanted to add *or a wife in his bed*, but thought better of it.

Arnold went directly to the commandant's office upon his return to Fort Lowell. Reporting to Colonel Haynes, he suggested that all the circumstantial evidence pointed toward Joe Holly, and that his recommendation was to charge the former lieutenant with the crime of armed robbery and attempted murder.

The colonel listened carefully to Arnold's report and pondered it for a few minutes when Arnold finished. "I suppose the best thing we can do is file charges and then try to make him confess," Haynes said.

"I think I have found out everything I can without questioning Holly himself."

"I doubt that would do any good. The best thing to do is have someone experienced with the law take over. We've done what we can, and now it's up to the federal prosecutor to handle the rest. You did the best you could, and we seem to have a case here."

"Thank you, Colonel Haynes. There is a matter I

must finish in Tucson. It is embarrassing to inform you that I lost my mount to none other than Geronimo. I rode a borrowed horse in from Holly's ranch and need to return it to Tyler's corrals."

"Willoughby, you seem to have trouble keeping yourself mounted. At least you didn't have to walk back like you did along the San Pedro. Do what you must and report back as soon as possible. In the meantime, I must send a troop out to try to find that rascal, Geronimo. I have a good idea. While you are in Tucson, contact the federal marshall and have him come out here for instructions on Holly."

"Yes, Colonel Haynes, it will be my pleasure to see Holly brought to justice."

"Remember, Captain, having the marshall arrest him doesn't mean Holly will be convicted. If your investigation uncovered enough evidence and the prosecutor sends a believeable argument to the jury, you might be able to celebrate."

"Yes, sir," Willoughby replied with firm voice, but in his thoughts he had doubts about the amount of evidence he had gathered. One thing he felt certain of: Holly would fail to account for the money he had spent on the ranch and horse purchases. He decided to leave for Tucson without checking on Betsy in case she was in some strange mood and wanted to join him.

Riding the new mount he had requisitioned from the Fort Lowell stable, he led Lucía's black gelding toward Tucson. Thinking on the colonel's remark about not being able to keep mounted, Arnold felt the heat of embarrassment return to his neck and face. "That Holly will get his comeuppance when he is behind bars in a federal prison," Arnold mumbled as he rode along the well-worn road to town.

Double Vengeance

Once on Congress Street and heading for Tyler's corrals by the river, Arnold looked around to see if he could spot the federal marshall. He wanted to give him the colonel's message about the charges right away. Reining the new horse north on Court Street, he rode to an adobe building where he had previously seen the marshall's sign on the wall by the doorway. He rode up to the hitchrack, dismounted and tied the two horses next to the bay gelding that stood hipshot in the early afternoon sun.

Knocking on the weathered wooden door, Arnold heard a voice from inside telling him to enter. Turning the tarnished brass knob, he opened the door and stepped over the worn threshold to find a red-mustached man with both feet on top of a battered wooden desk. Arnold noticed that both soles of the man's boots had worn through. The man's beaver-felt hat sat on the back of his bushy red hair and the badge pinned to his denim shirt looked like it had been years since it had seen polish.

"Are you the federal marshall?" Arnold asked.

The man pointed to his badge with the extended index finger on his right hand. "I sure am, Captain. Garvey's the name. What can I do for you?"

"I am Captain Willoughby from Fort Lowell. I have a message for you from Colonel Haynes about a man named Joseph Holly."

"I'm acquainted with Colonel Haynes. I'm afraid I can't place a Joseph Holly."

"Colonel Haynes would like you to come to the fort so that he can file charges of armed robbery and attempted murder against Holly. I have evidence that leads to Holly as the one who held up the army payroll heading for Camp Huachuca a couple of months ago.

The colonel has all the dates and particulars for you."

"All right, Captain Willoughby. I'll ride out to the fort in the morning. Can you give me some sort of description of this man Holly?"

Arnold told the marshall what Holly looked like. "The easiest way to find him will be to have J.Z. Tyler tell you when he shows up for the black gelding I have tied outside."

"Let's take a look at this horse," Garvey said, dropping his feet from the desktop and carefully pushing himself up from the swivel chair.

Arnold showed the marshall the black gelding and then mounted his horse to complete the ride to Tyler's place of business. Before leaving, he said, "If you want, I'll tell Tyler about letting you know when Holly comes for this horse."

"Much obliged, Captain. That will save me a trip down there."

Arnold rode away leading the black gelding. He spoke with J.Z. about letting Garvey know when Holly came for his horse and returned to Fort Lowell to see how Betsy had fared during his absence. When he told his wife about Haynes's intent to file charges against Holly for the payroll robbery, Betsy scowled and turned away from him.

Joe and Lucía enjoyed being together again at the ranch. The morning after his return from Arivaipa they sat by the kitchen window watching the sunrise as they sipped their morning coffee. Joe kept silent for a while and then reached across the table and took Lucía's hands in his. "I would like to marry you, Lucía," he said. "I love you."

"I love you, too. I have hoped that you would want to be married with me."

"Then let's go into Tucson and get it done."

"That is fine," she said, with a big smile on her face. "I have to get the black gelding from Senor Tyler before he charges a big feed bill."

"Do you want to be married in your church?"

"I do not think I have a church anymore. I almost feel married with you since we were in the wickiup in Arivaipa after Etazin gave me to you. I guess I have become Apache in many ways."

"It will be easier to get married by a judge than wait for the church to make up its mind about us."

"Then I will be Mrs. Holly, and when anyone comes out here to the ranch asking questions I can tell them I am your wife. I like that, Joe Holly."

"I do, too, Mrs. Holly."

They laughed and after breakfast, saddled two horses for the trip into town. As they approached J.Z.'s corrals in early afternoon, Joe reined up and stopped. "Let's ride back and get us a hotel for the night. We can have our honeymoon in Tucson."

"That sounds wonderful."

Joe and Lucía were married by Judge Moorehouse in his chambers. After that was taken care of, they rode to Tyler's and left their horses for the night. "We'll take the black gelding in the morning, Mr. Tyler," Joe said.

"That's fine, Mr. Holly. I do want a word with you right now."

"You can say anything you have to in front of Lucía. She's now Mrs. Joseph Holly."

"Well, congratulations," J.Z. said, removing his hat and giving Lucía a short bow. "What you need to know is that a Captain Willoughby who brought your black in, said for me to tell the federal marshall when you came to pick up the horse. I got no idea what this is all about, but I thought you should know."

"Thank you, Mr. Tyler. This is interesting. The good captain was at the ranch nosing around while I was gone. The reason he brought that black gelding of mine in was Lucía had to lend it to him. Seems Geronimo paid a visit and took his mount for dinner."

It was the first time Joe had seen J.Z. laugh. "That don't surprise me none. Willoughby don't strike me as havin' any more brains than a box a rocks. Incidentally, Holly, I have no intentions of giving Garvey any message from that Captain Willoughby. He come by here a while back askin' all sorts of questions concernin' the horses you were buyin'. I told him to get his information somewheres else."

"Thank you for your loyalty, Mr. Tyler. I appreciate you keeping our business our business."

"While we're talkin' business, are you goin' to be needin' more horses?"

"I'm glad you mentioned that, Mr. Tyler. A couple of those mares of mine have dropped their foals and even though they look mighty good, I'm thinking about breeding them back to a stud with a little more leg on him. The mares that have already foaled are bred back to that Steeldust horse you sold me and that's just fine. If you should hear about another stud for sale with more leg, send me some sort of message. I guess you could scribble out a note and give it to the Butterfield driver. I stop by the Steam Pump Ranch stage stop every so often."

"I'll keep my eyes open, and I know what you're a lookin' fer."

"Thanks, Mr. Tyler. I guess we best be seeing about

our honeymoon. We'll see you in the morning."

"You two have a nice honeymoon and congratulations again to both of you. The missus an' I been hitched for thirty years."

As they walked toward the Cosmopolitan Hotel, Lucía noticed a scowl on Joe's face. "What is all this business about a federal marshal?"

"That's what I would like to know. I'm wondering if I should find the marshall and ask him, except I don't trust Willoughby as far as I could throw the entire Arizona Territory. I have an idea he's trying to pin the payroll robbery on me. If that's the case, he's in for a really big surprise."

"What will you do, Joe?" Lucía asked, a worried tone to her voice.

"I can always tell him about his wife's partnership with the Clanton gang."

Approaching the hotel, Joe said, "Let's not worry about all this stuff until we have to. Tonight is our night, so to hell with Willoughby, the United States Army and the federal marshall."

After supper, they sought solitude in their room. Before, Joe felt hesitant to make love to Lucía, but he had lost all his former reticence now that they were married.

After getting dressed the next morning, they went to Tyler's corrals and saddled their horses for the ride back to the ranch. Leading the black gelding, Joe rode next to Lucía to Cafe Ronquillo.

At the breakfast table they sat smiling at one another until the waitress broke the spell with two mugs of coffee placed in front of them.

When they had finished their meal of eggs and cho-

John Duncklee

rizo sausage, Joe looked toward the entrance to see a tall red-headed man in a beaver hat come through the door and stop momentarily to look around the place. His eyes met Joe's, and he ambled over to the table. "I'm Marshall Garvey. Would your name be Holly?"

"Joe Holly, Marshall. Is there something I can do for you?"

"Mind if I sit for a spell?"

"Help yourself. This is my wife, Lucía."

Garvey took off his hat and extended his right hand toward Lucía. "My pleasure, ma'am," he said, before pulling out a chair and sitting down next to Joe. "I spotted that black gelding at the hitchrack. There was a captain in town tellin' me to go out to Fort Lowell to get information about you and a payroll robbery. Can you tell me anything about that? I don't cotton to those army fellers trying to run my job."

"So that's what Willoughby is trying to do. He has caused me more trouble than I deserve. First he got me drummed out of the army for, according to him, messing with his wife. Now he's trying to get me thrown in jail to keep me away from his wife. I have a wife of my own," Joe said, glancing at Lucía and smiling.

"I've already checked with old J.Z., and he seems to think highly of you. If he didn't, he would speak out against you quickly. He told me you bought the old Hicks place out by Cañada del Oro. Gonna raise Steeldusts, he says."

"That's what we figure to do. I bought some mares from J.Z., and they're dropping foals right now. In fact, we're in somewhat of a hurry to get back in case another foal decides it's time to come into the world."

"Well, Mr. Holly, I guess I know where to find you in case I need to."

Garvey stroked his red mustache with one hand and pushed his chair away from the table with the other. "A pleasure meeting you both," he said, and stood up.

Joe also stood and shook Garvey's hand. "When you're in our neighborhood, be sure to stop by for a visit anytime, Marshall."

"Thanks, I'd enjoy that. Hangin' around this dusty town gets pretty stale, even though there's enough trouble here for two marshalls."

They watched the marshall leave the restaurant, then looked at each other with eyebrows raised. "So Willoughby is after me," Joe said. "Too bad your friend Geronimo didn't take him somewhere and keep him out of trouble."

"If I had known what a *sangrón* he was I certainly would have asked Geronimo to take him," Lucía said.

"The Apache could make the captain talk in a high voice in a hurry."

"What do you mean by that, Joe?"

"It's just a joke. What it says is that if a man doesn't have testicles he's not a man and talks in a high voice."

"Oh, I get it. If I had given Willoughby to Geronimo to castrate, the captain would be talking in a high voice instead of trying to get you into trouble."

"That's close enough," Joe said, reaching into his pocket for money to pay their bill.

The dogs welcomed them back to the ranch. A quick look around told them that nothing had happened since their departure to Tucson. There were no strange tracks in the area around the house or in the barnyard.

Joe and Lucía discussed the possibility of the marshall arresting them on the charges being brought by Colonel Haynes. "I doubt if the charges will include you because they have absolutely no idea that you were there when Etazin held up the Clantons," Joe said. "If the marshall does arrest me, I know I'll end up in jail. Therefore, we need to stick close together. If I am sent to jail, you need to find a lawyer fast. Without a lawyer, I could rot in jail for months before a hearing is set."

"This does not sound fair to me, Joe."

"Who said it was fair? It's what happens when someone like Willoughby uses his place in the army to get revenge."

"Now I really wish I had given that *sangrón* to Geronimo."

"The way I have it figured out, nothing will happen except having to go through all the bullshit to satisfy the federal commissioner."

"I hope you are right, Joe. I am too happy now to live without you."

He took her into his arms and assured her that all would be well.

Chapter Seventeen

A week after they were married, Joe stopped by the stage station at Steam Pump Ranch to see if there might be a message from J.Z. about a stud prospect. Another mare had foaled a good-looking bay filly and Joe wanted to breed the mare back on her foal heat nine days after foaling. It was midafternoon when he rode up to the adobe building, dismounted and tied the sorrel to the hitchrack. Inside, he found the two horse handlers taking a break with mugs of coffee in front of them on the rough-hewn table where travelers took their meals.

"Howdy," one of the men said.

"Hello," Joe replied. "Do you happen to have any messages for Joe Holly?"

The man who had greeted Joe stood up, dug into one of the pockets of his denim trousers and brought out a somewhat wrinkled envelope. "This came in on the morning stage. We were in a big rush so I plumb forgot about it until you come in an' mentioned it. Sorry."

"Nothing to be sorry for. Thanks for taking care of it for me. I am Joe Holly, by the way."

"Homer Glenn and this *compadre* of mine is Benny Ward."

"I am pleased to meet you fellows. I am your neighbor up at the Rancho Tecolote, Ben Hicks's old place."

"I heard old Ben sold out. He was tired of givin' his cattle to them Apaches. What you gonna do out there?"

"I have some mares and a stud. I might get a few cows after awhile."

"Well, I hope you have better luck than old Ben."

"I hope so, too. I'd best be going back. Thanks for taking care of my message."

"Aw hell, anytime. Stop by again when you have time for coffee."

"Thanks," Joe said, and left.

Before mounting, he hurriedly opened the envelope and read the message from J.Z. Tyler. Stuffing the message back into the envelope, he slipped it into his shirt pocket and was astride the sorrel in moments, heading back to the ranch.

Lucía greeted him warmly at the corrals where she was gentling one of the foals.

"J.Z. sent a message. He has a four-year-old stallion from New Mexico he says ran well until he came close to foundering. He said he'd hold the horse a week for me to look at."

"When do we leave for Tucson?" Lucía asked cocking her head teasingly, knowing Joe would be anxious to look at the stud as soon as possible.

"I guess we might as well ride in tomorrow morning. Of course, we can start in tonight if you're in a hurry

214

to buy beans and coffee," Joe said, and smiled impishly at a laughing Lucía.

They got an early start the following morning and arrived at J.Z.'s corrals shortly after noon. Joe liked the looks of the stud horse, a dappled gray that stood at least two hands taller than the mares. He liked the canon bones and slope to the horse's shoulder. The gaskins showed strong muscling and together with flat leg bones showed Joe that the horse had a balanced strength that would hopefully be passed on to his progeny.

"What do you think of him?" Joe asked Lucía.

"He looks good to me, but you are the horse breeder."

"I know," Joe said, tipping his beaver hat back and scratching his forehead, "A fellow buys a stud horse that has the kind of characteristics he wants in the offspring from his mares. Then he breeds the horse to the mares and waits eleven months for them to foal. That is if nothing goes wrong and the foals get born. So the foals look good and have the characteristics they're bred for. After they reach three years old, you break them to the saddle and train them to do what you want them to do. That is unless there's an outlaw in the bunch. There might be more than one unruly one among the crop of foals. Of course, during the three years you wait for them to grow enough to use, a cougar or something else might rob you of the best one of the bunch, or maybe more than one. There are always the human robbers to watch for, too. What am I telling you all this for? You know what raising livestock is all about."

"I do not know what you know, Joe. I am interested in what you say."

215

John Duncklee

"After I said it I'm wondering why anyone would want to be in the horse business. I guess I might as well buy this stud horse and see what he can do. Let's go see how much J.Z. thinks he can get out of my pocket."

They both laughed as they turned and headed for horse trader's whittling bench. When Joe asked him how much he was asking for the stallion, J.Z., without taking his eyes from the piece of cottonwood branch he was carving, told Joe he wanted two hundred dollars. They wrangled around for a while until making the deal for one seventy-five.

After paying J.Z., Joe and Lucía went down the alleyway to where the stallion stood nibbling at his hay. Joe opened the gate to enter the corral and to put a halter on the horse when he heard his name called. He looked around and down the alley and saw Marshall Garvey walking toward him.

"I think we've got trouble," Joe said to Lucía in a whisper and closed the gate.

Garvey approached with several sheets of paper rolled up in his hand. "I had a hunch I'd find you here, Holly. I've got the papers to serve you with. That Colonel Haynes did file those charges against you. That captain, uh, Willoughby brought it in to me this morning."

"What does this mean, Marshall?" Joe asked.

"I have to take you into custody. Do you have a lawyer?"

"I sure don't. I've never needed one," Joe said. "Do you know a good one?"

"I'd say Nat Grimes is the best one to get. It's still early enough to talk to the federal commissioner and get yourself released on bail. Bein' how you're a ranch owner, he'll probably let you out on your own recognizance."

"Well," Joe said, sighing. "I guess we'd better get things started. "Lucía, dear, will you find Nat Grimes and tell him what has happened."

"Where can I find this man?" Lucía asked the marshall.

"His office is on Fremont Street. Tell him your husband needs to go before the commissioner right away. Grimes likes to get his clients home as soon as possible."

"Where is Fremont Street?"

"North and west of the courthouse. His office is the second door from Church Street."

"Thank you, Marshall," Lucía said. "I'll hurry as fast as I can, Joe." Lucía left Joe and the marshall to go in search of Lawyer Grimes.

Accompanied by the marshall, Joe stopped to see J.Z., still on his bench, and told him that they might have to spend another night in town before taking their saddle horses and the stallion back to the ranch.

Joe and Garvey chatted about horses on their way to the courthouse and jail. Once there, Garvey told the deputy that Grimes would come see him shortly if Lucía found him in his office. The deputy escorted Joe to an empty cell without saying a word.

It was an hour before Grimes came in with Lucía to interview his new client. The deputy let Grimes into the cell and locked the door. "Mr. Holly, I'm Nathaniel Grimes. Mrs. Holly told me a little about your case, but I need to know a little more before we go in front of the federal commissioner. Incidentally, I made an appointment for four this afternoon. That's as soon as the commissioner will be free to hear my motion for your release on your own recognizance. Since you are a ranch owner, I don't anticipate any problems with my motion."

"Thank you for attending to this so quickly, Mr. Grimes. I have mares foaling at the ranch, and we just bought a stallion from J.Z. Tyler to breed the mares back on their foal heats. What is it you need to know?"

"Having quickly scanned the the charges being brought against you, I would like to know if you are aware of any evidence the army has gathered against you."

"I don't know if my wife has told you about a certain captain named Willoughby who really has it in for me."

Joe explained almost everything he could think of to the lawyer right down to his being drummed out of the army because of his unjust court-martial. The two things he left out were his witnessing Betsy talking to Old Man Clanton and the successful robbery of the Clantons by Etazin and his warriors.

"I think I'll enjoy whipping the army's hind end with this one," Grimes said. "They think they can rule the whole country around here. Your Captain Willoughby sounds like he needs to send his wife back where she came from before she gets pregnant with someone else's child. From what I can gather, there is very little, if any, hard evidence against you, Holly."

"I just hope you can get me out of this damn jail today. I have a lot to do at the ranch. I'd also like to go out to Fort Lowell and have a talk with Captain Willoughby."

"I would advise against any confrontation with the captain. It is obvious to me that the man is grabbing for straws to implicate you just because his wife was kissing you. Unless she told him, he probably has no idea about the fun you had with her in Tombstone."

"I don't even care if he does know. I have an idea he at least has a strong suspicion or else he wouldn't have followed me once and he wouldn't be so goddamn insistent about getting me sent to federal prison."

"I still wouldn't attempt to confront him until we get all this stuff over with."

Grimes pulled his Waltham pocketwatch from a vest pocket and looked at it briefly before slipping it back into its regular place. He then stood up facing the jailer's desk in the hallway. "Deputy Holloway, we have an appointment with Commissioner Andrews in ten minutes."

The deputy scraped his chair on the floor, pushed himself up and ambled back to the cell. "Where's Garvey. Isn't the marshall supposed to go with the prisoner?"

"I suppose you are correct, Holloway," Grimes said. "Is he anywhere in the courthouse?"

"I sure couldn't tell you. I don't see nothin' down in this hole."

"Well, let me out of here and I'll try to find him. His office is just a half block south of here anyway."

Grimes left the jail area and quickly returned with Marshall Garvey. The deputy opened the cell door and turned Joe over to Garvey for the trip upstairs to the office the federal commissioner used despite it being a county building. Grimes knocked on the office door and let himself in. "Your Honor, we are here for the hearing. Are you planning to hold it in the courtroom?"

"No, Mr. Grimes, I'll hear your motion right here in my office."

John Duncklee

"Very well. Your Honor, have you read the charges against my client, Mr. Joseph Holly?"

"Yes, Mr. Grimes, I have read the charges or else I would not be holding this hearing of your motion," Commissioner Andrews said, annoyance toward Grimes showing in his tone.

"Your Honor, may it please the court that Mr. Holly is a married ranch owner in Pima County, and I have no reason to believe he will be derelict in his duty to appear to defend himself against the charges brought by the United States Army. I sincerely ask that you release my client on his own recognizance."

"Where is your client's ranch, Mr. Grimes?"

"It is north of Tucson by the Cañada del Oro, Your Honor."

"How long has your client owned the ranch?"

"Your Honor, pardon me for a minute while I consult with my client."

"Go right ahead, Mr. Grimes."

Grimes turned to Joe and asked him how long he had owned the Tecolote Ranch.

"About two months," Joe replied.

"Two months is not very long to establish your client with much permanence," Andrews said.

Marshall Garvey leaned over to Grimes and whispered in his ear.

"Your Honor," Grimes said returning his attention to the commissioner. "Marshall Garvey informs me that my client has just purchased a stallion for breeding purposes. This should demonstrate a desire on my client's part to remain in Pima County on his ranch."

"All right, Mr. Grimes, I am releasing your client, Joseph Holly, on his own recognizance. You will be informed when a hearing date has been set."

"Thank you, Your Honor," Grimes said, and everyone, including the marshal, left the commissioner's office.

Once outside, Grimes left for his office and the others stood around while the marshall asked Joe about looking at the foals.

"Come by anytime, Marshall. We're at the ranch most of the time. Of course, this Willoughby seems to want me somewhere else," Joe said and chuckled. "By the way, do you have any idea where Willoughby might be?"

"He rode in on a big bald-faced sorrel horse with two white stockin' legs. I saw the horse tied up outside The Lucky Dollar when I went down to J.Z.'s lookin' for you."

"Thanks. Maybe he's still there."

"I think I'd leave him be for now, Mr. Holly."

"Don't worry, I don't figure to cause any trouble," Joe said. "I just need to talk to him for a minute or so."

"Suit yourself, but you might pick a better place to talk than The Lucky Dollar. I was surprised to see his horse outside there. The Lucky Dollar generally don't attract army officers."

"Come out to the Tecolote Ranch and take a look at the foals. I think I have a nice crop for you to choose from," Joe said, taking Lucía by the arm.

"Bye, Mrs. Holly. A pleasure meeting you," the marshall said and crossed Church Street heading for his office.

Back on Congress Street, Joe escorted Lucía to the Cosmopolitan and booked a room for the night. He gave his wife the key. "Wait for me in the room. I need to find Willoughby and tell him what will happen if he doesn't get Haynes to drop the damn charges."

"Be careful, Joe. He might be drunk and cause trouble like the marshall said."

"If he is drunk, I'll find out where he will be in the morning and put off talking with him until then," Joe said, and left Lucía in the lobby.

He could smell stale beer a hundred feet away from the entrance to The Lucky Dollar saloon in the chilly afternoon air. The bald-faced sorrel stood hipshot at the hitchrack. The saloon's door stood open, so Joe walked in without a moment's hesitation, going straight to the bar to order a beer. He wanted to appear casual and like he hadn't come to the bar with the purpose of finding the captain. From the corner of his eye he spotted Arnold Willoughby sitting at a small table against the far wall of the room.

When the swarthy Mexican bartender brought his glass of beer, Joe paid him and concentrated on sipping the brew. *I hope that bastard sees me and calls me over to his table. Otherwise, I'll have to go to him.*

Holly sipped his beer anticipating Willoughby's voice, but the captain sat in his chair without saying a word. With a half-full glass of beer in his hand, Joe turned away from the roughly hewn bar and ambled over to where Willoughby sat. "Good afternoon, Captain Willoughby. I'd like to have a few words with you," Holly said, hoping the captain was not too drunk to understand what he planned to say.

"Well, Mr. Holly, I thought you'd be in jail by now."

"I was in jail, Captain, but I'm lucky to have a good lawyer this time. Do you mind if I pull up a chair?"

"Be my guest, Mr. Holly."

Joe grabbed a chair from the empty table next to Willoughby's and sat down. "I hope you'll remember what I'm about to tell you, Captain."

"If you are inferring that I might be drunk, you are wrong, Mr. Holly. Say what you have to say and then please leave me alone. I have things to think about."

"When I'm through here, you'll have much more to think about," Holly growled. "First of all, I must tell you that Colonel Haynes, your present commanding officer, sent me to Camp Huachuca to investigate where the bandits were getting their information on payroll wagon schedules. He told me that he thought it might be coming from inside the post."

"Are you trying to tell me that I was your suspect?"

"No, Captain. I did not have a suspect until after I was court-martialed and drummed out of the army, thanks to your efforts. One day I followed your wife, Betsy, out to the Clanton ranch and overheard a conversation between her and Old Man Clanton. I discovered that Betsy was in cahoots with the Clantons and was providing them with information about the arrival of army payrolls to Camp Huachuca. She got the schedules from you as finance officer."

"Holly, this is absurd. My wife would never betray me like that!"

"Captain, she told me that as soon as her business paid off she was going to leave you and the army behind."

"What did she want to do, take you with her?"

"She mentioned that once, but I refused. After leaving the army I had decided to go into the horse business. That's what I have done. This business of charging me with armed robbery and attempted murder is absurd, Captain. Either you convince Colonel Haynes to drop those charges, or, when the case comes up for preliminary hearing, I'll tell Betsy's story to the United States commissioner."

"And you think he'll believe you?"

"I have no more idea than you do, Captain, but it will be interesting to see and hear his reaction to my information. Incidentally, I have said nothing to anyone except you and my wife. However, if the charges are not dropped, I'll be forced to relate the entire story to my lawyer. You can be sure that he will subpoena Betsy and she'll have to testify at the hearing. I am trying to avoid that for her sake."

"Why are you being so nice to my wife, Holly?"

"You have nothing to worry about between me and your wife, Captain. I'm happily married as you should know from your visit to Rancho Tecolote when you met Mrs. Holly. I'm trying to be nice to Betsy because I know why she did what she did."

"Well, Holly," Willoughby said. "You have a fantastically absurd story that will, no doubt, entertain the United States commissioner."

"I suggest you ask Betsy about her business deal with the Clantons. Perhaps you remember how many dresses she actually brought home from Tombstone. Most of her trips were to the Clanton ranch. Don't be stupid, Captain. Protect your wife from a lot of trouble. She wanted to leave the army, not you. She needs to be understood."

Marshall Garvey strode through the door of The Lucky Dollar and went directly to the bar, glancing around as he stood, waiting for the barkeep to serve him. Joe stood up and made his way toward the door, slightly nodding to the marshall as he passed by.

Back in the hotel room with Lucía, Joe told her what had been said and that Willoughby had caused no trouble. "I think he'll have no trouble remembering what I said about Betsy and the Clantons, but I could win a month's wages by betting someone that Arnold Willoughby will get staggering drunk tonight."

Chapter Eighteen

Arnold Willoughby awakened to a head-throbbing hangover. The conversation with Joe Holly the previous night had pushed him over the edge of near sobriety to a colossal drunk. His entire world seemed to be collapsing around him, and a fiery pain in his stomach caused him to bend over when the feeling seemed trying to reach some sort of zenith.

Sitting on the side of the bed in his hotel room, Willoughby thought over and over like a cow chewing its cud about what Joe Holly had said of Betsy being involved with the Clanton gang. It was difficult to believe and even harder for him to accept that the woman he loved would lower herself to banditry in order to get away from him and the army.

After breakfast, still nursing his aching head, he managed to reach Tyler's corrals and saddle his horse for the ride back to Fort Lowell. It was midmorning when he left Tucson and afternoon as he rode into the stable area and left his horse. He wondered what Betsy would say when he told her about Holly revealing her part in the payroll holdup. Maybe Holly was grabbing at straws to get out from under the charges Colonel Haynes had filed against him. Willoughby wished he could just disappear with Betsy over the far horizon and never look back. His entire life had become a quagmire that he felt he was sinking into faster and faster.

Before he reached the door to his quarters, he felt a sharp pain in his stomach that came close to giving him nausea. Pausing before opening the front door, he brushed the dust from his breeches and then turned the brass knob to let himself in. "Betsy, are you home?"

"Yes, Arnold. Where have you been for two days?"

"Tucson. I had a talk with Holly, and I'm quite disturbed about what he said about you."

Betsy came out of the kitchen and stood in front of Willoughby with her hands on her hips. "What are you talking about, Arnold? Why were you talking to Joe Holly in the first place?"

"I was minding my own business in The Lucky Dollar when he came in and joined me. He was very upset about the charges that I filed on behalf of Colonel Haynes."

"That doesn't surprise me. Of course he would be upset. Anyone would be upset to have charges filed against him," Betsy said, lowering her hands to her sides and moving toward the kitchen. "There's some coffee left from breakfast, Arnold. Do you want some?"

"No thanks. I need an answer to a question that has plagued me since last night."

"I can't answer it unless you ask, Arnold."

"Holly told me you were involved with the Clanton

gang in that payroll robbery I accused him of. Is that true?"

"For heaven's sake, Arnold, how in the world could I ever get involved with the Clantons?"

"That is what's bothering me. Holly said he followed you to the Clanton ranch and listened to a conversation between you and Old Man Clanton. He said that you were giving that bandit the schedule of the payroll wagon."

"For God's sake, Arnold, can't you see that Holly is desperate?"

Willoughby removed his hat and placed it on a table. Scratching his head with both hands above his ears he lowered his eyes from Betsy and in an almost murmur, said, "Holly said he would testify that you were in cahoots with the Clantons if he is forced to defend himself."

"Well, Arnold, it's his word against mine." She tilted her head and winked her right eye teasingly. "And who do you think the commissioner will believe?"

"For some reason I don't feel good about this situation, Betsy. Frankly, Holly is more convincing than you are."

"You can believe anyone you want to believe, Captain Arnold Willoughby," she sneered. "I'm sick and tired of you, the army and even Joe Holly. Now go do something somewhere because I'm going to have a drink. How does that strike you, Captain Willoughby?"

"It doesn't surprise me in the slightest, Betsy. You'd better ease up on the booze, or you'll end up killing yourself."

"Nobody would give a damn if I did," she said, and went to the cupboard for a glass. "Come have a drink with me, Arnold dear?"

"No, thank you. I'm afraid I don't feel up to such an early drink. Perhaps, later I'll be in more of a mood for drinking. I think I'll take a nap."

Betsy poured herself a drink of straight whiskey. Arnold took off his boots and stretched out on top of the bed in the back room. In spite of his concerns, he was asleep in minutes, sleeping soundly for three hours. Dusk had begun to settle and the winter chill invading without the fire in the stove to warm the house awakened Arnold from his nap. Shivering, he sat momentarily on the side of the bed trying to make sense out of the dream he had about riding from Tucson to Tombstone in a blinding blizzard.

Shuffling in his stockinged feet, he entered the living room to find Betsy sipping from her glass. He glanced at the bottle that she had nearly emptied. "Well, Captain Willoughby," she slurred. "Did you have a nice nap?"

"Dammit, Betsy, you've almost guzzled that bottle empty."

"You should've been here last night. By God, you should've been, and we could've had a party, and I wouldn't have drank so much."

"You're not making much sense, Betsy."

"All right, Arnold dear, see if you can make sense out of this."

She paused momentarily as if she needed to think about what she was about to say. "Holly's right. I did talk to Old Man Clanton. Good lord, Arnold, I talked to Old Man Clanton lots. I would've made a bunch of money and could have gotten the hell out of here if they had been successful."

"Are you saying that Holly was telling the truth?"

"I'm telling you that I was in cahoots with the Clantons. Dammit, Arnold, I needed the money to leave this godforsaken country. You can't seem to get it through your head that I hate Arizona Territory so much that I am beginning to hate you because you won't leave."

"Christ's sake, Betsy, I have to go where the army sends me."

"You wouldn't have to stay here if you quit the army, or hasn't that ever crossed your mind?"

Willoughby returned to the bedroom and pulled on his boots. As he passed through the living room to the front door he glanced at his wife as she emptied the whiskey bottle into her glass. "I have some business to take care of," he said.

Betsy lifted her glass as if toasting his departure. Arnold was out the door before she could make any further drunken comment.

By the time Joe led the dappled gray stallion into the corrals at the ranch, he showed enough lameness to cause concern. "I wonder if J.Z. knows how this stud comes up lame," Joe said to Lucía as he removed the halter to allow the stud to drink and feed on the hay Lucía had tossed into the manger.

"Whoever sold the horse to J.Z. seems to have been honest enough to mention the near founder," Lucía said.

"I'm afraid we'll have to bring the mares to him here in the corral because he might get too lame to breed out in the hills with them. That will keep us close to home until all the mares have foaled and are bred back."

"Suppose the captain's wife denies what you told her husband?" Lucía asked.

"That is not my main concern. What I want to happen is for Willoughby to convince the colonel to drop those charges against me."

"What if you are sent to jail for a long time, Joe? What should I do with the mares, this lame stud and the Rancho Tecolote?"

"It's probably best only to think about that if that situation arises. I think the best thing for us to do now is go about our business as if nothing was in the wind that might interrupt us."

A frontal system had made a mackeral sky to the west of the Tucson and Tortolita Mountains. The sunset made it all look like a sea of orange, red, purple and pink waves. Joe and the dogs had just ambled down the road from the corrals after feeding the stud and the sorrel saddle horse. The dogs spotted him first and went to barking as they sped toward the man riding in from the stage road. With the sunset at his back, the man looked like a silouette. Joe couldn't see who it might be until the rider pulled up his reins and said, "Mistah Holly, it's me, Mose."

"Well, I'll be a scared rabbit in a windstorm," Joe said. "Come on in, Mose. What are you doing up this way? I thought you were cowboying down in the Sulfur Springs country."

Mose rode up, dismounted and reached out and shook Joe's hand. "It's mighty good to see you, Mistah Holly. I be in the saddle one long time gettin' here."

"I'm really happy to see you, Mose. Welcome to Rancho Tecolote."

"Thank you, Mistah Holly. I was cowboyin' down there in that Sulfa Springs valley, but I done quit two weeks ago. Was a new feller from Tucson come to work on the roundup and he was a tellin' how you was in some kind a trouble. I figures to quit anyways, so I done quit an come on up here to see if you needed a hand. I be happy to work for nothin'. I just remembered how you was good to me, and I want to be good to you 'cause a what I heard 'bout the trouble."

Joe felt touched by Mose's statement of friendship and offer to work for nothing just to help out because of the trouble he was having with the charges brought by Colonel Haynes. He reached out and shook Mose's hand again. "Let me show you where to put your horse up and then we can have supper." Joe said. "I found a wife since I last saw you, Mose. You're going to like her."

They went up to the corral, took care of Mose's horse and returned to the house. Having seen Mose's arrival from the window, Lucía had set the table for three. Joe introduced her to Mose and told her about serving with him at Camp Huachuca. "Mose's enlistment was up right after I got drummed out," Joe said.

"When that happen, Miz Holly, all of us soldiers was mad. That chicken captain was lucky he didn't get his-self accidentally shot at night."

"Like I told you in Tombstone when we were all having breakfast that morning, the chicken captain actually did me a big favor. Just think, Mose, I wouldn't found Lucía or bought this ranch if Willoughby hadn't brought those charges against me."

"That's true, Mistah Holly. But what's he got to do with the trouble you're in? I heard he moved to Fort Lowell."

"I must admit that Willoughby has caused me a bunch of trouble. He caused the colonel at Fort Lowell to file charges against me for the payroll robbery a while back."

"I heard 'bout that when I was to Benson on payday. Someone says Geronimo done that."

"That's one rumor, Mose. Willoughby thinks it was me because I bought this ranch and a bunch of horses. But I have a lawyer in Tucson. He should be able to get the charges dropped."

Joe didn't say anything about his real hope that Willoughby would influence Haynes into dropping the charges after hearing about Betsy's part in the robbery. There was no sense in taking any chances that information might get out and damage Betsy unnecessarily unless it had to come from him should the charges remain in place.

"Whatever happen, Mistah Holly, I be happy to stay here and take care a things till you get over the trouble."

"Mose, you have no idea how much I appreciate that, and I'm going to take you up on your offer. The only change I'll make is that I'll put you on the payroll. What made you quit your job down there?"

"Mistah Holly, that man Connely, the foreman feller, he don't treat all us cowboys the same. He thinks maybe I'm still a slave. There is a bunch of us that is cowboys. When some of the Buffalo Soldiers get out of the army they gets jobs cowboyin'. I chopped weeds out of cotton fields when I was a kid. Then, I went to cowboyin' before I joined up in the army."

"Lucía, remember what we were talking about the other day? I think we have just the man to take care of that end of our business, what do you think?"

"I think he would be just right," Lucía replied.

"What you talkin' about, Mistah Holly?"

"Mose, Lucía and I were talking about adding cattle to the ranch instead of just relying on the horses to make us a living. We both seem to agree that you would

233

be just the man to take care of the cattle if you want the job. For sure, you know more about cattle than either of us."

"Mistah Holly, you knows I give anything to do that."

"The way we figure, horses take so long to mature to top value that we need something else on the ranch."

"You is right about horses takin' a passel of time."

"It takes a mare eleven months after she is bred to have a foal. Then it takes two years after that before you can start saddling and another year before the horse is old enough and strong-legged enough to run a race or work all day."

"You got to figure that half them foals is gonna be fillies, and there sure ain't many men wants to ride mares in this country. When they's in heat they's too nervous."

"Tomorrow, we can ride the country around here, and you might be able to figure how many cows I should buy."

"What you wants to do, Mistah Holly, run cows and calves or just buy and sell steers?"

"I don't have that good an idea about the cattle business, Mose. Here is where you can teach me something about what I need to know before we decide."

"When I see the country up close, I be better at figurin'."

"I would like to ride with you tomorrow," Lucía said. "I have never seen the high country."

"Tomorrow will be a good chance to see it because we'll be going up to the pine country on top."

"I will pack us a good lunch."

They enjoyed their supper of venison and beans. Afterward Joe broke out a bottle of mescal from which

Mose and he drank toasts to the raising of cattle on Rancho Tecolote.

When Joe and Lucía finally slipped into bed, Joe took her into his arms and said, "I'm very glad Mose rode in tonight. I cannot think of any other man I'd rather have working with me."

"I like seeing you happy. Mose seems like a nice man, and I am glad you have a good friend like him."

Riding cross-country to where the Cañada del Oro flowed next to a butte below a long *bajada* from the first row of rugged, rocky hills, they reached a trail that wound its way to the top of the butte before heading eastward to the mountain country. It was there that they watched the sun spill a new day over the tallest part of the mountain to bathe the *bajada* and permit the trees, shrubs and grass to cast long shadows on the land and on each other. A half mile farther and they reached the wall of a canyon. A large palo verde tree stood near the edge where a game trail had been made by the hooves of deer, javelina and the paws of cougar, coyote and wolves.

Joe reined in and the others followed. "Listen," he said. "You can hear water rushing down through the canyon."

They sat on their horses in silence, listening to the stream below cascading over the boulders on the canyon floor, carrying whatever had been in its way, flinging it along to lower elevations to be caught and made part of a different home than it had known before.

Proceeding upward over the trail that led to the top of the mountain, Lucía saw an Apache sign, part of a feather on an ocotillo, to tell others that water would be in a short distance. She told the others.

Joe said, "Mose, the army would love to have Lucía as a scout if she would tell them what she knows."

"I remember Frog Eyes good," Mose said. "I bet he could be one bad Apache if he need to be."

"I always wondered how much Frog Eyes really told the chicken captain about the Apache way," Joe said musingly.

The trail leveled out around a cone-shaped hill. Behind the hill, they no longer could view the valley, and a small ravine divided the hill from the rugged, rocky slope of the mountain proper. The horses worked hard getting up the narrow passage through the rocks and boulders. Finally the trail descended from a saddle between two masses of boulders to a swiftly running stream that had a musical sound as it followed its course through the massive rocks. A white-tailed buck and four doe jumped from the stream's edge and bounded away through the boulder maze. To the north they saw two large pools that the stream had formed through the millennia. "What a wonderful place for a bath," Lucía said.

"I think I'd wait for summer," Joe remarked. "That water must be as cold as ice in the dead of winter coming down from the snow-covered summit."

"A man could water whole lots of cattle here, Mistah Holly."

"What do you think about the feed so far, Mose?"

"Maybe better below, but I ain't seen the top a the mountain yet."

"We'll be up there in an hour or so, according to what I've heard about this side of the mountain. I didn't ride this far when I bought Rancho Tecolote because I was only looking for a place to run a band of brood mares."

The trail up from the canyon steepened considerably. They saw a band of mountain sheep high on a ridge. Their sleek, tan coats shone in the sun. Soon conversation among the three became impossible, interrupted by the noise of hooves scraping over rocks. Chapparal turned into pine, and they stopped to enjoy Lucía's lunch just as they found a grove of ponderosa pine. "What do you think, Mose?" Joe inquired. "Can we raise cows on this country?"

"Mistah Holly, I think this high country might do for summer pasture 'cause the grass seems strong here, 'specially under these trees. That canyon below is good water and all, but it's a long ways from up here."

"Well, we can talk more when we see all we can see of this mountain," Joe said.

After finishing lunch, they rode farther to the top of the mountain where they found a tall-growing grove of Douglas fir. The dead needles on the ground below the trees formed a brownish carpet with occasional grasses peeking through in an attempt to find sunlight. Joe reined the sorrel around and began the ride home.

As they rode through the last of the ponderosa pine going downslope toward the chapparal and the canyon of boulders and running stream, the sound of an animal crashing through the brush came to their ears.

"What the hell was that, Mose?" Joe asked.

Before he could answer Joe's question, Mose had spurred his horse toward the sound. The others watched as he reined up and sat in the saddle looking off in the distance. Joining Joe and Lucía again, he said, "That crashing sound was a big old brindle bull that's wild as a deer and big as a Missoura barn. He got a horn spread of 'bout eight feet look like."

"I wonder who owns him," Joe said.

"Mistah Holly, that bull done owns hisself. You can bet money on that. If someone tried brandin' that old renegade he'd make short reatas out of long ones."

"A bull as wild as that might be a hazard to working cowhands, don't you think, Mose?"

"That old wild feller ain't no hazard, he's plumb dangerous. You ain't going to catch this ex-Buffalo Soldier messin' around with him unless I have a Sharps carbine handy. Then I'd use the Sharps before I even thought about puttin' a reata 'round them horns. Lawdy me." Trotting his horse up alongside Joe, Mose leaned over so as to be out of earshot of Lucía and whispered, "Them horns is longer than a whore's dream, Mistah Holly."

"If we were to put mother cows up here, that old bull is bound to breed some," Joe commented.

"Breed some. Mistah Holly, that old feller will breed all the cows within bellerin' distance."

It was almost dark by the time they unsaddled and put their horses up with a feed trough amply loaded with hay and a pound of grain each in *morrals* made from gunny sacks that went over the horses' heads. That method kept each horse's ration separated so the dominant one didn't get all the grain. Joe and Lucía made their way to the house leaving Mose to wait for the horses to finish their grain.

After supper, Joe and Mose retreated from the kitchen to the front room where they could talk about cattle as Lucía cleaned the dishes, pots and pans. "All right, you've seen the country we have to graze. What do you think about getting into the cow business?" Joe asked.

"Mistah Holly, I think there's some mighty fine cow

country on this side a the mountain. But it's damn sure tough graze."

"What do you mean, Mose?"

"Well, from the foot of the mountain on up it's rough country. Lots of rocks, steep slopes and tough goin'. Down below it's easy enough living for a cow, but there ain't much bottom country."

"Is there any reason why we shouldn't raise cattle here?"

"You're going to have some losses from cougar. That you might as well figure on. I saw plenty of tracks up there. In fact, I'd bet a year's wages that there was at least one old lion a watchin' us when we was waterin' the horses at that stream. I saw some fresh, big tracks where the trail crossed the water."

"I figured I would lose some foals to lion when I bought the mares, but I mean about the feed here. How many cows should I buy to put on this ranch without hurting the grass."

"You are sure enough different than them fellers down in Sulfur Springs country. They'd be askin' 'how many cows can I buy' without any thinkin' of the grass.

"If I was you, I'd buy me some leggy Mexicans because of the rough high country you have to graze. They can walk farther to water than them short-legged Durhams like old Colonel Hooker or Herefords that the Scottish feller what owns that San Rafael outfit is bringin' in. They all say that those cattle bring higher prices, but I got the notion that a steer with more leg what can get around the rough country better will live longer when times are tough and it don't rain."

"Mose, for an ex-Buffalo Soldier, you sure have learned a lot about cows."

"Well, like I told you, I done a little cowboyin' before

I joined the army, Mistah Holly. And I kept listenin' to what cowmen was sayin'."

"From what I can gather, the cow business is changing quickly. I heard about those European breeds that are being imported. I also have an idea that since the railroad got here last March, big changes will come about. The long cattle drives to the railheads like Dodge City will be a thing of the past, and other markets will open up."

"Back to what you should ought to do on this here ranch, Mistah Holly, I think you needs to figure that this side of the mountain will feed a big bunch of cows. But if the Apache raiders find it easy pickin' you may lose a lot of 'em."

"The one thing I don't worry about is the Apache. Lucía has that situation covered very well."

"What you mean got that situation covered very well?"

"Just take my word for that, Mose. Someday, maybe I can tell you the whole story."

The two men sat looking at one another. Joe could see by the expression on Mose's face that he was puzzled. Then, as if he had put Apache raiders out of his mind, his brow unwrinkled and he rubbed his chin as if he had a beard. "How many cows you figure to buy?"

"That is what I am asking you, Mose. I'll have to borrow the money to buy them, so it kind of depends on how much money I can get from the bank."

"One thing you needs to remember is that whatever number of cows you buy, you needs to multiply by three 'cause you'll have the calves around for three years. Now, 'course that figure ain't really three cause you ain't going to get a hunderd percent calf crop, no way."

"How many calves can I expect from a hundred head of cows?" Joe asked.

"You be lucky to get sixty and half of 'em will be heifers. And, Mistah Holly, it ain't just Apache raiders what gets your cattle. There's a bunch of rustlers what goes around this country stealin' cattle wherever they finds 'em."

"You keep talking all the ways I can lose money on cows, Mose, and maybe I'll decide to stick with horses and to hell with cattle."

"I just don't want to see you get burned in the cow business. It takes a heap of money and just when things look like they is goin' your way, it don't rain and the damned old cows up and die."

"I'll ride into town tomorrow and see the banker. Hell's fire, he might not want to lend me a plugged nickel, and that would make my decision easy."

As he sat in front of Jonathan Beasley's desk at the Territory Bank and Trust, Joe listened as the banker lectured him about the perils of the cattle business. "Mr. Beasley," Joe interrupted. "I didn't come here to hear how bad the cattle business is. I came here to borrow money to buy cows with. Why not come to the point? Are you interested in lending me enough money for a hundred head of cows and eight bulls?"

"Mr. Holly, I am obviously in the business of lending money. However, with the federal charges pending against you, I must question the risk you present."

Glowering menacingly at Beasley, Joe pushed himself up from the chair. "Beasley, I came in here to hear what you might say to my request, knowing that you had a part in the charges that have been filed against me."

"What in the world are you talking about, Holly?"

241

"You seem to forget that you gave out my financial dealings to the commandant of Fort Lowell. I used to think that bankers kept confidential information about their clients to themselves."

"Uh, uh . . ."

"Now, please, Mr. Beasley, spare me the lame excuses you are trying to think up. You are one sorry banker, and I won't hesitate to say so to anyone who might ask about your ethics."

"Now, Mr. Holly, perhaps there is some way we can settle this in an amiable fashion."

"Beasley, you settled this before I walked in the front door of your establishment. Good day to you."

Joe turned abruptly and strode out of the building. Once outside, his face broke into a broad grin. *It isn't every day that I get to tell a banker to go to hell.*

J.Z. Tyler glanced up as Joe rode toward him, dismounted and tied the sorrel to the hitchrack. After recognizing his visitor, the horse trader returned his concentration to the piece of cottonwood he was whittling.

"How are you, Mr. Tyler?" Joe asked.

Without looking up, Tyler said, "I couldn't be any better unless you came in to buy more mares." His paunch wiggled as he chuckled at his own words.

"I don't need any more mares today, Mr. Tyler. I came by to ask you about cattle prices. I'm thinking about buying around a hundred head of mother cows and eight bulls to run on the Tecolote country."

"The price of cows depends on what kind of cows you're wantin' to buy. If you're wantin' them newfangled Shorthorns or Herefords, you're gonna pay a premium 'cause them fellers who is importin' them short-legged critters think they got gold in their tails."

"I'm interested in plain Mexican or Texas cattle. I'm told the west side of Frog Mountain is too rugged for those short-legged animals."

"Do you want cows with calves or just cows?"

"What is the difference in price?"

"Well, pairs'll bring around thirty and singles should go for a little less, maybe twenty-six."

"I think pairs would suit me better, Mr. Tyler. Most likely they would be bred back and I could go a season without bulls."

"I'm no cowman, Holly, but I think I'd get your bulls out there and let 'em get located good. Pairs are gonna be harder to drive than singles."

"I didn't think of that," Joe said.

"You're probably less of a cowman than I am."

Joe ignored J.Z.'s remark. "Do you know anyone who might have a hundred cows for sale?"

"There's an old boy out in the Altar country who I heard wanted to sell out and go back to East Texas. He's runnin' around a hundred fifty head up in the Sierritas. I'll try to find out about those cows if you want."

"I'd appreciate that, Mr. Tyler. I'll have to find another banker besides Beasley. I just came from him, and he thinks the charges the army filed against me present too big a risk."

"That little runty sumbitch ain't worth a fart in a windstorm as a banker. Tell him something you're thinkin' 'bout doin' an' the entire town knows 'bout it in a half hour."

"That's what I discovered. I wish you and I hadn't used him as an agent with the money I bought your horses with."

"That's partly my fault. I never figured that sumbitch would pull the crap he did on you. One of these days, he might be lookin' up at the sky from the bottom of a well. Trouble with that is water's too dear around Tucson to ruin."

"Can you recommend a different banker, Mr. Tyler?"

J.Z. looked up into Joe's eyes for the first time since he had dismounted and walked over to the bench. "I'll tell you what," he said. "I'll lend you the money for your cows and calves and a little extra for expenses. All you gotta do is sign a mortgage to that ranch and a note for the cows and mares."

"You may be sorry if those damn lawyers toss me in jail."

"I'll have your ranch, mares and cows."

"I doubt that my wife would let that happen. She'd run things very well until I got back."

"You're a lucky man, Mr. Holly."

"I feel that way, Mr. Tyler. The people who are trying to make me unhappy are not very happy themselves. What is it—envy, jealousy?"

"Beats me. But it seems to happen a whole bunch."

"Back to these cows you say are for sale. Why is the rancher selling them?" Joe asked.

"He's got a dry outfit up there in the Sierrita Mountains, and the only time he has stock water is when it rains. He's figurin' to quit cows and calves and run steers after the rains fill up his represos. When he located out there he took a couple of fresnos and some stout work teams out there and dug out two good represos. Trouble is, the rains don't come right for cows. Steers is easier to move when you have to move them."

"I think I'd like to have a look at these cows," Joe said, tipping his hat back with his thumb. "Can you arrange for that?"

"I expect I'll see that feller sometime today. He left

his saddle horse here yesterday. He's generally in town for a day this time of the month."

"You can send word to me at the Cosmopolitan. I'll be spending the night there."

"Before you take off outa here, I've got the rest of those horses in the back corral. They came in yesterday. Go have a look-see and tell me if they're all right for your order."

"I paid you for twenty-five head. Are they all back there?"

"There's twenty-eight so you can cut back three of 'em."

"I'll take a look. When do I have to take delivery without a feed bill?"

"Aw hell, I'll go easy on you. I'll give you a week seeing how they came in sooner than I thought they would."

Joe mounted the sorrel and trotted back to the large corral in the rear of the complex. Looking over the estacada fence, he saw the conglomeration of horseflesh J.Z. had put together. Spotting the three smallest of the bunch, he made a mental note of their descriptions to tell the trader which ones he wanted to cut back.

Leaving the sorrel tied to the hitchrack, Joe ambled back to tell J.Z. which of the horses he wanted to refuse and then headed afoot for the hotel. He thought about taking delivery on the horses destined for Arivaipa Canyon in the morning, but by the time he reached the Cosmopolitan Hotel, he had decided he might as well get them out to the ranch and then to Etazin before all the legal stuff began again. Getting cows bought would just have to wait, but he felt good that J.Z. had offered to be his banker.

Shortly after he had sat down for supper in the hotel

dining room, a grizzled-looking man who, by the nature of his clothes, Joe assumed was a cowman introduced himself as Harry Garrity and said that J.Z. had sent him. "He said you were in the market for a hundred cows with calves."

"I am, Mr. Garrity, but it will be a week or so before I can look at them. I have some horses to deliver, and that will take at least five days."

"A week's no problem, but I need to get them off the ranch as soon as possible because the represos are near dry."

"I understand. How do I get to your place?"

"Once you get to the north end of the Sierritas, you ride south a couple of miles and then go west until you hit the wagon road. It will take you right in to my headquarters. The cows are mostly in the south part before you get into Palo Alto range, so you probably won't see many on your way in."

"I'll get out there as soon as possible, Mr. Garrity."

"I'm either at the ranch or in town. J.Z. can tell you if I'm here in town 'cause I always leave my horse with him."

"Fine, Mr. Garrity. I look forward to seeing your cows and calves."

Chapter Nineteen

Tired from all the business he had conducted in Tucson and from the ride north driving the twenty-five horses over the Butterfield Stage Route, Joe was happy to see them safely in the corrals at the Tecolote headquarters. The thought of seeing Lucía and holding her close sparked him into sitting taller in the saddle as he booted the sorrel into a trot toward the house. The dogs came out to meet him barking their friendly greeting and wagging their tails frantically. It seemed they were trying to tell him something. His face broke into a broad grin when he saw Lucía come from the ranch house and walk quickly out to meet him by the hitchrack.

He dismounted, tossed the reins over the pole of the rack and took her into his arms. "How are you, Mrs. Holly? It is sure nice to see you."

"I am glad to see you, too, Joe. We have a visitor."

"Oh?" Joe said, tilting his head quizzically.

"It is your father. He rode in yesterday afternoon."

"Oh my God. What the hell is he doing here?"

"I think he is upset about the charges the colonel made on you. He does not smile much, and he seems to think I am your maid."

"Didn't you tell him you're my wife?"

"I tried to, but he doesn't allow me to talk much. Joe, I am really glad to see you. I am not happy with the way your father is."

"Let's go inside and see what I can do with him."

Just as they turned to walk to the house, Nathan Holly emerged from the old adobe ranch house, his empty sleeve, despite being pinned up, slightly flapping in the breeze coming in from the west. Joe and Lucía halted their steps toward the house, watching wordlessly as Joe's father approached. "Hello, Son," the elder Holly said. "I expect you are surprised to see me here."

Joe looked at his father, discovering that in spite of the relatively short time he had been away from him, the gray in his hair had become dominant and the lines in his face more pronounced. "I have to say that I didn't expect to see you, Father. What brings you to Arizona Territory?"

"Colonel Haynes, Jeffery, my old comrade from Gettysburg wrote about your being drummed out of the army. I was quite disappointed to hear that bad news. However, his telegram about you being charged with armed robbery of an army payroll detail concerns me greatly. I started west as soon as I got my luggage packed."

"I suppose I should have written to you, but we've been very busy with all sorts of things, especially since my decision to buy some cows for the ranch."

"Why stay out here in the wind?" Lucía asked. "I have coffee heated."

Joe proceeded to open the door for Lucía and his father. When the two men were seated in the living room, she brought them each a steaming cup of coffee. "I will put your horse up, Joe, and then I will have supper ready in a short time," she said, leaving for the kitchen and shutting the old wooden door behind her.

"I see you have managed to find a good housekeeper, Son. Lucía has made me comfortable here while you were in town."

"Lucía is not my housekeeper, Father. She is my wife," Joe said emphatically as he gave Nathan Holly a steely glare.

"Good grief, boy, what in hell are you saying?"

"Lucía and I are married. We love each other," Joe said.

"Why in hell did you marry a Mexican?"

"I never gave any thought to her being Mexican because she isn't a Mexican."

"Come now, Son, don't tell me you've lost your sight as well as your mind."

"Lucía was born here in Arizona Territory, and that makes her an American just as much as I am."

"You certainly have gotten some funny ideas out here."

"I like this country, and I like living on the frontier."

"Well, let's get to the point, Joseph. I had a long talk with Jeff Haynes before I came out here. He gave me the details about you and this Captain Willoughby. Jeff said Willoughby brought charges against you at Camp Huachuca for striking him, a superior, and conduct not becoming an officer. Jeff thinks that he can get the court-martial decision reversed on that. Of course, that would depend on how you survive this latest trial in federal court. I must say, Joseph, I fail to understand how you get yourself into such predicaments. Do you have no concern for the family reputation?"

"Father, I'm going to be very frank with you, and I think it would behoove you to listen very carefully. I've thought a lot about what you refer to as a predicament and a lot about what you refer to as family."

"I'm not sure I like the way you are talking to me, Joseph."

"I'm sorry, but I cannot help the way you feel. First of all, you can tell Colonel Haynes that I would not accept any sort of reinstatement in the army. I wouldn't even accept an appointment as General of the Army of the West. I don't like the army. I'm overjoyed to be away from it."

"How in hell are you going to make a living on this dried-up country full of rocks and cactus?"

"I'm not sure yet, but I do know one thing, and that is, I'll be happier in failure here than I would be in the army with every promotion possible."

"You had a great future in the army, Joseph. You're just too rebellious to realize that."

"That brings up another point that I must mention. I might ask you the question, why do you think I got to be rebellious? Do you have any idea how I felt being constantly in second place to Edward in everything at home?"

"I'm afraid I don't understand you."

"All my life, except when you were off to war, I've taken second place to my older brother. You always greeted him first when you came back from trips. You always put him in charge of the farm while you were away. You always put him in charge of me, even when you were home. He was always the one to get the best colts to ride. I always had to ride the bad ones. In that respect you did me a favor because I learned how to train colts much better than Edward ever did."

"Edward is very good with horses. I don't think you have cause to criticize him."

"Christ's sake, Father, I'm not criticizing Edward. I feel sorry for the poor bastard."

"What do you mean?" Nathan Holly said angrily.

"It's very simple, Father. I am free. Edward is stuck with that goddamn rock pile of a farm in Maine where the winter will freeze the balls off a moose. He's under your thumb in spite of being thirty years old. Did he ever get married?"

"Not yet, but he's seeing the Blanchard girl. She teaches school down in Kittery."

"How long will you be staying with us, Father?" Joe asked.

"I cannot stay long. Edward will be choosing the colts to train for polo and those that go to the Boston Police Department. I should get back to help him with that."

Joe cleared his throat and pondered how he should proceed. He slapped both his knees and said, "Father, you have just substantiated what I told you about why I feel sorry for Edward."

"What are you talking about, Joseph?"

"When I asked you how long you plan to be here, the first thing that comes to your mind is getting back to Maine to help Edward make a decision about the horses. If you don't allow him to make decisions now when he's thirty years old, he'll never be able to decide anything once you are gone. You must realize that someday you will die. If Edward hasn't made any decisions by himself by then, how do you suppose he'll manage without you?"

"I guess I'd like to think about that for a while," Nathan Holly said, obviously shaken by the confrontation.

Joe and his father sat in silence, each thinking about the previous conversation. Their spell broke when Lucía opened the door to the kitchen and announced that supper was on the table. The men rose from their chairs and proceeded to the kitchen. Just as they began taking their places, Mose came into the room, having ridden in from his day's work looking after the mares. "Mose, have you met my father, Nathan Holly?"

"Yes, Mistah Holly. I met him yesterday when he got here," Mose replied, and turned toward Joe's father. "I hope you is enjoyin' yourself, Mistah Nathan."

"Thank you, Mose," Nathan said. "It is good to see my son again."

"Did that gray mare foal yet, Mose?" Joe asked.

"Not yet, Mistah Holly. I got a good look at her today and she ain't waxed yet. What's them horses in the corrals?"

"I drove them out from Tucson. I have to deliver them over in the San Pedro country. Lucía and I can handle that business."

He glanced over to his wife and caught the look of excitement in her eyes. "I thought about starting out in the morning, but I had no idea that you were here, Father. Now that you are, I think you'd enjoy the ride over into that country."

"I don't know about that. After what you said, I don't want to get in your way when you're doing business."

"Don't worry about that. The business is all taken care of. You might enjoy meeting the people to whom I am delivering the horses."

"All right then, count me in," Nathan Holly said.

Joe wondered what his father's answer would have been had he known that the ride they would begin in the morning would take them into an Apache stronghold.

Before retiring for the night, Lucía wrapped supplies that would go into the panniers on the pack saddle. Joe busied himself with other preparations, including thoroughly cleaning his Sharps carbine for hunting. He wanted to give his father a taste of the West in addition to the sights and experience that he would remember for the rest of his life.

The sun had broken through the clouds of a storm coming in from the west by the time they had everything ready for the trail drive. Mose helped get the bunch started and when they were lined out and used to being on the trail again, he said good-bye and turned back to Rancho Tecolote, still not knowing his boss's destination with the horses. Riding back to the ranch, he remembered listening to the elder Holly's comments after seeing the horses in the corral. "Who in the world wants a bunch of junk horseflesh like this, Son?"

"When we get there, you will understand better."

"I wouldn't have a single one of these nags on my place. Someone might think they were the kind I raised."

"You noticed that I'm not keeping them in the corrals longer than overnight, don't you?"

"True enough. How far is this place you are so secretive about?"

"Two days. Two full days driving seventy-five head of horses, so with only twenty-five head to drive, we'll hopefully get there tomorrow afternoon if nothing happens to hold us back."

Mose tried to figure out where Joe was heading and came up with a total blank despite his knowledge of the territory south of the Mongollon Rim. Arriving back at the Tecolote corrals, he headed out to check the mares.

Joe, Lucía and Nathan kept the horses moving north toward the small mining village called Oracle that had recently been established. The name came from the ship that brought the founder around Cape Horn, not the place in ancient Greece where the future was told. Joe planned to spend the night in the vicinity of the village and, in the morning, descend the steep *bajada* to the San Pedro River.

As they drove the horse herd, there was little opportunity for conversation. Joe continued to wonder how his father would react to suddenly being in the middle of the Apache settlement. Riding point, Joe could not see much of his father, who rode behind the bunch with Lucía. When they arrived at Oracle, Joe hobbled the sorrel and put a small bell around the neck of a tall bay mare that seemed to be a good leader. He chose a sheltered area that had plenty of grass and a small stream that meandered down the south slope of the mountain.

Around the perimeter of the meadow Joe noticed that the manzanita and sotol had been blackened by a fire sometime in the past. The oak trees had also survived in spite of their bark being charred around the bases of the trunks. Joe could see that his father was curious about the trees because he went up to one and looked intently at the leaves. "Do you know what these trees are, Joseph?"

"The one you're looking at is an oak. Most of the

trees around here are oak, but there are a few mesquite and juniper."

"The oaks here don't look like the ones we have back east," Nathan said.

"From what I've seen, Arizona Territory doesn't resemble the East in the slightest. Maybe that's why I enjoy being a part of the frontier."

"Frontiers are risky places to make a living, Joseph."

"I suppose that's the challenge that attracts me to this one. After all, Maine was a frontier not so long ago."

Lucía had been listening to father and son discussing her country like it was some strange place. "I do not understand why you think this is such a wild place. My family has been around Tumacacori as long as anyone can remember," she interjected.

"Where did your family come from?" Nathan asked.

"My father told us that our ancestors were originally from Spain, but through time we became Mexican like most who were here before you people came. There are still more Mexicans in Tucson than any other people."

Having no desire to pursue that conversation, Nathan asked Joe how far he planned to ride the following day.

"We should reach the canyon by the middle of the afternoon. It is a very beautiful place with tall cottonwoods, sycamores and a stream of cold, clear water."

Pointing across the valley toward the canyon, distinguishable by its multicolored cliffs, Joe showed Nathan their destination.

"That doesn't look far away. Are you sure it will take that long to reach it?"

"Out here the distances are very deceiving, Father. From here on the mountain, the canyon looks a whole lot closer than it really is. You'll see what I mean tomorrow."

The horses seemed reluctant to leave the meadow the following morning. Joe discovered why when he spotted a cougar lying on a rounded granite boulder to the west, watching the horses. "That big cat up there is looking for breakfast," Joe said, pointing toward the feline. "If we had any foals in this bunch he wouldn't be lying down."

"Will they be a problem with your foals at the ranch?" Nathan asked.

"I imagine we'll lose some now and then, but that's to be expected in this country according to some of the old-timers I have talked with."

"Why don't you shoot the sonofabitch?"

"I suppose I could since everyone seems to regard the cougar as an enemy, but there's something rather regal about that big cat. I'd hate to be responsible for killing him."

"You'd think differently if that regal cat had one of your foals by the jugular," Nathan said.

"Maybe," Joe replied, and yelled at the horses trying to start them out of the meadow and down the long, steep slope to the river.

"I will ride the point in front," Lucía suggested. "That way you will have a chance to talk with your father."

Not wanting to disgruntle his father, Joe agreed, but underneath he was happier to be out of earshot of Nathan Holly, especially when the older man started talking against Arizona Territory as a dried-up rock pile.

They arrived at the west bank of the San Pedro shortly after midday, watered the horses and proceeded to cross the stream to head north along the bases of the

foothills of the Galiuro Mountains. Joe noticed that between the hills the arroyos were sandy dry and he wondered how much water was coming down Arivaipa
Creek. He thought about the time he and Frog Eyes
had set Arnold Willoughby afoot to walk all the way to
Benson and how he had given Etazin Willoughby's
horse. When he gave that gift, Joe had no idea that
Etazin would give him Lucía in return. He recalled his
feelings of near panic and embarrassment then, and as
he watched her riding at the head of the procession of
equines he felt a yearning to take her into his arms.

Reaching the mouth of Arivaipa Creek close to
where it emptied its precious cargo of water into the
sometimes fiercely flooding San Pedro, Joe rode around
the flank of the bunch to chat a moment with Lucía.
"If my father looks like he is going to panic when he
sees who my so-called customers are, you may have to
help me calm him down. I'm going to take his pistola
just in case."

"Good idea. I will tell Etazin right away that he is
your father. That will ease the mind of Etazin because
he does not trust anyone since the massacre."

Joe rode back and reined the sorrel alongside Nathan's bay. "I need to take your Colt, Father. The people we are delivering these horses to would not take
kindly to a stranger riding in here armed. I'll explain it
all to you later."

"Now after keeping me guessing where we're going,
you want me to surrender my weapon. What's going
on here, Son? This is making me feel very uneasy."

"I'm sure it's difficult, but soon you'll know everything, and I am sure you will find this an interesting
experience."

Nathan took the Colt out of the holster and handed

it to Joe, who stuffed it into the waistband of his denim trousers. He continued to ride next to his father. After two days on the trail, the horses didn't need any extra urging and followed Lucía like she was their leader.

The first guard stood up when he recognized Lucía in the lead. She hailed him by waving her hand. The guard held his carbine up over his head.

"What the hell is going on, Joseph? That man in the rocks looks like an Indian. What's he doing with a rifle?"

"Do not fear, Father. He recognized Lucía out in front. The others will do the same. They are guarding the canyon from intruders. A few years ago, a bunch of Tucson merchants and some Papago warriors came in and slaughtered over a hundred people, mostly women. I need to find out more about that, but it seems the perpetrators were brought to trial in Tucson and the jury aquitted them. I don't have much faith in justice out here in the territories."

"And these are your customers?"

"Yes, Father. They're a band of Apache called Arivaipans. A man named Etazin is their headman. He and I are friends."

"How can you be friends with an enemy of your country, Joseph?"

"Father, these people did not choose to be enemies of the United States. We came in here and took their lands. Would you let someone come in and take your farm in Maine?"

"But the Apache are savages."

"I once thought the same, but I have changed my mind. The Apache are not savages just because they are different than we are. Here is something you might consider: In doing business with Etazin, I have never written anything out on a piece of paper. When I deal with a customer in Tucson, I have to have a receipt to make a deal legal. Etazin is a man of great honor and I trust him implicitly."

"You are as different as the Apache since you were drummed out of the army."

"I certainly hope so, Father. I didn't fit in the army."

"But, this Etazin you speak of, how do you know you can trust him?"

"For one thing, he has done everything we agreed on. But more importantly, Father, it was Etazin who gave me Lucía, who he regarded as a daughter."

"How the hell did he come by Lucía? I thought she was a Mexican."

"He captured Lucía six years ago and raised her like a daughter. Lucía is very fond of him."

Another guard stood up and waved his rifle. Lucía responded again with a wave.

"There is a lot I don't seem able to understand. On one hand, you say that this Etazin captured Lucía, and on the other hand, you say she is fond of him. It doesn't make much sense to me."

"I've wondered about that myself. Lucía was twelve when the Apache raiding party swooped in on her family's place in Tumacacori. They were after horses and cattle, but when Lucía's father tried to defend his holdings the raiders killed him, his wife and two sons. Lucía was hiding under a bed and they spared her. However, Etazin took her back to Arivaipa as a captive, probably so she would not be able to identify the band that killed her family."

"I still can't understand how she came to be fond of your friend Etazin."

"When you meet the headman, you might understand better. He treated her like a daughter from the time she was twelve until she left Arivaipa with me. He protected her against the Apache men who wanted her. She was also excited when she learned that I might take her back to Tumacacori to see her uncle, aunt and cousins."

After a two-hour ride farther up the canyon and passing several sentries, they came within sight of the settlement of wickiups on the mesa above the floodplain. "We are almost there," Joe said.

"I'm not sure I like being here," Nathan said. "I have read and heard a lot about these Apaches and they do not seem like a friendly people, quite savage as a matter of fact."

"You have probably read more about them than I have, but I know the people here and would not be bringing you along if I thought for a minute I would be putting your life at risk. From what I can gather, the Apache situation is far more complicated than our people realize. For one thing, there are different clans and bands. Some Apaches do not get along with other Apaches. Our army thinks one Apache is the same as all the rest, but that is not true at all."

"Where do you get all these ideas, Joseph?"

"From Lucía, mainly. She knows them very well. When you hear her speak their language, you might understand her better, too."

Lucía continued at the point and led the horses up the trail to the mesa. The people had watched them approach the village and had opened the gate to the corral. Once the horses were inside, Lucía rode out of the enclosure and reined her horse over to where Joe and his father had stopped and remained mounted near

Etazin's wickiup. The headman appeared from inside the wattled structure and approached the three visitors with a smile on his face. He spoke to Lucía.

"Etazin says welcome," she interpreted. "I told him that we brought your father with us and he welcomes him also. He says for you to please dismount."

The three handed their horses to two young boys, who led the animals to the corral and began unsaddling them. Etazin offered the guests seats on cottonwood logs around the large fire circle in the middle of the plaza.

"Tell Etazin that I am happy to see him again and that I now have a ranch where he is always welcome."

Lucía turned to speak again with the headman.

"Etazin thanks you. He also says that he is pleased to see that I am more beautiful than when he saw me last. He gives you credit for taking good care of me."

"Tell him that there is never a day that passes that I do not feel his friendship when I look at you."

She conversed again with the headman. "Etazin welcomes the father of his friend," she said looking at Nathan.

"Tell him thank you," Nathan said nervously.

The conversation continued as two women stirred the coals in the fire circle and added mesquite wood. The fire soon flared and as the sun began to leave the canyon, the women placed some meat on green willow skewers on the fresh coals.

Joe turned to his father. "They are preparing a feast for us, Father. How are you feeling? Still nervous about being here?"

"I can't say that I feel completely comfortable. However, if Lucía is interpreting acurately, the headman, as you call him, is friendly to you."

One of the women brought a bottle of tiswin from the wickiup and handed it to Etazin. He took a swallow and handed it to Lucía to give to Joe.

"Etazin asks if your father is acquainted with tiswin. I told him I did not think so because he is a new arrival to Arizona Territory. He wants to know from where your father came."

"Tell him that my father is from the East Coast, where he raises horses."

Lucía relayed the information as Joe took a swig of tiswin and handed the bottle to Nathan. "What in hell is this stuff?" Nathan asked.

"It's a drink they make from corn. I don't drink much at a time because it can be pretty strong."

The women served the skewered broiled meat to Etazin and his guests. The last thing the three trail drivers had had to eat was some jerky while they were watering the horses at the San Pedro. They ate the meat with relish. Nathan lifted his eyebrows in approval as he tasted the first morsel. When he had finished a sizeable chunk, he asked what kind of meat it was.

"Horse," Joe informed his father. "The Apache consider horse meat a delicacy."

"I'll be damned. I never thought I'd ever eat horse meat," Nathan said.

"I'll wager that you never thought you'd be eating it in the company of Apaches either."

"I am afraid that is quite true, Son."

Joe was happy to see that his father was beginning to relax. For some reason that Joe did not completely understand, it was important to him that his father enjoy the experience rather than fear it.

Etazin had been watching Nathan the entire time when he wasn't conversing with Lucía. Joe could tell by the way the headman looked back and forth from his father to Lucía as he spoke that he was saying something for Lucía to translate to Nathan.

"Etazin says that he notices your father's nervousness and that, perhaps, a woman in his bed might help to calm him."

"Absolutely not," Nathan exclaimed, scowling. "I am a Christian and do not believe in that sort of behavior."

"Mr. Holly," Lucía said, "Etazin did not mention any sort of behavior in his offer to you. It was his offer of friendship."

Somewhat subdued by Lucía's admonishment, Nathan told her to thank Etazin but that he preferred to sleep alone. A quizzical look appeared on Etazin's face when Lucía spoke for Joe's father.

Continuing the conversation after the feast and then showing Nathan where he could spend the night, Joe and Lucía went into the wickiup they had shared their first night together. In spite of the distance between Nathan and them, Joe and Lucía kept their voices at a whisper.

"Does my father still look nervous to you?" Joe asked.

"He seems a lot less nervous than when we arrived. I thought he was going to start shaking."

"I can understand him being nervous. He's never been around anyone except his own kind before. There are Indians in Maine, but they were placed apart from the whites a long time ago. He has also read about Apaches by white writers who consider them savages just because they are different in skin color and customs."

John Duncklee

"One of the reasons I love you, Joe, is that you are different from other white men I have seen."

"I love you because you are the way you are."

"Etazin can see that we are in love with each other. He said so, but I did not interpret all that he said, especially about the robbery."

"My father does not need to know about that party we had with the Clantons."

"Etazin refers to your father as 'Bird With Broken Wing.' I did not want to say that either."

"Is there anything that Etazin said that you did not translate that I might want to hear."

"I have told you everything. We talked a little about Rancho Tecolote. I told him where it is so he can find it easily and assured me that he knew where it was. From my description he recognized it."

"He probably raided the cattle and is therefore a major reason for me being able to buy the place for a good price."

"I did not think of that, but what you say is probably quite true," she said.

"Well, Mrs. Holly, my father may not care to relax, but I would."

"Joe Holly, you are a good man."

As they rode back toward the ranch, a winter storm rolled in from the west, buffeting them with wind and a snowstorm that came horizontally at them. The temperature had dropped enough to keep the snow from melting. By the time they arrived at the cluster of new buildings that had recently been dubbed Oracle, two inches of snow had accumulated and the horses' steaming breath looked like smoke.

Without stopping at the village, Joe reined the sorrel

southward to Cañada del Oro. Within an hour of hard riding they escaped the snowstorm, as darkness started earlier than usual because of the clouds.

"I think we should keep going and not stop until we get to the ranch," Joe said. "If it gets too dark for us to see the way, the horses will take us there without any directions from us."

"Just so they don't go under any low tree limbs that will rub us off their backs," Nathan said.

"If we stay away from the arroyo we won't meet up with any trees," Joe replied.

"Look at the sky, Joe," Lucía said. "The clouds look like they are breaking. Maybe we will have moonlight to ride by."

Joe and Nathan looked up to see the clouds swirling in the dusky sky. "It does look like the storm is moving out, but it will be awhile before the moon makes its way over Frog Mountain so we can see," Joe said.

"We have another half hour until it's dark," Lucía said. "How far is the Butterfield road? If we can find it before dark, it will be easy to follow whether there's moonlight or not."

"You are sure enough right about that, my dear. The only thing I was thinking of back at Oracle was to get down below that snowstorm as soon as possible. Now that we're out of it, you are right. We can head west until we hit the stage road."

Joe, in the lead, booted the sorrel into a trot to try and find the stage road before total darkness engulfed them. The clouds broke and rose above the mountain. Just as they reached the rutted stage route and reined southward, they saw the moon reflected from the bottom of the cloud layer.

From the bunkhouse by the corral, a sleepy Mose carried a lit coal-oil lamp when he was awakened by their arrival. After putting up the horses, they headed for the ranch house. Lucía started a fire in the stove and soon had a platter of bacon and eggs set on the kitchen table. Approaching his chair, Nathan pulled his Waltham pocketwatch out and glanced at it. "Well, we are either having an early breakfast or a late supper," he said and chuckled. "It's two in the morning."

Joe and Lucía laughed with him and all three sat down to satisfy their hunger.

The storm had disappeared and the sun was high by the time they climbed out of bed the following morning. Joe felt obligated to keep his father entertained during his visit so he suggested that they ride out to have a look at the mares. Knowing that Joe and Lucía would probably sleep late, Mose had not stopped in for breakfast. Instead, he had saddled up and ridden out to find the mares.

Finishing their breakfast, Joe and Nathan left Lucía at the ranch house and went to the corrals to catch their saddle horses. Within an hour they found Mose on a butte that overlooked the arroyo. He was sitting on his horse, watching the mares and their foals grazing. "The gray mare done had a little filly, Mistah Holly," Mose said as Joe and his father approached. "They're over behind that hill," he said, pointing. "Looks to me like she didn't have no trouble and her filly has the look of a strong one."

"That is good news," Joe said. "I am glad she had a filly. We already have four colts and only one filly besides the new one."

"Fillies can run as fast as geldings or stallions," Nathan commented.

"And, like you always said, Father, good mares are harder to come by than mediocre geldings."

"Geldings might be easier to sell, but for a man in the breeding business, starting out like you are, getting a good band of mares together is very important. Let's have a look at that newborn foal."

They left Mose with the mares and rode around into a small vee, where an arroyo came down from bisecting the hills. The mare looked up as they approached and nickered at the foal that was laying on the sand resting from its efforts at nursing. The filly struggled to a standing position, looked at the two men, and on wobbily legs, searched for her mother's leathery bag.

"Give that filly a couple of weeks and you'll be able to tell what she'll look like," Nathan said.

"She has her mama's long hip and her leg bones are nice and flat," Joe said.

"Good shoulder on her, too," Nathan said.

They watched the filly nurse and then rode away. "I need to ride over to the Sierrita Mountains tomorrow or the next day to look at some cows and calves," Joe said. "Would you like to join me, or do you think you need to get back to Edward?"

Nathan scowled at Joe's manner of invitation. Then with his left eyebrow arched, he said, "I dare say I would enjoy watching you deal for cows and calves."

"I figure to have Mose come along with us. He knows cattle better than I do."

"You certainly put more faith in that man's abilities than I would, Joseph."

"Mose might fool you with what he knows about cattle. He is also damn good with horses."

Chapter Twenty

The muddy streets of Tucson, pockmarked from the horse traffic during and after another winter storm, were crowded when Joe, Mose and Nathan arrived on their way to look at the Garrity cows on the Sierrita Mountain *bajada*. At the hitchrack for Tyler's Corrals and Livery, J.Z. stopped whittling as soon as he saw them and, with a look of mild urgency in his eyes, watched them gather around the bench. Without waiting for any greetings to be exchanged, J.Z. tapped his knife against the piece of cottonwood. "Have you heard the good news?" he asked with more excitement in his voice than Joe had ever heard.

"It depends on what news you are talking about, Mr. Tyler."

"Well, hell, it's all over town. The federal commissioner has dropped those charges against you."

"That is good news, Mr. Tyler. I wasn't aware the town knew about all that."

John Duncklee

"Hell's fire, Holly, this town is alive with rumors and gossip like a nest of cockroaches. That lawyer Grimes is tellin' everyone that he's the one got you off the hook."

"He is my attorney. Maybe he's figuring on sending me a large bill."

J.Z. smiled at Joe's remark. "I try like hell to never need a damn lawyer. They always end up costin' more damn money than they're worth."

"I guess I'd better ride by his office later," Joe said. "We're heading out to Garrity's to look at his cows and calves. How do you want to handle this if we buy them?"

"The best way is to have him drive the cows you buy in here and you take delivery in my corrals. That way you'll have 'em here to brand 'em and I can give ol' Garrity his money. You can sign the mortgage we talked about once that is all done."

"That sounds good, Mr. Tyler."

"You might think about going out there tomorrow startin' early 'cause it's pretty much a day's ridin' to get there."

"We'll take your advice, Mr. Tyler. I want to hear what my lawyer has to say anyway."

"From what I hear, you can listen to what Grimes has to say and then believe half of it," J.Z. said. "Those lawyer fellers pull more words outa the sky than I knew were in existence."

Unsaddling their horses and putting them in an empty corral, the three made plans for the following day. "Mose, my father and I will be at the Cosmopolitan. We might as well meet here at the corrals just before sunup."

"That be fine with me, Mistah Holly. I could use a

270

bit of my wages for Maiden Lane. I can stay with Emmy Lou 'long's I give her a dollar."

Joe reached into his pocket and withdrew some coins, handing Mose a double eagle.

"Thanks, Mistah Holly. I'll meet you at the corrals just before sunup tomorrow."

Joe and Nathan started for Grime's office to learn what they could about the charges being dropped. The lawyer shook their hands enthusiastically when they arrived, and Joe introduced him to Nathan. "I suppose you have heard the good news that I had the charges against you dropped by the federal commissioner," Grimes said after he sat back down in his swivel chair behind his oak desk.

"J.Z. Tyler mentioned it," Joe said. *This bastard really is a liar at heart. I wish Father weren't here, so I could tell this lawyer who really got the charges dropped. I guess things are working out for the best. If I told Grimes the truth of the matter, that would fly around town. J.Z. is right about this nest of cockroaches.* "Is there anything further I must do about this?"

"No, Mr. Holly. I have taken care of everything. However, if you would like to pay me the balance, I wouldn't mind."

"What is the balance, Mr. Grimes?"

"I think a hundred dollars should cover it."

"Mr. Grimes, I think a hundred dollars is about ten times more than your efforts were worth, but I'll send it to you as soon as I return from a cattle buying trip."

"Why, Mr. Holly, you could have been languishing in jail if I hadn't talked sense into the commissioner."

"Mr. Grimes, I told you that I would honor your bill."

John Duncklee

With that, Joe turned to Nathan. "I think we need to take care of some other business, Father."

Taking the cue from his son, Nathan said, "That's right, Joseph, and we'd better get on with it."

They left the lawyer's office and went to the Cosmopolitan Hotel to arrange for a room. Once sitting at a table over their coffee in The Cattlemen's Cafe, Nathan raised his eyebrows and laughed softly. "You really don't like your attorney, do you, Joseph?"

"He tarnishes the truth, Father. He's the kind of lawyer you want on your side if you're in trouble. I thought well of him before today, but I do think he set me up for a larger-than-normal charge for his services."

"I am becoming rather confused by all this," Nathan said. "When I talked with Haynes, he seemed dead sure you were guilty of robbing that payroll detail. Now, out of the clear blue sky, he drops the charges that he had filed against you. Somehow, it doesn't make any sense."

"Father, I am not guilty of robbing the payroll detail. I may not like the army, but I wouldn't think of endangering the lives of my former companions. I'm just happy that Colonel Haynes finally came to his senses, and I am sure Lucía will be happy about the good news, too."

"Speaking of Lucía, she is quite a woman. The way she can speak that Apache lingo is quite something. I must say I wasn't very enthusiastic about you marrying a Mexican girl, but I can see why you are attracted to her. I haven't given much thought to women since your mother passed on."

"I am glad you feel differently about Lucía from when you arrived."

They sipped their coffee, keeping their thoughts to

themselves until Nathan cleared his throat, more than anything to get Joe's attention. "Son, it is all well and good about the charges being dropped, and I can understand your feelings about that captain taking a swing at you, but there is one other matter that keeps bothering me."

"And what might that be, Father?"

"I still wonder about where you got the money to buy your ranch, the mares and that old lame stud horse."

"Can't you see that I've made friends out here?"

"Oh yes, I can see that Mr. Tyler thinks highly of you. It's just that I can't see him furnishing money for your business endeavors."

"I think it best that you stop wondering about where I got money for whatever I've bought. As I've told others, it is Lucía's and my business."

"I must say that you have changed a great deal since you were a boy in Maine and left for the army, Joseph."

"I reckon you might say that I am no longer a boy, Father."

Harry Garrity looked surprised to see the three riders approach his corrals as he trudged back to the ranch house from the barn. He stopped and waited to see who his visitors were. When Joe, Nathan and Mose had crossed the arroyo that drained much of that part of the *bajada,* Harry recognized Joe as the man who had inquired about his cows after hearing about them from J.Z. Tyler.

"Mr. Garrity, I am Joe Holly. This is my father, Nathan Holly, and Mose Handley, my foreman. Remember, we talked in Tucson about your cows?"

"Yes, Mr. Holly, I remember giving you directions to

the ranch here. Looks like they were good directions 'cause you found me."

Garrity chuckled nervously at his joking.

"We've come to look the cows over if they're still for sale," Joe said.

"They're still for sale. I haven't had any runoff to fill the tanks, and besides I'm ready to move on. Mrs. Garrity passed away last year, and I get awful lonely way out here without any company except the dogs."

"I expect it's too late to see them today, but we'd appreciate looking them over in the morning."

"They should be easy to look at 'cause I've only got one tank with any water in it, and they'll be in around midmorning. You'll be able to see them all. Some of the calves might be out with a nanny cow."

"I'm afraid I don't understand what you mean by a nanny cow, Mr. Garrity."

"A nanny cow takes care of several calves while their mothers go in to water. Then when those cows come back to nurse their calves the nanny leaves her calf and goes in to the water hole. I never could figure out how they come to the agreement on who is going to be the nanny and who gets to water first. Them old cows must have some sort of way to talk out stuff with each other."

"I think horses have ways of communicating, too," Joe said.

With their horses put up in the corrals, Joe, Nathan and Mose strolled down the wagon road to the ranch house, where Garrity stirred the fire in the old cast-iron cook stove and heated a pot of coffee as he started warming up a kettle full of stew.

The following morning, they all rode out to a large represo that contained some water that Garrity explained would be gone before May if the winter rainy season didn't bring a storm with enough moisture in it to cause runoff.

As Garrity had predicted the evening before, the cows began arriving at the water hole around mid-morning. The men stayed behind some mesquite that grew off to one side so that they wouldn't spook the cattle. Mose looked at all the cows closely, shifting his eyes from one to another and then back to have another look. "Mose, you're looking at those cows so hard you're probably seeing what's inside their stomachs," Joe said.

"Well, Mistah Holly, I gotta see what kinds of cows we is lookin' at to buy. See that one old brindle cow over next to that black calf?"

"Yes, what about her?"

"See that one big tit she's got?"

"Yes, after you pointed it out, I can see that it looks a bit swollen."

"Well, that's one tit that ain't goin' to give no milk. Other than that, she's a fair-lookin' cow, but I'd say not to buy her with a swollen tit like that."

"That's why I brought you along, Mose. I probably wouldn't have noticed that and bought a spoiled cow."

"I wouldn't have noticed that either," Nathan added.

They stayed at the water hole until noon. Joe and Mose stayed well away from Garrity and Nathan so they could have a talk about the cattle. Mose had good thoughts about the quality of the cow herd and what calves he saw looked thrifty. "I'd say that you cain't do much better than these cows, Mistah Holly. They got enough leg so's they'll graze that Frog Mountain,

275

and the calves show that the mamas is givin' good milk."

Back at headquarters they sat down at the kitchen table, while again, Garrity heated the coffee and stew.

"I reckon we might as well get down to business," Joe said. "What are you asking for your cows, Mr. Garrity?"

"Well, Mr. Holly, my cows are good breeders, and I've been careful pickin' good heifers. I think they're worth thirty dollars and those with calves should be worth thirty-three."

"That sounds a bit on the high side, Mr. Garrity," Joe said.

"They're damn good cows," Garrity said defensively.

"I'm not doubting that a bit. I just think you're too high for the market these days."

"Then why don't you make me an offer I can't refuse, Mr. Holly?"

"I can do that. I want a hundred pairs of cows and calves. I want all pairs and we get to choose. I'll give you thirty dollars a pair and you deliver them to J.Z.'s corrals."

Joe knew that Garrity was in no position to refuse an offer like he was making, especially after looking at the amount of water in the represo where they had spent the morning. If Garrity insisted on more money, Joe was determined to get up from the table and start to leave.

"How about giving me thirty-two for a straight run?"

"As J.Z. might say, do you think your cows have gold strands in their tails? I think I'll let my offer stand and if you want to accept that, come out to the Rancho Tecolote. If I haven't bought any cows by then, I might still be in the market for yours, Mr. Garrity."

Joe rose from his chair. "Father, Mose, I reckon we might as well head back to Tucson. It will be dark by the time we get there."

Nathan and Mose also stood up ready to leave.

"You had better stay for some stew, gents," Garrity said. "It's a long ride to town."

Joe glanced at his father and Mose. "I suppose we might as well. Thank you, Mr. Garrity."

Garrity ladeled out the stew into four bowls and filled the coffee cups before sitting down to eat. The four ate in silence. Joe wondered what was going on inside Garrity's head. Certainly, he would not get a better offer before the represo went dry.

When he had finished the bowl of stew, Garrity filled his old briar pipe that had a piece of the stem missing. Taking a sliver of wood from the woodpile next to the stove, he opened the fire box, lit the wood and brought it flaming up to the tobacco. After getting it started and filling the kitchen with a bluish hue from the smoke, Garrity sat back down in his chair.

"All right, Mr. Holly. You have me over a damn barrel and you know it. I know what the market is, but I also know these cows are worth more than average. I'll take your offer, except that you must help me deliver these hundred cows to J.Z.'s corrals. I'll have to pay J.Z. fifty cents a head commission for the sale."

"Do you have any neighbors who might help you round up?"

"There's old Manuel down at the Cuero Quemado. He would either help out or send me a cowboy or two."

"All right, let's do it this way. I need to go back to town with my father because he is leaving soon. I'll leave Mose here with you to help round up the cows so he can make the cuts for me. Tell me when you'll have them at J.Z.'s, and I'll be there to see that you get your money. And, Mr. Garrity, I will pay the commission."

"That sounds like we have a deal, Mr. Holly. I will have the cows at J.Z.'s in one week unless a storm comes in and keeps us from working the cattle."

Chapter Twenty-one

Leaving Mose to help Garrity round up the cattle and make the cut of a hundred pairs, Joe and his father rode out of the ranch headquarters toward the north point of the Sierrita Mountains. "When do you plan to leave on your return trip to Maine, Father?" Joe inquired.

"I'm glad you brought that up because I've done a lot of thinking lately. I have decided that Edward can handle matters by himself while I'm here."

"You are talking in a much different tone than you were when you came here."

They rode abreast over the trail used by the ranchers in the Altar Valley. Joe looked over at his father perched on the McClelland saddle cinched to the lanky bay gelding he had bought from J.Z. on his arrival in Tucson. He had noticed that his father's initial icy attitude had begun to thaw, especially after they had returned from Arivaipa.

"Well, Son, I think maybe I haven't given you enough

credit for growing up to maturity. I probably have been lacking in that respect with Edward, too. So, as we rode out there with Garrity, looking at his cattle, I decided that it might be fun to help you drive your cow herd from Tucson to the ranch. I'd like to help with branding, too."

"I never thought I'd hear you wanting to have anything to do with cows, Father."

"Now don't get me wrong, Joseph. I'm not saying I like cows or anything like that. But I've read about those long trail drives from Texas to Dodge City to the railhead. Mind you, I would never think about joining one of those enterprises, it's just interesting to read about."

"Driving a hundred pairs of cows and calves from Tucson to Rancho Tecolote won't be anything like those Texas trail drives."

"Oh, I know that. I just think it might be fun to experience driving cattle."

"I don't know how to drive cattle either, but I'd guess it's not much different from driving horses, except it might be slower."

"Whatever it might be, would you mind if I joined you when you take your cows home?"

"Father, I would like nothing more than to have you help us drive the cows to the ranch. And, you're welcome to stay with us as long as you care to."

Nathan Holly looked straight ahead. Finally he turned toward his son. "Thank you, Joseph. I appreciate feeling like I'm welcome."

"You have always been welcome, Father. Perhaps it has been your feelings toward yourself that have made you maintain your distance."

"You are probably on the right track there."

Joe felt a new affection for his father. He felt his eyes begin to fill with tears as they rode together around the mountain and saw Tucson's huddle of muddy brown adobe buildings mixed with those whose residents thought well enough of to plaster and whitewash with lime and water.

Before leaving their horses with J.Z., Joe told the horse trader about buying a hundred cow/calf pairs from Garrity and that he was expecting to take delivery on them in a week.

"Are you using Hicks's brand, or do you have another?" J.Z. asked.

"The T bar O came with the ranch, so we will use it," Joe said.

"I know a couple of good Mexican cowboys who can always use a few pesos. Do you want me to hire them to help with the brandin'?"

"That would probably be a good idea, Mr. Tyler."

"Did you buy any of Garrity's bulls?"

"No. Mose, my foreman, thinks it's better to find some younger animals that will be easier to locate up on Frog Mountain. You seem to be my source for just about everything, Mr. Tyler. Do you know about any young bulls that I could buy at a reasonable price?"

"Harvey Fletcher has some yearlin' bulls he drove over from New Mexico awhile back. He's out Tanque Verde way with 'em."

"What are they like?" Joe asked.

"Ya know, Holly, I haven't seen 'em. Ol' Harv stopped in a month or so ago an' was a tellin' me 'bout his pretty black bulls. All I knows is they're black. Knowin' Harv, they could be the ugliest sumbitches in the world an' as long as Harvey Fletcher owned 'em he'd call 'em pretty."

"I know Mose recommends cattle that can travel mountain country easily. Where can I find these bulls to look at them?"

"Harv runs 'em just east of Sabino Canyon. He's got some heifers, too. He headquarters at the old Cebadilla place. Just ride out that way and there's people around can tell you how to get there."

"Thank you, Mr. Tyler," Joe said, and turned to Nathan. "While we're buying cattle and are here already, we might as well ride out and have a look tomorrow."

"What about Lucía alone out at the ranch?" Nathan asked.

"I have no worries about my wife taking care of herself and the ranch. She understands more than most men would give her credit for."

"I must agree with you. You are very fortunate to have found a woman like Lucía, Son."

After an early breakfast, Joe and Nathan began the ride east to the Tanque Verde area to find Harvey Fletcher and his "pretty" black yearling bulls. By noon they rode up to an adobe ranch house outside of which a group of children played some game of chase. As they approached, the children stopped their play and told Joe that Fletcher lived a half mile farther to the east.

Harvey had just ridden into the corrals when Joe and Nathan arrived. Instead of dismounting, Harvey rode out to meet them by the house.

"What can I help you with, fellers?" Harvey asked.

"We are looking for Harvey Fletcher," Joe said.

"You've found him. I'm Harvey."

"Joe Holly. And this is my father, Nathan. J.Z. Tyler told us you might have some yearling bulls for sale."

"Well, J.Z. told you the truth. I've got the prettiest

black bulls from New Mexico you will ever see."

"Can we have a look?" Joe asked, almost laughing after hearing "pretty" mentioned.

"Sure thing. Let's catch a bite to eat and then I'll take you on up the canyon. I rode through most of 'em this morning."

With their hunger satisfied, the three men rode up a canyon that came down from the mountain to empty into the Tanque Verde arroyo. After a half hour's ride they spotted the first bunch of bulls grazing alongside the small stream that trickled with water from the recent storm.

"How big will these bulls be when they grow to maturity?" Joe asked as they watched them nibbling at the new weed growth.

"I brought a few cows with them so they'd drive easier. There should be a couple of them a little higher up. I saw two of them this morning. They should give you an idea of how big these bulls will get."

They went farther into the canyon and soon came to a place where the stream had eroded enough of the canyon walls to form a small meadow. The black cows raised their heads when they heard the horses approach.

Joe saw the cows were taller than the Garrity cows he had purchased. He knew that Mose would approve of a deal with Harvey Fletcher. "How much are you asking for your bulls? I'm looking for eight to be delivered to the Tyler corrals by next Wednesday."

"I'm askin' thirty dollars a head, Mr. Holly."

"I reckon we rode up this canyon for nothing, Father."

"These are right pretty bulls, Mr. Holly," Fletcher said.

John Duncklee

"They could be the prettiest bulls in the world and still not worth thirty dollars a head. I just bought a hundred cow and calf pairs for thirty dollars."

"Hell's fire, I drove these critters plumb from New Mexico."

"A market is a market, Mr. Fletcher. I don't see any gold strands in your pretty bulls' tails, so I'll offer you fifteen dollars a head and take eight delivered to Tyler's Wednesday next."

"I'll get thirty easy by spring."

"Then as long as you have plenty of feed, I would certainly keep the pretty bulls until spring. The cows I bought are all bred back, so I'm in no hurry to buy bulls anyway," Joe said. "Let's be riding back to the ranch, Father."

"I'll be right behind you, Son."

"Now wait a minute, fellers. Don't be rushin' off so damn quick."

Joe reined up the sorrel and looked back at Fletcher. "You heard my offer. I think we are much too far apart for a deal."

"Are you wantin' your cut or will you take a straight run?"

"I'll accept a straight run as long as the bulls are uniform and look like the ones we have just seen here in the canyon."

"All right, I'll take your offer, Holly. You sure as hell drive a tough bargain."

"Just remember, there are no gold strands in their tails."

After a night at the Cosmopolitan, father and son rode back north to the ranch. Joe told Lucía about buying the cows and bulls and was happy to see her. Every-

284

thing had gone smoothly at the ranch during his absence.

"I rode around some and noticed there are a lot of spring weeds beginning to sprout," Lucía said. "There's quite a lot of filaree coming up."

"What is filaree?"

"After good winter rains the filaree will sprout and grow quickly. It is the best spring feed there is. I will show you some tomorrow. You can tell it by the leaves that are like mesquite and then there are purple flowers."

"I have three days to spend here. Then I must take delivery on the cattle at J.Z. Tyler's. Mose is with Garrity, and J.Z. is hiring a couple of cowboys to help us brand the cows, calves and bulls."

"The gray mare looks like she is coming into her foal heat," Lucía said.

"Have you seen her near the stud horse?" Joe asked.

"Yes, I checked the mares this morning when they came in for water, and she seemed quite friendly to the stud horse through the corral fence."

"Maybe we should get her bred in the morning or just turn that horse loose tonight. He's bound to find her if she's ready."

"By the way she acted this morning, I think she can wait until tomorrow."

"I guess it wouldn't hurt to saddle up early and bring the mares in to make sure we get the gray bred on her foal heat," Joe said.

"This is a good example of why I don't like cattle," Nathan said emphatically.

"What do you mean, Father?" Joe asked.

"We should have been here watching that mare in-

John Duncklee

stead of traipsing around the countryside buying a bunch of four-bellied bovine."

"I think we did the right thing by getting those cows, calves and bulls. Until I can build a reputation for top racehorses, I will need to make money some other way, and the cattle business seems logical for what I need. Besides, Mose knows cattle and can manage them very well."

"I can understand your concern about earning money until you can establish yourself in the horse business, but I am not sure I would count on Mose. Suppose he decides to up and quit?"

"I reckon I'll cross that canyon only if it ever gets in my way."

The stud horse nickered and paced along the corral fence as Joe and Nathan arrived with the mares the following morning. With the mares all in the large corral, Nathan rode in, keeping his eye on the gray mare as Joe closed the corral gate. "Let's wait for them to get their fill of water and then I'll catch the gray. Then we can turn the rest out while I let the stud tease the gray."

Dismounting, Joe grabbed a halter he had previously hung on one of the corral posts and proceeded to catch the gray mare. She could sense that she was Joe's target and spun around to get away from him, almost knocking her foal over in the process. Joe followed her to the corner of the corral and by shifting quickly when the mare made a move to try to escape, he wore her down and she gave in to being haltered.

"Are you ready for the gate?" Nathan asked.

"Yes. See if you can let them leave as slowly as possible. I don't want the gray's foal to get in with the main bunch."

Double Vengeance

Nathan opened the gate and rode outside the corral, stopping about a hundred feet away. The mares watched him as they walked out of the corral, switching their tails and making sure their foals were with them. With the corral empty except for the gray, her foal and Joe, Nathan returned, closing the gate behind him.

"Let's see if this mare is hot enough to breed," Joe said, leading her up to the fence that divided the stud horse's pen from the large one. The stud switched around, nickering loudly as he smelled the mare's nose through the mesquite poles. Then Joe turned the mare around so that her rear end backed up to the fence. The stud neighed loudly and reared up on his hind legs. The gray mare lifted her tail, squatted and urinated. The stud horse had fire in his eyes and shook his head as he neighed and nickered.

"She looks ready to me," Joe said.

"She's as hot as any mare I've ever seen," Nathan commented.

"I think the best way to get this darling bred is to turn them both loose in this large corral. When he's finished, I can cut him back into his own pen."

"How many times will you put her with the stud, Son?"

"I'll keep the gray mare up today and then tonight we can tease her again."

"Sounds like you learned something about horse breeding back in Maine."

"I learned all I know back there, Father. You are a good teacher."

Joe unbuckled the halter and slipped it from the mare's head. Having dismounted, Nathan opened the gate into the barnyard, led his horse through, and closed the gate behind him. "Who knows, that stud might not appreciate this gelding in the same pen where he is making love to his sweetheart of the day."

"Good thinking. Now we will see just how hot the gray mare is this morning."

Joe ambled over to the gate between the two corrals and opened it. The stud horse pranced out with arched neck, nickering, calling to the mare. She stood in the middle of the large corral as if waiting for him. He first touched his nose to hers, then quickly lunged to her rear where he smelled her. The mare raised her tail and urinated again. The stud raised his head and flipped up his upper lip showing his teeth. Quickly, he moved to her side and began biting her neck around her withers. Again the mare squatted and urinated. "She damn sure is a hot one," Joe said.

"I'll say," Nathan commented. "She couldn't be much hotter or she'd burst into flames."

Joe laughed at his father's humor. The stud horse's organ extended in hardness as he mounted the mare and searched for his target. Thrusting, he found her opening and entered as the mare struggled to keep her legs under her. His head came down on her neck as he exploded inside. He let himself slide out with the end flared like a large pink blossom dripping with milky liquid. The mare had arched her back and stood quietly without noticing the foal running nervously around her head.

"We can tease her this evening," Joe said. "But I'd bet he got the job done just now."

"You never know, but it looked like a good breed," Nathan said.

The nine-day-old foal searched under its mother for her bag. Finding it, the little one encircled one of the two nipples with its mouth and nosed the bag upward as the mare slightly lifted the hind leg on the side where the foal had decided to nurse. The mare looked back at her baby as it found warmth and nourishment.

Joe drove the stud horse back through the open gate to his pen and closed it. "I need to give them both some grain. Then we can unsaddle our horses and call it a day until we come up here to tease her again."

"Don't let me get in your way if you have something to do, Joseph."

"I'd just as soon go to the house and talk. It isn't every day that you are here. Today is Tuesday, and the cattle will be at J.Z.'s day after tomorrow. We'll have to ride to town in the morning."

"I have been thinking that I will leave for Maine after we get the cattle home here."

"Only you know what you need to do, Father. You are certainly welcome to stay as long as you like."

"I appreciate that, Joseph. I have been thinking a lot about what you said about letting Edward learn to make decisions on his own. Well, I have decided to move away from the farm and get a place in town. If that isn't far enough away to be out of the way, then I'll move somewhere else."

"What will you do with your time if you are not around the horses?"

"I was thinking about that on the ride back from buying the bulls," Nathan said, rubbing the stubble on his chin. "I never showed you the diary of the war I kept. I think I'll write a book about those experiences and the thoughts I had while I didn't know how many breaths I would have left as the rebel ordinance flew at us."

"When you get that one finished, you can write a book on horsemanship that could become a classic."

"Joseph, I have no idea where you got that idea, but I was thinking of writing about horses after I deal with the war story."

"I reckon there's no need for me to be concerned about how you'll spend your time if you don't have the horses to take care of."

Joe and Nathan arrived at Tyler's corrals in time to see Mose riding point with the hundred cows with their calves strung out behind him. Mose returned Joe's wave as he led the herd through the gate to the five-acre holding pasture behind the estacada corrals. Riding the drag, Garrity brought up the rear, keeping the cows moving so they had little chance to think about breaking away from the herd. Once the first of the cattle were inside, Mose left the lead and rode over to one side. Joe watched him count the cows as they pushed through the gate, their long horns clicking as they crowded together.

Once Mose had closed the gate, he rode over to where Joe and Nathan sat on the top of the estacada corral. "They's all here, Mistah Holly. Do you like 'em?"

"You did a great job, Mose. They may be all colors of the rainbow, but every one looks like a good cow. I like the calves, too. Incidentally, I bought eight black yearling bulls. They should be getting here today."

Mose smiled, showing his bright white teeth. "You seen that brindle cow leadin' the bunch?"

"Yes, she has a nice big calf if I'm seeing right," Joe replied.

"Yeah, that big brockled-faced heifer is hers. She's a good lead cow, so we gotta make sure she's out in front when we goes to the ranch. I'd keep her heifer for a replacement 'cause that cow's a good milker. I can tell that by how thrifty her calf be."

The cattle milled around the enclosure once they were no longer being driven. Cows bawled for their calves and calves sang out for their mothers. It was not long before all the calves had mothered with the cows and Joe watched as some nursed and others found spots to stand with their offspring.

"How long will it take to brand?" Joe asked Mose.

"Depends on how many hands we got."

"J.Z. said he had hired a couple of cowboys to work tomorrow."

"We might get done tomorrow if we starts early," Mose said. "Have two ropin' and the rest on the ground with the irons. Be a long day, no matter how you looks at it."

"If it takes more than a day, it takes more than a day," Joe said.

"I'd like to get done tomorrow and get these cows home as soon as we can. There ain't no feed in this here holdin' trap."

"You have a good point there, Mose. I will talk to J.Z. and see if he can find a couple more cowboys."

"That be good, Mistah Holly."

Joe found J.Z. sitting on his bench, as usual. "Got all your cows and calves?" the trader asked.

"All accounted for, Mr. Tyler."

"I walked out there and took a look at 'em. Your man has a good eye. He got the best of old Garrity's cows. I've known that bunch for a long time. Bought his steers a couple years back."

"That's good to hear. I'm wondering if you can hire two more cowboys to work tomorrow so we can be sure to get everything branded in a day."

"I'll send word out. You should have all the help you need in the mornin'."

"Thank you, Mr. Tyler. Another thing, Garrity wants his money as soon as possible so he can go home."

"That Garrity wants his money so's he can head for The Lucky Dollar. Tell him I'll have it for him in the mornin' after the bank opens."

As Joe headed back to the holding trap, he saw Harvey Fletcher driving eight black bulls down the road leading to the holding trap. Mose had the gate open and was standing to one side, keeping the cows from leaving and out of the way so the bulls would go through the gate without spooking.

As darkness invaded and the coal oil lamps winked on in the windows of Tucson, Joe and Nathan left Tyler's to spend the night in the Cosmopolitan. Mose had insisted that he sleep by the holding trap to make sure the cattle would all be there in the morning. "You never knows who might decide to open that gate," he had said.

Chapter Twenty-two

Mose had the branding fire blazing away before Joe and Nathan reached the corrals. The first morning light had just begun to seep into the Tucson basin. Right after Mose said, "Now all we needs is some fast ropin' cowboys," four *vaqueros* rode in.

Mose greeted them in Spanish and told them how he wanted to work. He then turned to Joe. "Mistah Holly, I figure to have these men rope. You and me can work the irons. Maybe your father he can keep the irons hot for us."

Overhearing Mose's suggestion, Nathan agreed and went over to the fire, tossing on some mesquite with his one remaining hand.

"We might as well get started, Mistah Holly, 'cause it's gonna be dark when we gets done."

Mose called to the *vaqueros* to begin with the cows. Joe watched closely as the first team, Pedro and Antonio, shook out their rawhide reatas, building large loops, and began riding toward the herd. Pedro reined up before arriving where the cattle milled around. He waited for Antonio to rope the first cow around her horns. Antonio chose the animal he wanted, swung the loop once around his head to build the loop and threw. Just as the loop encircled the animal's horns, the cowboy quickly pulled up the slack in the reata and the loop snugged tight. With his right hand still grabbing the reata, he wrapped it around the saddle horn three times in a dally, and, simultaneously reined his horse away from the cow with his other hand as Pedro rode in swinging his loop before tossing it in front of the cow's hind legs. As the bovine stepped into the loop, Pedro jerked on the reata so that it tightened around the legs. And, in another simultaneous move, as with Antonio and the cow's horns, Pedro reined his horse away from the cow as he dallied his reata around his saddle horn. Stretched between the taut reatas, the cows lost footing and fell to the ground bawling. The cow's right side faced up so Pedro reined his horse, keeping the reata tight and turned so that he flipped the cow over for branding on the left side. Joe watched and, in his mind, filed away a question he would later ask Mose.

Mose sprang into action with the hot iron as soon as the cowboys had their target on the ground in the proper position. High across the left hip, he drew a three-inch-long *T*, then a straight bar three inches long, and before the iron cooled he had made an "O" on the right side of the bar. With a second hot iron he drew an "L" on the left shoulder to vent, or cancel, Garrity's "G/" that was low on the left hip. Finished, Mose nodded at Antonio who rode toward the cow causing his reata to slacken. Mose grabbed the reata and loosened it further so that he could slip it off the horns. Tossing the reata away, Mose started back to the fire for hot irons to brand the next cow that Luis and Jaime had roped and stretched out. As soon as Antonio's reata was free from the cow's horns, Pedro rode toward the cow to loosen his reata around her legs. The cow struggled to her feet stepping out of Pedro's loop. The cowboys coiled their reatas again and built loops for the next cow.

Joe had followed Mose out to the first cow to see what had to be done and how to do it. "I'll brand the next one, Mose," Joe said. "Just keep an eye on me in case I mess up."

"You ain't gonna mess up, Mistah Holly. Just do what I done."

Joe hurried out to the third cow while Mose branded the second one. After applying the brand and the *L* vent, he called to Mose for an inspection. "Not bad, Mistah Holly, but I would burn a tad deeper 'til you see the same color as was on the first brand I did."

Joe took another hot iron and burned the brand a little deeper. Then he nodded to Luis to slacken his reata from the horns. The seven men, including Nathan, who made sure there were always hot irons, worked steadily until early afternoon. The mother cows had all been branded when a young Mexican boy appeared with a parcel wrapped in old flour sacks and a blue enameled pot with six matching cups wired together and attached to the handle of the pot.

Mose told the boy in Spanish to put the things by the fire.

"What's all this?" Joe asked Mose.

"That's dinner," Mose said. "I ordered it brought down here so's we wouldn't have to take out too much time to eat."

John Duncklee

"You seem to think of everything, Mose," Joe said.

"I heard you call me your foreman. Foremans got to think of everything. You needs to pay Manuelito four pesos, Mistah Holly."

Joe pulled some coins from his pocket and handed the waiting boy enough for the bill and a generous tip for his work in bringing the food. After watering their horses, the men gathered around the fire and enjoyed the meal of chile con carne wrapped in flour tortillas, washed down by the rich black coffee made from beans roasted in sugar.

As they ate and rested, Nathan also kept the fire going. Joe remembered the question he wanted to ask Mose. "Why are brands on the left side of the cattle?"

"That's 'cause when cattle is millin' around, they generally go from right to left. So if a feller is standing there lookin' for strays, the brands are on the left side and you don't have to turn the cattle around so they mill in the wrong direction."

"Damn, there are lots of little details that a cowman has to know about," Joe said.

"It's the same with horses, Mistah Holly. You is a horseman and you knows all those little details that some cowman might not know unless he's a horseman, too."

"I suppose you're right, Mose. I wish I had more questions, but I really don't know what to ask."

"You'll probably think of some more," Mose said, then turned away to announce to the cowboys that they had eight bulls and a hundred calves to brand before sundown.

They worked the calves differently because of their size. There was no need to have two ropers head and heel to stretch out the calves. It took one roper heeling the calves and dragging them to the men with the irons near the fire. The shorter the distance the men branding had to walk, the faster the job got done. Therefore, three men on horseback roped and Pedro joined Joe and Mose with the branding. After finishing the calves as the sun reached the far western horizon, they teamed up again on the eight yearling bulls.

Finally, Joe thanked and paid the men for their day's work before heading out to the hotel with Nathan. J.Z. waited on the bench. "I have the totals for you, Holly," he said, handing Joe a piece of paper with numbers written in columns on it. "I paid Garrity and that crazy Fletcher. You can meet me in the morning and I'll have that mortgage ready for you to sign."

"Thank you, Mr. Tyler. We'll be here early to drive these cattle to the ranch."

"That'll be fine. It won't take but a second to sign the papers unless you have a longer name than I think you do."

They laughed together and Nathan joined in appreciating J.Z.'s dry humor.

Mose had joined the four cowboys and left the corrals for the center of town. Joe, weary from the day's work stretched out on the bed in the hotel room. Nathan, also tired from working all day, found comfort by relaxing in an overstuffed chair that had part of the wool exposed from many years of use and no effort to repair a rotting seam in the seat cushion.

"I reckon I'll feel like I'm more in the cattle business once we get the herd to the ranch and located in the mountains," Joe said, his eyes closed as he remained on his back on the bed.

"I don't know anything about the cow business out here," Nathan commented. "But those cows you bought sure as hell look different than the cows in Maine."

"The cows in Maine are mostly dairy cattle. Western cattle are mostly raised for beef. I have seen some milk cows here and there in the West."

"These cattle you bought are quite wild," Nathan said. "What if they all run away?"

"That's why Mose is here. He will make sure they are as safe as possible."

"How much did you pay for all the cattle, Joseph?"

"The cows, calves and bulls came to three thousand, one hundred and seventy. That is what I am borrowing from J.Z."

"What would you say to my paying for the cattle instead of having J.Z. hold a mortgage on your ranch."

"Thank you for the offer, Father, but I think I have it figured out all right."

Nathan dropped the subject. They dined and went to sleep shortly afterward.

Joe and Nathan arrived at the corrals as Mose was catching the horses. J.Z. came in driving his buggy. As he climbed out of the vehicle, he carried a battered leather briefcase that looked like it might have been used by Caesar. He sat down and put the briefcase next to him on the bench.

"Is everything ready?" Joe asked as he finished tightening the cinch on his saddle.

"Got it all here," the trader said, patting the briefcase.

Joe left his horse tied and went over to look at the papers he was to sign. After glancing at the total amount of the mortgage, he took the pen J.Z. handed him and signed his name. Handing back the pen and the document, Joe shook Tyler's hand. "Thank you, Mr. Tyler."

Double Vengeance

Joe and Nathan joined Mose at the gate to the holding pen. "We shouldn't have no trouble with 'em gettin' started. I shut the gate on the water trough corral last night, so we be driving these cows to water instead of away from water. They drive a whole lot better that-away."

"Good," Joe said. "We sure don't need a stampeding herd going through Tucson at five in the morning."

"I think it be best if you and your father go in and start them out. I be waiting for 'em outside here to turn 'em in the direction we want 'em to go. When we gets 'em started and that lead cow out in front, I'll ride point and you two keep 'em movin' and bunched. Any of 'em gets the notion to break away from the rest, you can chase 'em back."

"Sounds good, Mose," Joe said. "We might as well get these critters moving."

Mose opened the gate. Joe and Nathan rode to the back of the holding trap and started the cows and calves toward the outside. Even though they tried to be quiet as they rode up on the cattle, the mother cows, knowing instinctively that something was happening, bawled for their calves as they nervously began trotting for the gate. Mose sat on his horse, strategically located so the cows turned north and headed for Frog Mountain without going through Tucson streets.

The lead cow and her calf quickly made their way forward, and Mose smiled as they arrived at their position of authority. He rode with his right hand on the cantle and looking back to the herd as it traveled along, making sure that they followed and none tried to break away. Soon they were trail broke again so Mose turned around and faced forward. Joe and Nathan took the drag behind the herd. In this manner the T bar O cows, calves and young, black bulls plodded steadily toward their new home on the ranges of Rancho Tecolote.

As the herd reached the destination, the sunset through the sparse cloud layer displayed a beautiful array of reds, oranges and yellows as if the sun had exploded on the western horizon.

Mose booted his horse into a trot to reach the wire gate to the wrangle-horse pasture. Dismounting, he quickly opened the gate and tossed it back on the ground behind the fence. Mounting again, he led the herd through and then on to the corrals for water. Joe and Nathan followed and sat on their horses watching the thirsty cattle gulp the water.

"We can get them up on the mountain country in the mornin'," Mose said. "Since there's no snow there the cows can find feed all right."

"How long will you need me?" Nathan asked.

"Be easier with three of us ridin' and if Missus Holly can ride, too, we should be gettin' these here gals up to the water by noon. After that I can go up there every day to make sure they get located all right."

"I just wanted to know when I could start back to Maine."

Lucía happily joined the work of driving the cattle into the mountains. As Mose had estimated, the sun was high when the herd reached the mountain stream. "They should stay up here all right," Mose said. "There's plenty of feed and water, but there is bound to be some of the cow brutes that will drift back down. Them that does is goin' to run into me."

After arriving home from the drive, Lucía had pre-pared a supper of steak smothered with salsa and with *frijoles de la olla* that she had simmered on the stove the day before. Before sitting down to eat, Joe and Nathan sipped tequila together. "Father, it has been a real pleasure having you visit us."

"Well, Son, I've enjoyed it, too. I have also learned a lot that I didn't know before this trip. I am quite proud of you, as a matter of fact."

"That means a great deal to hear you say that, Father. I hope you can come out here again very soon."

After a substantial breakfast, Joe joined his father at the corrals to saddle their horses. "I can pick up your horse at Tyler's the next time we go to town," Joe said.

"That sounds easy. I wish you could ride to Tucson with me, but I know those cattle need attention right now."

Lucía arrived at the corrals. "I hope you have a safe and pleasant trip back to Maine."

"Thank you, Lucía. I must tell you that I am very happy you are my son's wife."

"Gracias," she said.

Nathan mounted and waved to them as he reined around to head out to the stage road.

"That was certainly a surprise," Joe said, watching his father disappear behind the low hill near the ranch house. "I reckon we both learned a lot about each other. I think I might even miss the old fellow."

"He changed a great deal from the time he arrived and treated me like I was a maid."

"He wanted to pay for the cattle."

"What did you tell him?"

"I told him I have everything figured out."

"Is he planning to return here some day?"

"I hope so. I wouldn't have felt that way before."

"Be careful up there in the mountains today. I do not want anything to happen to you, Joe Holly."

"I'll be just fine, my beautiful Lucía."

He stepped over to his horse, mounted and rode off to meet Mose for the day's work making sure the cattle were not drifting off the mountain.

After two days of accompanying Mose, Joe decided it was time for him to tend to the mares and stallion. The first chore he had seen necessary was to trim the stud horse's hooves.

Suddenly the dogs vaulted from their slumber in the shade beneath the old mesquite tree by the corral. Tails going in circles, they sped down the road to the house, arriving just in time to greet a lone rider with their bedlam of barking. Between the barking and furious snarling, the rider remained mounted, waiting for the appearance of someone to calm the guards with assuring words. From the door, Lucía called out, *"callense perros!"* The dogs lowered their tones to short yips, but remained circling the rider until Lucía walked into the yard. "Capitán Willoughby," she said with her arms akimbo. "What brings you to Rancho Tecolote? Are you trying to get my husband into more trouble again?"

"No, Mrs. Holly. In fact, I am here to apologize to Joe. Is he around?

"He is up at the corrals. I will go tell him you are here."

"I can ride up there and not bother you."

"It is no bother, Capitán. I think it is best that I go because he might not appreciate being surprised by you, not knowing why you are here."

"Suit yourself, Mrs. Holly. I'll wait here."

With a quick pace, Lucía hurried to the corral where

Joe was trimming the stallion's hooves. She almost didn't recognize the captain in civilian clothes. "Joe, Capitán Willoughby just rode in," she said over the estacada corral fence.

"What the hell does he want this time?"

"I asked him the same thing, and he told me he is here to apologize to you."

"Apologize? What the hell has come over him? He must be sick or something."

"What do you want me to tell him?"

"Oh, tell him to come on up here. I'm nearly finished on the last hoof."

As he applied the heavy rasp to the stallion's right rear hoof, Joe wondered why Willoughby had told Lucía he had come to apologize. Apology of any sort seemed completely out of character for Arnold Willoughby. Joe shook his head with disbelief after releasing the finished hoof. He watched Willoughby approach. For a moment he contemplated retreating to the tack room to grab his carbine from the scabbard on his saddle. "I cannot say that I am not surprised to see you here at my ranch, Captain, especially wearing that outfit instead of your uniform."

Willoughby had reined up and waited for Holly to invite him to dismount. Still wondering about Willoughby's purpose in visiting him, Joe stood next to the tethered stallion.

"I rode out here to talk to you, Holly. There is something I need to say before I leave the territory."

"Well, get down and we can sit a spell on the bench under the mesquite. I'll turn this stud loose and be with you in a minute."

As Willoughby dismounted and wrapped his reins around the hitchrack by the corral, Joe took the halter off the stallion and took it over to the barn where he hung it on a hook under the overhang. Exiting the corral through the barn, he then removed his chaps and tossed them over the grain bin. All the while he pondered Willoughby's visit.

Sitting next to the captain on the bench, Joe tipped his beaver hat back on his forehead. "What did you say about leaving the territory?" Joe asked.

"It's quite simple, Mr. Holly. I am no longer a captain in the United States Cavalry. I have resigned my commission."

"What in the world made you decide to do something that drastic?"

"All right, I'll start at the beginning. At least, I'll start at the beginning of what made me decide to resign. When you told me about Betsy being involved with the Clanton gang and the payroll robberies, I was dumbfounded."

"That's strange to hear. You sounded like you didn't believe me," Joe interjected.

"I guess I did that for appearances. Anyway, I went back to Fort Lowell the next morning and questioned Betsy. At first she denied everything, and I almost believed her. I suppose I wanted to believe her, but I continued interrogating her. I must admit that I tricked her into her admission. I told her I would resign and take her back to Philadelphia if she would only tell me the truth. Holly, she confessed everything about her liaison with the Clanton gang. She also reaffirmed what you had said about her doing all that to get enough money together to leave me and the army."

"What are your plans, and why are you here telling me all about this?"

"To answer your first question, Betsy and I are returning to Philadelphia as I promised her. We leave day after tomorrow. I have no plan once we get there. My family has a business that I once rejected to join the cavalry. I will see how the waters are running in that direction. As for the second question, I rode out here to offer you my sincere and heartfelt apologies for all the grief I have caused you."

"I must say that your efforts to have me thrown out of the army and then jailed for robbery and attempted murder haven't made me feel any friendship toward you."

"The court-martial was unjust. I know now that it was as you maintained at the very beginning. It was Betsy who kissed you and not the other way around. She admitted even that."

"But nobody realized that I was glad to be out of the army. I had planned to resign as soon as possible. The court-martial just speeded things up."

"I've talked to Colonel Haynes, and he has agreed to try to get you reinstated with your commission and nothing on your record."

"Thank you, but no thank you," Joe said. "I never want to get into another uniform. Being in the army is definitely not on my list of desires."

"I wasn't sure what you thought about getting drummed out. I wanted to do my best to get you reinstated if that was what you wanted."

"Well, Willoughby, I appreciate your thoughts in that direction, but there is no way I would even accept a general's commission. There's too much about the army that I find abhorrent. For starters, the court-martial was a joke. That was not your fault. That was just the army's way of justice, and I don't agree with that at all. You should be happier away from the army, too."

"As long as Betsy is happy away from it I will be, but the army was my life until I realized I had to resign. For several reasons," Arnold said, and dropped his eyes to the ground.

"While we are considering all these past happenings, did you really follow me down the San Pedro to try and kill me?" Joe asked.

"To tell you the truth, I was so angry about you and Betsy that my purpose was to kill you and leave you for the buzzards. In fact, I was just about to pull the trigger when that Apache jumped me. You really embarrassed me with that long walk to Benson from Arivaipa Canyon. What were you doing there with Frog Eyes?"

"Let's say we were riding down the river," Joe replied. *Willoughby might say he is here to apologize, but I don't trust him any more than I ever did.*

"I didn't ride out here to investigate your past activities, Holly. I'm just curious."

"You'll have to stay curious, Willoughby. An apology is one thing, but intrusive questions are another."

"On the way out here, I thought about asking you all about you and Betsy, but I won't."

"I am glad you won't, because you wouldn't get an answer to that either. The best thing you could do about Betsy is what you are doing. Get her back to Philadelphia and start your life with her over again if you can."

"I hope I am not doing all this in vain."

"Me too, but I wouldn't want to be in your boots," Joe said.

"I'm hoping you will accept my apology, Holly. That would mean a great deal to me. I also would like to reassure myself that you won't say anything about Betsy and the Clantons to anyone."

"I told you that when we were in Tucson at The Lucky Dollar. I keep my word, Willoughby. As far as your apology is concerned, I accept it."

Joe reached over and shook Willoughby's hand. "That must have been tough for you to do, Willoughby. Maybe some day we can be friends."

"I sincerely hope so. If you ever find yourself in Philadelphia you will always have a place to stay."

"Well, thank you. I don't expect I'll get any farther east than the Rio Grande, but one never knows. I might have a racehorse someday that will win the derby."

"Good luck with your horse business."

"Thank you. Why don't we go down to the house and see what Lucía has for dinner."

After the noon meal, Willoughby and Joe returned to the barn area where Arnold led his horse into the corral for water. Ready to leave for Tucson, Arnold turned to Joe before mounting. "Well, Holly, you turned out to be the winner, and I am the loser."

"You are not a loser, Willoughby, you just need to make a new start and that's what you are doing. Many of us have done just that, make a new start. Good luck and have a safe trip back to Philadelphia."

Joe watched the former captain mount his horse and begin the ride back to town. Willoughby stopped after a hundred yards, turned in the saddle and waved. Joe returned the gesture as he wondered if Betsy would behave differently once she and Arnold were away from the isolation of army posts in the West.

Chapter Twenty-three

Joe saddled the sorrel to ride to the stage stop to check on any mail that might have arrived. He expected a letter from a man in New Mexico who had written earlier expressing interest in the foals as soon as they could be weaned. Selling any that young was not what Joe wanted to do, but if the price was high enough he would sell the entire crop of colts and fillies.

The stage had just left for Florence as he rode in and dismounted. The horse-handler ambled back from the corral after seeing that the tired horses had hay enough. "Howdy there, Holly," the man welcomed.

"Hello," Joe said. "I just rode by to check on any mail I might have."

"There's two letters came in yesterday. I'll get 'em for you."

"Thank you," he said, and waited as the man went into the adobe building and returned with the mail.

"Here you go, Holly. How are things at the Tecolote? Them Apache leavin' you alone?"

"So far so good," Joe said. He thought it best to keep his friendship with Etazin to himself because he did not know who around the vicinity of Tucson had been involved in the Camp Grant affair.

"I see you drivin' some cows and calves in the other day."

"They're already up on the mountain. Have to make a living somehow."

"Well, good luck. I hope those Apache raiders don't get wind of all that beef to eat."

"I hope not, too," Joe said, and mounted the sorrel. He was anxious to open the letters, especially the one with "N. Holly" written in the upper left corner. "Thank you for the mail."

"You're welcome, Holly. See you next time."

Joe stuffed the envelopes into his jacket pocket and rode off. After reaching the trail along the base of the foothills, he reined in the sorrel to have a look at the unexpected letter from his father. After opening and taking out the contents of the envelope, he read the short note:

Enclosed, please find the mortgage on your ranch marked paid in full. I know you had everything figured out, but I wanted to do something. Love, your father, Nathan Holly.

Joe looked at the mortgage that he had signed to J.Z. Tyler and, sure enough, J.Z. had written "Paid in full" and signed his name. He put the letter and mortgage back into the envelope, returned it to his pocket and opened the other letter from the horse buyer in New Mexico. The man wrote that the prices Holly had quoted for the foals was more than the man cared to pay, but he would be interested in them later.

With both letters back in his jacket pocket, Joe booted the sorrel into a trot for the short ride back to headquarters. He was anxious to speak with Lucía.

Arriving at the house, he hurriedly dismounted and strode through the front door. "Lucía," he called.

"In the kitchen," she replied.

Continuing his way into the kitchen, he took the envelope out of his pocket and handed it to her. "This is the mortgage that I signed to Tyler for the cattle money he lent me. My father paid it off. See, it's marked 'Paid in full' and signed by Tyler. Then read his letter. Goddammit, I told him I had things figured out all right. Why did he go and pay this off anyway?"

Lucía read Nathan's letter, refolded it, returned it to the envelope and gave it back to her husband. "Joe, he wants to help in the only way he knows how. Maybe you should allow him to make his amends the way he sees fit. He really is proud of you and he stopped talking about your brother, Edward, after the first day he was here."

"I hadn't thought about it in that light, Lucía. Thank you for being the way you are."

He took her into his arms and kissed her fervently. She put her hands on his chest, tilted her head back and looked into his eyes. "You are such a good man, Joe Holly. I have news for you."

"What are you talking about?"

"If I am not mistaken, all signs tell me that we are going to be parents."

Graciela
of the
Border
John Duncklee

Jeff Collins knows horses. He works as a horse trainer on the Sierra Diablo ranch in Arizona, and he is mighty good at it. But he wants more. He's dreamed for years of having his own ranch. He sees his chance when he wins a blue roan in a high-stakes poker game. This isn't just any roan; it is carrying the foal of a great racehorse, and that foal is Jeff's ticket to his dreams. When that roan is stolen and herded along with other horses toward the Mexican border, Jeff knows where he has to go. But he doesn't know what will be waiting for him when he gets there. The border is a dangerous place, a harsh land filled with bandits and outlaws—and the woman who will change his life . . . Graciela of the border.

__4809-4 $4.99 US/$5.99 CAN

Broken Ranks

Hiram King

The Civil War just ended. For one group of black men, hope for a new life comes in the form of a piece of paper, a government handbill urging volunteers to join the new Negro Cavalry, which will soon become the famous Tenth Cavalry Regiment. But trouble begins for the recruits long before they can even reach their training camp. First they have to get from St. Louis to Fort Leavenworth, Kansas, a hard journey through hostile, ex-Confederate territory, surrounded by vengeful white men who don't like the idea of these recruits having guns. The army hires Ples Butler, a grim, black gunfighter, to get the recruits to Fort Leavenworth safely, and he will do his job . . . even if it means riding through Hell.

___4872-8 $5.99 US/$6.99 CAN

DARK TRAIL

Hiram King

When the War Between the States was finally over, many men returned from battle only to find their homes destroyed and their families scattered to the wind. Bodie Johnson is one of those men. But while some families fled before advancing armies, the Johnson family was packed up like cattle and shipped west—on a slave train. With only that information to go on, Bodie sets out to find whatever remains of his family. And he will do it. Because no matter how vast the West is, no matter what stands in his way, Bodie knows one thing—the Johnsons will survive.

___4418-8 $5.50 US/$6.50 CAN

Man From Wolf River

John D. Nesbitt

Owen Felver is just passing through. He is on his way from the Wolf River down to the Laramie Mountains for some summer wages. He makes his camp outside of Cameron, Wyoming, and rides in for a quick beer. But it isn't quick enough. While he is there he sees pretty, young Jenny—and the puffed-up gent trying to get rude with her. What else can he do but step in and defend her? Right after that some pretty tough thugs start to make it clear Felver isn't all too welcome around town. Trouble is, the more they tell him to move on—and the more he sees of Jenny—the more he wants to stay. He knows they have something to hide, but he has no idea just how awful it is—or how far they will go to keep it hidden.

___4871-X $4.50 US/$5.50 CAN

Dorchester Publishing Co., Inc.
P.O. Box 6640
Wayne, PA 19087-8640

WILD ROSE
of
RUBY CANYON
JOHN D. NESBITT

At first homesteader Henry Sommers is pleased when his neighbor Van O'Leary starts dropping by. After all, friends come in handy out on the Wyoming plains. But it soon becomes clear that O'Leary has some sort of money-making scheme in the works and doesn't much care how the money is made. Henry wants no part of his neighbor's dirty business, but freeing himself of O'Leary is almost as difficult as climbing out of quicksand . . . and just as dangerous.

___4520-6 $3.99 US/$4.99 CAN

Coyote Trail

John D. Nesbitt

Travis Quinn doesn't have much luck picking his friends. He is fired from the last ranch he works on when a friend of his gets blacklisted for going behind the owner's back. Guilt by association sends Quinn looking for another job, too. He makes his way down the Powder River country until he runs into Miles Newman, who puts in a good word for him and gets him a job at the Lockhart Ranch. But Quinn doesn't know too much about Newman, and the more he learns, the less he likes. Pretty soon it starts to look like Quinn has picked the wrong friend again. And if the rumors about Newman are true, this friend might just get him killed.

___4671-7 $4.50 US/$5.50 CAN

Dorchester Publishing Co., Inc.
P.O. Box 6640
Wayne, PA 19087-8640

Please add $1.75 for shipping and handling for the first book and $.50 for each book thereafter. NY, NYC, and PA residents, please add appropriate sales tax. No cash, stamps, or C.O.D.s. All orders shipped within 6 weeks via postal service book rate. Canadian orders require $2.00 extra postage and must be paid in U.S. dollars through a U.S. banking facility.

Name_____
Address_____
City_____State_____Zip_____
I have enclosed $_____ in payment for the checked book(s).
Payment <u>must</u> accompany all orders. ❑ Please send a free catalog.
CHECK OUT OUR WEBSITE! www.dorchesterpub.com

Behold a Red Horse

Cotton Smith

After the Civil War, Ethan Kerry carved out the Bar K cattle spread with little more than hard work and fierce courage—and the help of his younger, slow-witted brother, Luther. But now the Bar K is in serious trouble. Ethan's loan was called in and the only way he can save the spread is if he can drive a herd from central Texas to Kansas. Ethan will need more than Luther's help this time—because Ethan has been struck blind by a kick from an untamed horse. His one slim hope has come from a most unlikely source—another brother, long thought dead, who follows the outlaw trail. Only if all three brothers band together can they save the Bar K . . . if they don't kill each other first.

___4894-9 $4.99 US/$5.99 CAN